A Trust Betrayed

Also by Candace Robb

You can also visit Candace Robb's website at
www.candacerobb.com

A Trust Betrayed

Candace Robb

WILLIAM HEINEMANN: LONDON

First published in the United Kingdom in 2000 by
William Heinemann

1 3 5 7 9 10 8 6 4 2

Copyright © Candace Robb

The right of Candace Robb to be identified as the author of this work has been asserted by her
in accordance with the Copyright, Designs and Patents Act, 1988.

William Heinemann
The Random House Group Limited
20 Vauxhall Bridge Road, London, SW1V 2SA

Random House Australia (Pty) Limited
20 Alfred Street, Milsons Point, Sydney, New South Wales 2061, Australia

Random House New Zealand Limited
18 Poland Road, Glenfield
Auckland 10, New Zealand

Random House South Africa (Pty) Limited
Endulini, 5a Jubilee Road, Parktown, 2193, South Africa

The Random House Group Limited Reg. No. 954009
www.randomhouse.co.uk

A CIP catalogue record for this book is available from the British Library

Papers used by Random House are natural, recyclable products made from wood grown in
sustainable forests. The manufacturing processes conform to the environmental regulations of the
country of origin.

Typeset in Caslon 540
Printed and bound in the United Kingdom by
Mackays of Chatham plc, Chatham, Kent

ISBN 0 434 00902 4

CONTENTS

In memory of Nigel Tranter,
who invited me to tea and inspired me to walk with my muse

ACKNOWLEDGEMENTS

Elizabeth Ewan has been so generous with her expertise and time, enthusiastically helping me create and recreate the world of Margaret Kerr. No question regarding Scottish history and culture was too quibbling. Her suggestions have made it all the richer. My friend Joyce Gibb has been a patient, calming and encouraging sounding board and reader, working miracles with tight deadlines. Kate Elton did a wonderfully provocative final emotive edit.

Claudia Noyes advised me on vertical looms and card weaving, even giving me hands-on experience with the latter – it is much more difficult than it looks. Alan Young provided me with a balanced bibliography for the Wars of Independence. Brian Moffat spent a cold, blustery Easter Monday atop Soutra Hill sharing his knowledge of the great medieval hospital with my husband and me. And Charles Robb has made good use of our explorations to provide the maps. As ever, I'm grateful to my colleagues and friends on Chaucernet and Medfem and all who participate in the annual International Congress of Medieval Studies at Kalamazoo.

And my especial thanks to Lynne Drew, Sara Ann Freed, Evan Marshall and Patrick Walsh for their wisdom and encouragement, and for believing in Margaret when she was just an idea.

HISTORICAL NOTE

Scotland and the Scots have been the subjects of so many popular tales that readers often come to works about them with set ideas – which may be contrary to the people and the country depicted in *A Trust Betrayed*. I mention plaids, but no clan tartans – they had not been formalised at this time. Also, although I pepper the speech of my characters with some Scots words, I do it with a light touch. Scots lowland speech was much closer to that of northern England in the late thirteenth century than some might expect, and the majority of the lowland Scots could not understand the Gaelic of the highlanders.

Nor were the Wars of Independence a simple two-way battle, Scots vs English, at this point. To explain the complication I must go back to the death of the Maid of Norway, the last member in the direct line of kings of Scotland from Malcolm Canmore. After her death, two major claimants arose – John Balliol and Robert Bruce – but eventually ten additional claimants stepped forward. In an effort to prevent civil war, the Scots asked King Edward of England to act as judge. In hindsight, they were tragically unwise to trust Edward, who had already proved his ruthlessness in Wales. Edward chose John Balliol as king, and then proceeded to make a puppet of him, which is somewhat puzzling considering the powerful Comyn family to which Balliol was connected by his sister's marriage.

Robert Bruce, known as 'the Competitor' to distinguish him from his son Robert and his grandson Robert, still seething under the lost opportunity, handed over his earldom to his son, who was more an Englishman at heart than a Scotsman. He in turn handed over the earldom to his son, who would eventually become King Robert I. Through the 1290s this younger Bruce, Earl of Carrick – the Robert Bruce who appears in this novel – vacillated between supporting and opposing Edward. When he at last resolved to stand against Edward, he was not doing so in support of John Balliol, but was pursuing his own interests.

As for William Wallace, he was in 1297 and thereafter fighting for the return of John Balliol to the throne. He was never a supporter of Robert Bruce.

The reader might at first be puzzled by the small size of Edinburgh in 1297. Until the siege of the town of Berwick, it had been the jewel in the Scots crown. Edinburgh did not come into its own until the fourteenth century, and largely because of the fate of Berwick. At the time of this tale what is now called the Old Town was all that existed of Edinburgh, and truly just the bare bones of that.

The Bishop of St Andrews was essentially the head of the Church in Scotland: there were no archbishoprics in Scotland.

The treachery of Adam, Abbot of Holyrood, is fact, though the particulars in this tale are speculation.

Scotswomen did not take their husband's family name, so a woman would be known by her own family name, the exception being when she was widowed. Then her status was marked by her late husband's surname, as in 'Widow Sinclair'.

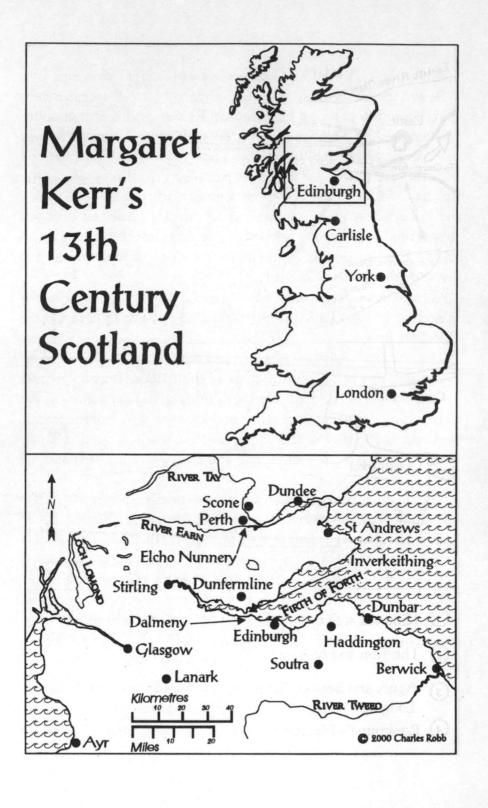

Margaret Kerr's 13th Century Scotland

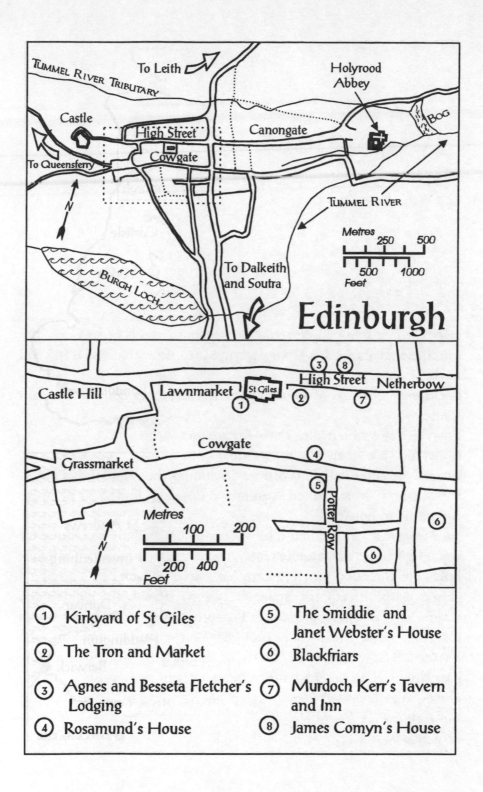

Edinburgh

To Leith

Tummel River Tributary

Castle

Holyrood Abbey

Canongate

High Street

Cowgate

To Queensferry

Bog

Tummel River

Metres
250   500
500   1000
Feet

N

To Dalkeith and Soutra

Burgh Loch

Castle Hill

Lawnmarket   St Giles

High Street   Netherbow

Grassmarket

Cowgate

Potter Row

Metres
100   200
200   400
Feet

N

---

① Kirkyard of St Giles

② The Tron and Market

③ Agnes and Besseta Fletcher's Lodging

④ Rosamund's House

⑤ The Smiddie and Janet Webster's House

⑥ Blackfriars

⑦ Murdoch Kerr's Tavern and Inn

⑧ James Comyn's House

GLOSSARY

arles   when two people strike a bargain in goods or services, the purchaser gives arles, a money payment to show that she is in good faith.

backland   the part of a burgh plot that stretches behind the main house.

bowyer   one who makes bows for archers.

brewster   a woman who brews ale.

canon   in some religious orders, including the Augustinian order, the priests were called canons; Holyrood and Soutra were Augustinian houses.

card weaving   also called tablet weaving, an ancient technique for weaving bands that predates loom weaving. A set of cards with four holes are threaded for the warp, each hole in each card carrying a single warp thread; the space between these holes creates the shed. As the cards are turned one-quarter, individually or in clusters, new threads are brought to the surface making the pattern. The warps twist, or twine around the weft, completely covering it. The cards are often made of bone or wood.

close   a pathway between burgh properties larger than an alley but not public (see 'wynd').

cruisie   an oil lamp with a rush wick.

Edward Longshanks King Edward I was long-legged, hence the nickname.

factor one who buys and sells for another person; a mercantile agent; a commission merchant.

flyting scolding.

gate street.

gey very.

gooddaughter daughter-in-law.

goodmother mother-in-law.

kirtle a gown laced at the bodice that served as an undergarment.

lugs ears.

lyke corpse.

lykewake the watch over the corpse.

merrills a popular board game with a board containing holes and pegs that the players moved in the manner of tic-tac-toe or noughts and crosses.

Pater Noster beads rosary beads.

pattens wooden platforms attached to shoes for walking in mud.

plaid vari-coloured wool cloth, precursor to the tartan but linked to an area only by the dyes available to weavers.

port gate.

queyn girl.

Ragman Rolls an oath of fealty to Edward I signed by Scots, dated 28 September 1296, Berwick.

scarlett the finest cloth, not necessarily red in colour.

scrip a small bag, wallet, or satchel.

siller money (from 'silver').

smiddie smithy.

trencher a thick slice of brown bread a few days old with a slight hollow in the centre, used as a platter.

tron the marketplace weigh beam for weighing goods.

wean baby.

wynd a more public alley between burgh properties than a close.

❦ 1 ❧

A Wake and a Burial

Dunfermline, 26 April 1297

Sleet drummed against the parchment window beside the door. Logs sizzled and popped in the fire circle. A water jug stood ready for dousing embers that might fly outside the ring of stones. After devoting so many hours to the altar cloth neither woman wished to chance any damage. The firelight picked out the colours on the long linen draped across the women's laps, a paschal lamb sitting at the foot of a crucifix, a crown of thorns in the grass beside him. Margaret leaned away from the fire, towards the oil lamp on a small table at her side, preferring its steady light for the fine needlework. Now and again she glanced up at Katherine, smiled unsteadily if she caught her goodmother's eye, then bent back over her work. Katherine did likewise. Each forced a brave face for the other. Each saw the questions, the sorrow, the fear in the other's eyes.

Roger Sinclair – Margaret's husband, Katherine's son – had been gone more than five months. And now his cousin Jack, who had departed in search of Roger three weeks past, had been brought home in a shroud.

Margaret pricked her finger for the third time and judged it best to put her work aside before she stained it with her blood. She cut her thread and tucked her needle into a cloth in the basket at her side. Rising, she sucked at the puncture as she opened the street door, stepped out into the chill, wet evening, lifting her face and spreading her arms to the icy drizzle.

'The draught, gooddaughter,' Katherine said.

Margaret stepped back over the threshold, shut the door. 'It is so warm by the fire I cannot breathe.'

The unhealthy flush of her goodmother's face made Margaret feel even hotter. Nor could Katherine mask her sweaty odour despite all the lavender water she wore.

'My old bones enjoy heat.'

Old bones. Katherine would not have said that before Roger disappeared. She had aged in his absence. And today she had received another blow with the news of Jack's death. It was more than the loss of a nephew – Katherine had raised him as a second son.

Margaret resumed her seat, taking care not to wrinkle the cloth as she lifted it. She considered Katherine's fleshy body – her goodmother indulged excessively in food as well as heat – and judged her shoulders more rounded than they had been the past summer, the joints on her hands more knobbly. Perhaps there was more grey in her brows.

'You are not old.'

'I ken my own body, lass.' Katherine did not look up.

Margaret picked up her basket as if to take up her needle again, but she could not sit still. 'I'll sit the lykewake this evening.'

'It is over cold in that hut,' Katherine protested. 'I lasted but a few short prayers – me, with all this flesh protecting my bones from the cold. And you are so much thinner.' She shook her head at Margaret. 'I cannot allow it. What would Roger say if you lost fingers or toes keeping vigil over his cousin?'

What would Roger think? Margaret could not guess. Out of their two years of marriage she could count on one hand how many months he had been home. She hardly knew him any better than she had at their betrothal. Before her marriage she had dreamed of their life together – she would share in the concerns of his shipping business, entertain the prominent burgesses of Perth, bear children, run an efficient household, comfort Roger and the young ones through their illnesses. Instead, she was commonly alone, the burgesses gossiped about her husband's long absences, and as for children, there were none – they had little chance of being conceived. She did not know which possibility was more frightening – that Roger was caught up in the fighting against the English king, perhaps lying injured somewhere, or that he was away from her this long while by choice.

And since learning of Jack's violent death an even greater fear gripped her – that Jack had been killed because he was searching for Roger, which meant her husband was in danger.

Katherine moved from fretting about Margaret to reassuring her. 'Celia is out there, ready to affright any evil spirits with candles.' Celia was Katherine's maid.

'A member of the family should keep the lykewake,' Margaret said.

She regretted her words when she saw Katherine's small frown. Her goodmother had been kind to her, welcoming her warmly at Yuletide and again at Easter, weeks when Margaret's house in Perth would have echoed with her loneliness.

'*I* should keep the lykewake, not a mere servant – that is what I meant,' Margaret appeased. 'Not that *you* should do it. You must ready the house for those who will come for the burial.'

Katherine relented when Margaret promised to wrap herself in two mantles, her coarse plaid one over the fine wool one her goodmother had given her at Christmas.

The ground in the frosty evening yard gave Margaret pause. It was rough and slippery, sleet washing over the frozen ruts in the packed earth. The hut was not far. Light from the lantern she carried already danced on the door of the small building. But she would last no longer than Katherine if she had wet feet. She took time to strap wooden pattens over her soft, worn shoes, then she gathered her skirts in hand to cross the expanse.

Margaret slowed as she approached the hut. When she had last seen Jack he had been bright-eyed and laughing with the prospect of a journey. Her burden of dread had lifted a little with the possibility that the months of waiting, of uncertainty, might be about to end, that she would learn what had delayed Roger. At least something was being done. But if Jack had discovered anything he had sent no word before his death. Margaret knew no more than before, and now had lost the person who had seen to Roger's business in his absence – Jack had been his cousin's factor, representing Roger at the port of Perth, arranging sales of the goods in the warehouses. He had also been a good friend to Margaret.

The shed was lopsided, made of mud and twigs, roofed with old thatch. When Margaret pulled at the door it stuck and she had to yank it, rattling the flimsy structure.

The maid jumped up with a cry. Shielding her eyes from the lantern's bright glow, she cried, 'Who comes here?'

'It's Margaret.' She fumbled at the lantern shutters with frozen fingers.

'I was feart you were an evil spirit,' said Celia.

'As I would have been,' said Margaret, shutting the door. 'That is why we are here, to keep the evil spirits from Jack's departing soul. Though I think his soul must have passed before he came here.' He had been found in Edinburgh three days earlier.

Celia hugged herself as a gust of wind from the open door blew out a candle.

'It is a night for spirits,' said Margaret.

'Aye, it is.' Celia lit the candle from another. 'And a cold one.' The mantle she wore looked warm – Katherine treated her servants well – but as Celia turned from the candle and shook out her skirt Margaret saw that it was damp from the rivulets that criss-crossed the packed-earth floor.

Margaret held out the lantern. 'Take yourself off to bed. I shall watch till dawn.'

'You are kind, Dame Kerr, but my mistress told me to bide until sunrise.' Celia settled back down in her chair in the corner, tucking a loose strand of dark hair into her cap and patting it primly. She was a tiny woman of an age with Margaret, not yet twenty, with a pale complexion and dark eyes under heavy brows. 'I'll not disturb your prayers.'

Celia answered only to her mistress, and even then she was very stubborn – a trait tiny people often had, it seemed to Margaret. She did not bother to argue with Celia. Neither did she intend to let the woman interfere with her farewell to Jack.

The sputtering candles burning at both ends of the shrouded corpse scented the air with beeswax but could not mask the other, stronger odour of decay. Dried herbs had been added to Jack's shroud before it had been sewn shut, as was the custom, but they were no longer equal to the task.

Sewn shut. Margaret had only her brother Andrew's terse description of Jack's wounds – the slashed stomach and throat, related dispassionately. Not that Andrew had reason to sorrow, no more than for any man's death. Her brother, a canon of Holyrood in Edinburgh, had brought Jack's body home, but she doubted the two had ever spoken more than a few cordial words of greeting. It seemed to her that someone who had cared for Jack should witness his wounds. In fact, having had so little acquaintance with him, Andrew might even have made a mistake in identifying the body as Jack.

'How can I know it is him?' Margaret whispered as she stood over the shrouded figure.

'Father Andrew said as much, Dame Kerr,' said Celia.

Andrew had taken his vows before Margaret met Roger and his family. He had come to her wedding, where he would have met Jack, but she did not know of another time he might have seen him. A mistake was possible. Still, the prospect of opening the shroud filled her with dread.

If she had her mother's gift of second sight she might spare herself this added grief of seeing Jack's handsome face transformed by hideous death. But though Margaret looked much like her mother, she did not have her gift. She must deal with the world more directly. She must see the body.

'Bring my sewing basket to me, Celia. Make sure that my scissors and a good needle are in it.'

She saw Celia's uncertainty. 'I pray you, go.'

'Widow Sinclair will wonder why you want your sewing things.'

'Tell her I must occupy my hands.'

Celia looked doubtful, but with a nod she departed.

Once alone, Margaret knelt beside the bier and bowed her head. She prayed that God would not take offence at what she was about to do. She prayed, too, for Jack's soul. And, as always, that Roger was safe. 'Bring him home to me, dear Lord.'

Celia returned with the basket.

'I shall need the lantern,' Margaret said. 'You are free to cross back to the house if you like, though it will be dark.'

Celia shook her head. 'You need someone to hold the light for you if you mean to take the stitches out neatly.'

'It is best that no one knows of this but us.'

'I don't gossip.' It was a statement, not a vow.

But Margaret was grateful. 'God bless you, Celia.'

'Where would it be best for me to stand?'

Margaret indicated a place near the head of the shroud. 'I need see only his face.'

Silently, Celia took her position. Margaret was grateful the maid asked no more questions. And why should she? It was reasonable to have some small hope that Andrew had made a mistake.

The stitches at the top of the shroud were tiny and even. Margaret worked to keep her hand steady. There was no cause to let others know she had unwrapped the corpse. As she picked at the stitches in the dim light and the cold, her sight blurred and her fingers grew clumsy. Celia took the scissors and handed Margaret the lantern.

'The lantern warmed my hands,' Celia said. 'If you hold it while I finish the tearing out, you will have warm fingers to sew.'

The lantern did warm Margaret's hands. And when Celia stood back, proclaiming the stitches all undone, Margaret thought herself ready to look at Jack, then sew the shroud closed. She pulled back the cloth.

The sight of him shattered her. Jack's blond lashes should have rested on pale, high cheekbones. Instead they were almost invisible in the folds of bloated eyelids, cheeks. Yet she could not stop there. She tugged further at the shroud with stiff, impatient, careless fingers.

Celia grabbed her hands, but Margaret struggled to free herself. 'I must see his wounds. I must see them.'

'Let me do it,' Celia said. 'You will tear the shroud.'

His body was unrecognisable, the flesh discoloured, the wounds gaping perversions of the body's form, obscenely intimate, exposing the inner maze of blood and tissue. The odour made Margaret gag. Why had she done this? This was not Jack, but his lifeless, bloated shell. She lifted the shroud to begin rewinding it, caught his right hand in a fold of the sheet. Something slipped from his hand – a small stone with a hole in the centre. She plucked it from the sheet, tucked it up the tight sleeve of her shift.

'Shall we add more dried herbs?' Celia asked quietly.

'What does it matter?'

Silently they bent to their work in the candlelit shed, the wind moaning and pushing at the fragile hut, the rain drumming overhead.

That Jack's good deed should come to this. Margaret remembered the day, just over a month past, when the plan had been hatched. She was at home in Perth, making use of a rare dry afternoon in March with a tolerable wind. Margaret and her servant had strung rope in the garden between two apple trees and hung out the bedding to air. She was hanging some of Roger's clothes as well. Five months he had been gone, and the clothes in the chest smelled musty. If the airing did not help, she would add them to next week's laundry. Margaret's hands were soon stiff with the cold, but the sunshine cheered her.

An errand, she could not recall what, brought Jack to the house. He strode into the yard, graceful and twitching with energy like a fine horse, wearing his best clothes, a green tunic with a white shirt beneath, brown leggings, soft blue shoes with long points and matching felt hat. How fine he looked. And she could tell by his posturing that he knew it.

'I am bidden to dine with Alan Fletcher.' Jack looked smug. Alan was a wealthy and influential merchant in Perth, and Jack had ambitions. 'I told him that I thought it high time I went in search of Roger. Master Fletcher has proposed a bit of business for me to do in Edinburgh and will provide the horse for the journey.' A welcome offer. With no shipping from Berwick or Leith since the English had seized the ports the previous summer, the coffers were almost empty, and hiring a horse for such a journey was out of the question. Margaret needed her mare here.

Still, she had been puzzled. She had worried about Roger all this time, but all the while Jack had assured her Roger was not headstrong and he could take care of himself. 'Why now?'

'I did not want— God help us, Roger is home.' Jack had just noticed the hanging clothes. 'No wonder I confuse you.'

'No, Roger is not home. Tell me more about your plan.' Easter was upon them. Perhaps she might ride south with him to Roger's mother in Dunfermline for the holy day.

But Jack said he must leave at once, and Margaret had much to do for the household before she could depart.

'Why this haste?' she asked.

'Seize the opportunity.' He had glanced round, then lifted her hand and kissed it. She pulled away from him, her face burning, and Jack grinned. 'I cannot kiss my cousin?'

'It is good you take such an interest in searching for Roger,' she said rather more loudly than necessary, 'but why search for him in

Edinburgh? He would not ship from there.' His purpose in setting out had been to find an alternative port now Berwick was in English hands. He had said he would begin with Dundee.

Jack still teased her with his eyes. 'It was from Edinburgh he wrote to you. I may find a trace of him.'

It was true – she had received one letter from Roger in late November saying he would be home by Yuletide. The messenger had come from Edinburgh. 'And if his trail leads you beyond Edinburgh, will Alan Fletcher approve your continuing with his horse?' Her father and Fletcher had long ago fallen out over the man's miserly ways. He would expect a full accounting from Jack.

'Such a fuss! Do you not wish to find Roger?'

'Sweet heaven, you know that is not why I ask.'

But it had been the way of arguments with Jack. Teasing, playful. He had been such a vital presence.

And now here he lay.

Margaret's vigil began in tears. But as the hours slipped by her eyes dried, her sorrow replaced by a more selfish emotion. Fear. For herself, for Roger. Whoever had so savagely murdered Jack might be after Roger. After all, Jack's business had been Roger's business, Jack's kin were Roger's kin.

In the early morning Margaret's brother, Father Andrew, relieved her at the watch. After Celia took her leave, Margaret watched Andrew for a sign that he noticed the shroud had been opened and resewn.

He knelt beside it, said a prayer, then settled on the stool Celia had vacated, rubbing his hands together. 'I don't need to tell you it's a cold morn. You must have frozen in here all the night.'

'I preferred that to warming the lyke. Jack is four days gone.'

'Aye.' Andrew ran his hands through the dark hair that curled round his tonsure. He could be handsome if his mouth did not have such a downward curve, if his deep brown eyes met one's own more often.

Margaret was relieved he noticed nothing untoward. He had grown into such a humourless and judgemental man. She did not know whether she could have explained herself to his satisfaction. And she did not have the stomach for a sermon.

'Be off with you,' Andrew said. 'Fergus awaits you in the house.'

Fergus was Margaret's younger brother, whom she had left in Perth to see to the business and take care of her house. 'How can that be? It is at least a day's ride here.'

'I sent word with a messenger from Edinburgh before I began the journey.'

'It was good of you, Andrew.' If anyone could empathise and in doing so cheer her, it would be Fergus. The brothers were perfect examples of the melancholic and the choleric – Andrew cold, Fergus hot; Andrew dark in mood and appearance, Fergus aglow in all things.

'He can escort you home.'

'Home? But I cannot leave at a time like this. Roger's mother needs me.'

'You have much to do in Perth. Find a new factor.'

'Fergus has been doing the work since Jack left. He will continue.'

'Uncle Thomas expects him in Aberdeen.' Their father had arranged for Fergus to become secretary to his uncle, who had a fleet of merchant ships.

'He will not go now.' He could not. He *must* not. 'He will be Roger's factor.'

'He is too young, Maggie. Younger even than you. He wants training,' Andrew replied firmly.

Margaret felt her face growing hot. Fergus *was* young, seventeen. But Margaret had no money with which to pay a factor. 'It is not for you to decide.' The Church saw to all Andrew's material needs. He knew nothing of what the merchants suffered with the English blocking the shipping. He could not possibly understand her situation.

Their eyes locked. Margaret prayed Andrew could not see how close she was to tears.

He was the first to look away. 'Go, break your fast, Maggie. The burial is set for nones.'

Fleeing the hut, she slipped on the rutted ice, steadied herself against the wall. The morning was cold but dry. She stood a moment in the sharp air, letting it cool her burning cheeks. She must calm herself and think what to do.

Fergus jumped up from his seat by the fire circle to embrace Margaret.

'I am so sorry, Maggie. Jack was a good friend to you.'

Fergus had thought Jack a difficult boss, ever finding fault, never praising, but he was aware how much Margaret had valued her husband's cousin.

'You should come back north with me,' he continued. 'Far as you can away from the English soldiers. Better yet, close up the house and come to Aberdeen. Aye, that's best.'

It was good advice, but Margaret was not free to agree to it. 'How would Roger find me?' She fought tears, but they already streamed down her face. She was tired, hungry, frightened.

'Oh, Maggie, I didn't mean to make you weep.'

But as he stood before her she saw that Fergus was truly a very young seventeen, not yet experienced enough to handle the responsibilities of a factor without guidance. He did need time with Uncle Thomas. She did not know how she was to manage without either Roger or Jack.

'Have any ships come through while I've been away?' she managed to ask.

'Nay. Things are no better than when you left.'

Perhaps it did not matter. She was not likely to find a factor even had she the money to pay one. All the young men were slipping away to fight the English. Another good reason to tie Fergus to the business – he might yearn to be a soldier, but he would not desert her.

By late morning the sun shone on mud brittle with frost. Jack's coffin was to be placed in one of the shallow winter graves until the earth thawed and he could be moved to a permanent grave. Standing in the doorway of her goodmother's house, Margaret shivered and pulled her plaid mantle close about her, shifting from one foot to the other in an attempt to keep some feeling in her toes. She said good morrow to some neighbours and a priest from another parish, pressed the hands of an elderly goodwife in tears.

'Dame Kerr.' It was the hoarse voice of Jack's father. Will Sinclair bowed his shrivelled head to her; the stench of stale wine lingered in his wake as he entered the house. Jack had hated his father, a drunkard who had begotten eight children on two wives, both of whom had died of his neglect. Then he had worked two daughters so hard they, too, had fallen with fevers. Being the youngest, Jack had been taken in by his aunt Katherine.

The mourners had been congregating without the house after expressing their sorrow to the family. There was not room for all of them within. Now they milled about, soberly greeting neighbours.

Margaret's good mantle was suddenly placed on her shoulders. Fergus squeezed her shoulders and whispered, 'No need for you to freeze, Maggie. Jack is on his own now, doing his own penance.'

'What do you mean?' Margaret asked rather sharply.

Fergus moved beside her. 'Surely he has not become a saint in your mind now he's dead? If ever there was an unsaintly man it was Jack with his schemes and his small lies, his flirtation with all females younger than Mother. But no, I recall he even flirted with Mother for a time, until she had a damning dream about him.'

Margaret blushed at the memory.

'Look at all the females in this crowd, eh?'

'Aye,' Margaret whispered.

'Well?' Fergus asked. 'Why did you snap at me?'

'I am tired, that is all. And I do mourn him, Fergus. He was a great help to me and a good man.'

'Oh, aye, I know that. But he was a knave as well.'

'I'm much better since you joined me. And warmer.'

'Your goodmother should have thought of the mantle.'

Folk came up to speak with them, but Margaret responded with only half her attention. She kept looking for Roger's arrival at the edge of the crowd. Had he heard about Jack's death, he would have come. So he did not know. She would not let herself think of the other possibilities, that he was prevented from coming by illness or death.

The tolling bell stilled the voices, calling the mourners to the kirk. It kept the pall-bearers' steps slow and steady. The priest's incense spiced the wintry air.

In the kirk Margaret's breath rose in frosty clouds as she prayed, steadying her goodmother beside her.

Once more the pall-bearers lifted Jack. Katherine straightened, shook her head at Margaret's offer of support. For this last walk with her nephew she would be strong.

The hard clods of frozen earth dropping on the coffin sounded like hoof beats in the quiet kirkyard. How they must thunder within Jack's coffin. Margaret shivered. Fergus put an arm round her.

It should have been Roger who comforted her.

❧ 2 ❧

THE CROSSING

Monday brought iron grey clouds, winds that found every crack in the walls, every loose shingle, and a chill that threatened to turn the rain to snow. It was not a day to travel. But Andrew, having wasted Sunday in Dunfermline, was determined to lose no more time in returning to Edinburgh, and Margaret was not about to be shaken off by his haste.

As she had walked back to the house from Jack's grave on Saturday she had decided what she must do. Once the guests had departed she had urged Katherine to retire to her chamber, then gathered her brothers round the fire circle in the main room. She warned Andrew and Fergus to speak softly, that the elderly woman's hearing was quite sharp.

'What do you not wish her to hear?' Fergus had asked, glancing uneasily at Andrew.

'She will know on the morn, but for now I would have her sleep.' Margaret took a deep breath. 'I am accompanying Andrew to Edinburgh.'

'What?' Andrew came to attention.

'I must find Roger.'

'You don't know when he was last there,' Fergus said.

'If you do not mean to support me, hold your tongue,' Margaret snapped.

14

Andrew shook his head. 'Edinburgh Castle is crowded with Edward Longshanks' soldiers, Maggie. The town is no place for a young woman.'

'There is no other way. No one else will search for him with English soldiers about.'

'Aye. Nor should you.'

'You are on good terms with the English.'

'Why do you say that?' Andrew looked offended by the comment.

'They let you have Jack's body. You said you knew the sheriff.'

'Do you?' Fergus asked.

'It is true I studied at Oxford with Sir Walter Huntercombe's son. His son, mind you,' Andrew said. 'I cannot protect you, Maggie. And what will you do with Roger when you find him – demand that he come home?'

It was perhaps foolish to go, but it was better than what she had done so far – worry and pray. She was sick of it.

'Where would you stay?' Andrew demanded.

'With Uncle Murdoch, at his inn.'

'Heaven help you.'

'I am decided.'

They had argued until they woke Katherine, who had heard enough by the time she came out of her chamber that she needed no explanation.

'Of course you must go, Margaret,' she said in the tone of one who suddenly understands. 'That is how your mother's prophecy will be fulfilled.'

'You believe Mother's vision?' Margaret said.

'Wise men and women go to her for advice. The Abbess of Elcho was happy to receive her. It means pilgrim offerings for their abbey.'

Margaret's mother had withdrawn to Elcho Nunnery on the Tay after Margaret's marriage. With her father's blessing. Malcolm Kerr said his wife's notoriety in the town made his fellow merchants uneasy, which was bad for trade.

When Margaret had last visited Elcho Nunnery her mother had told her of two visions of her daughter's future. 'I saw you standing over a table, studying maps with two men. One was giving you and the other orders, concerning a battle.' Margaret had laughed at that. But her mother had solemnly continued. 'On another day I saw you holding your baby daughter in your arms, your husband standing by your side, watching the true King of Scots ride into Edinburgh.'

Christiana MacFarlane, Margaret's mother, had grown up on the north shore of Loch Long. Her family had been perplexed by her fasts and visions even as a child, and her parents undertook the difficult journey to St Andrews to pray at the shrine of the apostle for guidance. Christiana's flux began while they were there, and her parents decided it was a sign she was to be wed and bear children. On their way back to Loch Long they stayed in Perth, where Malcolm Kerr first set eyes on her. He thought she had the face of an angel, but he did not know whether he liked the idea of marrying an angel. Or a saint. So he did not make his feelings known to her parents. A year later, when he understood that he had discarded all the marriageable women in Perth for not being the beautiful Christiana, he took himself off to Loch Long.

Christiana's visions had ceased until Fergus was born, and then she began to inform neighbours of her dreams about them. Margaret had grown up with the unpleasant expectation that being her mother's only daughter, she would very likely also have visions. When she showed no sign of doing so, she felt people wondered what imperfection cursed her.

'I shall rely on my own strength in this,' Margaret said to her goodmother. 'On my own certainty that God guides me.' She turned to her brothers. 'Is that not better than relying on our mother's pronouncements?'

Andrew did not answer, but sat staring into the fire.

Fergus looked uncertain. 'I thought them strange visions at the time, but now that you've chosen to go to Edinburgh and feel so sure of it, I wonder. She might have foreseen all this.'

'There,' said Katherine, satisfied. 'Now Margaret must get her sleep, so good night to you, Father Andrew, Fergus.'

This morning, Katherine paced about and hovered over Celia's preparations – she insisted Margaret have a maid on the journey. Celia was a vain woman and tidy to the point of sinfulness – though Katherine claimed it to be an excellent virtue in a maid. Margaret was not pleased with her goodmother's gift, but she knew it was meant kindly and so accepted Celia's presence – for the time being.

Eventually the household began to calm and settle into the morning routine.

Then Andrew announced that his servant, Matthew, waited without with the horses. It was time to depart.

The widow threw back her head and pressed her palms together. 'Blessed Mary, Mother of God, watch over them.' She lowered her eyes to Celia. 'Take care of Margaret. What you do for her, you do for me.'

Celia forced a smile. Margaret did not like the tension she sensed beneath the maid's attempts to appear calm and wondered whether Celia was less pleased at the prospect than she had claimed the previous night, whether she had agreed to do this to please the widow. No doubt she was afraid. Faith, she would be wise to be fearful.

The scent of lavender water and the sour breath of one who has been weeping for days assailed Margaret as her goodmother gathered her in a farewell embrace. 'Find our Roger, my dear. Let your mother's vision of your future give you courage.'

Margaret pulled back far enough to look into her goodmother's eyes.

The widow smiled through tears and hugged Margaret once more. 'God go with you.'

'May God watch o'er all of us,' Margaret whispered.

Father Andrew loved his sister, but he did not want her in

Edinburgh. So close, within a comfortable walk, sooner or later she would hear of his shame.

He had watched her this morning, rushing about, her red-gold hair loose, tumbling in long waves down her back, her freckles making her look too young to be a wife. She should not witness what the troubles had done to her fellow man. Neither should she endanger herself for a husband who so regularly disappeared.

Yet even Perth was not safe. King Edward had touched it, as he had touched so much of this land. Margaret was strong boned and strong willed. She would no doubt survive the disillusionment. In faith, he only angered her when he tried to guide her. Sooner or later Margaret would know anyway.

All through the ride to Inverkeithing the wind tore at Margaret's hood. The rain soaked through two pairs of gloves, the outer pair made of leather.

But worse than the weather was her belated fear. Saturday night she had been so sure this was what she must do. But that clarity had abandoned her, replaced by the clamour of all she had heard about the cruelty of Edward Longshanks, his governors and soldiers. If they were behind Jack's death, she did not know what justice she could hope for.

Her uncertainty about her husband haunted her too. Though Roger had been horrified by the slaughter in Berwick, she was uncertain what he might be willing to do in exchange for an English governor's turning a blind eye as his ships approached Scotland. She would never have wondered but that one of his ships had arrived in Dundee in early autumn. Roger had proclaimed it a sign of a good captain, no more, and set his sights on Dundee as an alternative port, but folk had whispered at his long absences and the ease with which he had found a solution. And the longer Roger was away the more Margaret brooded on his contradictory behaviour. He had cursed Edward Longshanks when his army slaughtered the people of Berwick, but then he had subscribed to the Ragman Rolls, swearing his loyalty to the English king. He had been summoned to swear, it was true, but he was no one of importance, the King of England would not have wasted troops to pluck him from Perth if he had not gone. He need not have sworn loyalty to the murderer.

She glanced at Celia to see how she fared.

Katherine had not warned Margaret that Celia had little experience on horseback. The maid had required assistance this morning in mounting and staying astride. On the journey her hood had been blown back and her white headdress was askew. Her horse flicked his tail and danced. Celia fussed nervously with the reins. Despite all this, her expression was one of determination.

As they approached Inverkeithing Matthew spurred his horse and rode ahead for news of the ferry. The timing of the crossing was unpredictable in the stormy weather, and with the English occasionally shutting down the ferry. In a short while, the lad reappeared, sodden and flushed by the ride, shaking his head at Andrew's shouted query. The news drew a curse from Margaret's impatient brother.

'Do we return to Dunfermline?' Celia asked Margaret tremulously.

'That would be foolhardy,' Margaret said. 'My brother will have arranged a room at a hostel near the ferry landing.' He was nothing if not organised. 'He knows how uncertain the crossings are in this season.'

'But he did not plan for us.'

'We may all four crowd in one room, Celia. It is the way of travellers. Matthew will wake early and take up watch on the ferry landing.'

Margaret was gey glad when they gained the inn yard, looking forward to dry clothes, a fire, and something warm to drink. Dismounting, she took the reins from Celia's icy hands. Andrew's servant, Matthew, assisted the maid in dismounting.

'Forgive me for my awkwardness,' Celia said to Margaret. 'I shall improve.'

'You sat your horse all the way – I applaud you,' said Margaret. 'Now – do you have Pater Noster beads?'

Celia shook her head.

'I shall loan you mine. I want you to pray for God's help in calming yourself while we cross in the morning. Your mount senses your fear. That is why he dances.'

'I am not afeart.'

'You cannot lie to a horse.'

Celia turned away, tidying her cap as best she could. It was not easy. The linen was limp and damp.

The hostel was small, and crowded because of the storm. Margaret did not see many of their fellow travellers, for Andrew hastened them into a private room, arranged by a letter from the Abbot of Dunfermline – the landings for the ferry had been carved from his lands, the ferry operated on his munificence. The four huddled round a smoky brazier, steaming in the welcome warmth.

Though she was already so deeply chilled that even changing into dry clothes did not abate her shivering, Margaret vowed to be first awake in the morning. She was disappointed in that. Sleep held off until just before dawn, and then she fell into a deep slumber from which Celia had to shake her awake. It added to Andrew's already foul mood regarding the delayed crossing, and as he rode beside her to the landing he leaned over every few feet to urge her forward. 'The ferry approaches.' 'Let us make haste.' 'You might have caused us to miss it.'

'I did not even stop to break my fast,' Margaret snapped finally. He was so impatient. He had a schedule and all must fall in line. No doubt he thought unless she strained forward in the saddle she was being too easy on the horse.

The stormy day afforded no view of Dalmeny on the far bank. A huddle of cloaked figures, some with carts, a few horsemen, stood on the ferry landing. Seagulls circled above them, their cries a bleak accompaniment to the wind and the crashing waves. The large ferry, oars lifted, bobbed on the choppy water of the firth. Soon she would be bobbing with it, colder yet than she was now. She thought back to her days seated before her goodmother's hot fire working on the altar cloth and wondered when next she would be so warm and dry.

They dismounted at the edge of the crowd.

'Matthew will tend your horse until we reach Dalmeny,' Margaret said to Celia's back.

The maid nodded, securing her hood over her cap. She seemed quite subdued this morning, and moved stiffly.

The vessel bumped against the dock, frightening some of the horses. A man on the shore called to those waiting on the landing to open a path for those disembarking, then he hurried forward to take the ropes, tie up the ferry. The passengers came off, a bedraggled dozen, stumbling on the solid earth. Two horses were led off by servants, one of the men wearing the evidence of a weak stomach on his mantle.

Margaret glanced round at her fellow passengers. There were several merchants, fat-bellied and well dressed – no ostentation in their garb, of course, no need to call attention to themselves in such times; an elderly couple, with a boy of ten or so who complained loudly that his boots were wet, all three wrapped in fine mantles held shut with silver brooches; two servants who accompanied the three; two clerics, both quite humble, one a lay priest in patched clothing, the other a Dominican friar; several young men with the stony expressions of soldiers – Scots, but as they were heading south perhaps hoping to join the English.

The friar stood beside Andrew. They had talked a little, as strangers do in such places, discussing the weather, the crossing. The friar's hood was so wet it clung to his head, and it and the rest of his black habit was mud-stained and much mended. He was unshaven and encrusted with more dirt than the rain could rinse away.

'You have journeyed far, Brother?' Andrew said now.

'What is far to one of my order, Father? Dominicans travel everywhere there are souls to save.'

One of the seven crew members stepped out onto the dock, eyed the waiting crowd, and shouted for attention – he had to shout to be heard above the wind, the crashing waves, the shrieking gulls.

'All you who would board this ferry be ware. This is a treacherous water.'

One of those disembarking said to the friar as he passed, 'Some might find the English soldiers at Dalmeny a greater danger than the sea.'

'Soldiers at Dalmeny?' a woman moaned.

Had she no sense? Of course the English would guard the ferry – they would be fools not to.

A man armed with a broadsword withdrew from the cluster waiting at the dock. Margaret had noted the weapon when the wind caught the man's cloak. It had been covered quickly. Now one of the men who had disembarked bowed slightly towards the armed man and joined him. A murmur went through the crowd.

'The man with the broadsword is William, the younger son of Malcolm Wallace,' said Andrew, speaking softly. 'He has been at St Andrews. Bishop Wishart and James the Steward have had words with him.'

Margaret followed the man's progress through the small crowd, saw yet another man join him. It was a moment before she registered her surprise. 'The Bishop of Glasgow and the Steward of Scotland? What would they want with a thief like William Wallace?'

'Thief?' Andrew looked down at Margaret, droplets of rain falling from the edge of his hood to his beaked nose. 'You have confused him with someone else,' he said.

Margaret thought it rewarding to know something Andrew did not for once. 'He robbed a wealthy widow of Perth of food and ale. His slow companion was caught. He named his accomplice as William Wallace.'

Andrew grunted. 'Young Wallace a thief? Foolish talk. I do not believe it.'

Margaret felt the friar's eyes upon her. He studied her so closely she dropped her head, sorry to have spoken.

Fortunately, they had begun to board the ferry. Andrew and Matthew took charge of the party's horses, coaxing them aboard and into the enclosed space for beasts, where they could be restrained with harnesses. As they boarded, a wave caught the vessel, panicking Celia's horse. The friar, leading his horse behind them, called out to the foot passengers to help. One grabbed the reins of the other horse in Matthew's charge.

Margaret pushed through the crowd, climbed up onto the deck of the bucking vessel. 'Matthew, let me have the reins while you cover his eyes.' She took the bridle firmly in hand, talked to the horse, calming him as Matthew blindfolded him with a strip of cloth.

The cold rain stung Margaret's face and the fierce wind that carried it tore at her breath. She was grateful to have both cloaks and held them close to shield her face, but she lost hold of them whenever a wave tossed the ferry and she was thrown against Celia's horse. The beast had responded to her gentling murmurs and did not panic again, God be praised. Margaret glanced round to see how others fared. Celia stood beside the elderly woman and boy, all three hanging on to the side of a cart. She seemed to ride the rolling boat well. There was hope for her.

Turning the other way, Margaret found the friar's eyes on her.

He nodded. 'That was brave, what you did. You have a calming way with a horse.'

'It is what was needed. I thank you for your concern.'

The friar bowed slightly. 'Travellers help one another. You are kin to Father Andrew?'

'His sister.'

'He escorts you to some happy event?'

'No, he does not.' She turned away, not liking his interest. Friars were known to prey on women and to be the confidants of thieves. Fortunately, Andrew was making his way to her, balancing himself like quite the seaman. He looked grave.

'You heard that there are soldiers at Dalmeny. Keep your eyes downcast, speak only to answer *if* necessary.'

'What are you afraid I shall say? Tell me of what I should not speak.'

'It is best to let me speak for you.'

He was so solemn he frightened her. 'I shall be silent. But I cannot learn what is unsafe if you tell me nothing.'

'Just do as I say. And if a horse frights while we are in their sight, let the men handle it.'

Andrew was angry she had come to the rescue of his servant? Sweet heaven, he could be such a fool. But Margaret was too uneasy now to argue or ask more questions.

Her wet, cold clothes clung to her. Doubt churned her stomach. She dreaded their arrival in Edinburgh – the soldiers, the occupied town, the uncertainty of Uncle Murdoch's reception.

As a child in Perth she had been a favourite with her uncle, and he with her. He understood how much her mother's fits frightened her and took the time no other adult had taken to explain that Christiana was seeing things that were occurring at another time, like a vivid memory, but in the future. All Margaret could see was that her mother would stop in mid-gesture and stare, sometimes shake her head and speak gibberish, sometimes laugh or weep, occasionally shout or scream. Murdoch Kerr had been living in Perth at the time. He told her that he for one thanked the Lord that his little Maggie was not to follow Christiana's path.

It was because of that long-ago kindness that Margaret now expected her uncle's cooperation in her quest. He would be proud of her taking action like this; he would commend her on being so much more practical than her mother. Andrew seemed compelled to remind her that she had not seen much of their uncle since his late wife's family drove him away from Perth. Smuggling was fine when their kin were reaping the rewards, but once Murdoch's wife was dead his reputation embarrassed them. Still, Margaret believed that Murdoch was a man constant in his affections.

'Time will tell whether you can count on him, Maggie,' Andrew had said just before shuttering the lantern last night. She blamed on him her wakefulness.

❧ 3 ❧

WE ARE NOT SO FINE

The road from Dalmeny led round Castle Hill to the West Port gate of Edinburgh. Andrew showed his abbot's letter of protection, as he had when they disembarked. Margaret kept her eyes downcast and let Andrew answer the soldiers' queries about her and Celia. She wondered whether all who came to the town must submit to this, if all townspeople who had business without the town faced such inquisitions at the portals. She felt like a sheep being tagged and herded from field to fold.

Once within the gate, Margaret lifted her eyes, curious to see the Grassmarket lacking stalls, tents, crowds, livestock. To her, Edinburgh had always meant fairs and feasts. This Edinburgh she had never seen. The knoll was rutted and pitted and puddled. In one corner a siege engine warped in the rain. The echoing emptiness seemed diminished and ugly. It felt as if the market had been reduced to its other function – the place of execution – yet even the gallows tilted drunkenly.

'Where are the people?'

'In their houses,' said Andrew.

Celia stumbled as she craned her neck to gaze up at the battlements. 'It is a dreary place.'

Margaret wished they had entered the town at the far end, away from the castle. Murdoch Kerr's inn was at the bottom of High Street, just before Netherbow and the Leith road across which the burgh of Canongate began, in which Holyrood Abbey ruled. But Andrew had said the English might be suspicious if they skirted Edinburgh coming from Dalmeny, which was the direction they watched most carefully.

His anxiety heightened Celia's and spread to her horse, who whinnied and danced. The town was eerily silent. Margaret imagined every head in every house glancing towards the horse's whinny, though the wind and the rain might muffle much of their passing. She was glad when Matthew took the reins and steadied the animal, quieting it.

Many houses below the castle were damaged, some blackened and stinking of charred wood, others lacking doors or shutters. Bits of furniture lay strewn about the doorway of one of the burned houses. The front wall of another was stained with blood. A baby's cry sent chills down Margaret's back. This was no place for a child. Armed men moved about their business, as did some townsfolk, though Margaret saw no children and few women.

At St Giles' Kirk she handed her horse's reins to Matthew and invited Andrew to step within to say a prayer of thanksgiving for their arrival.

'We are not yet at the inn. You can walk up to the kirk later,' Andrew said with a shake of his cloak as if to remind her that he, too, was soaked to the skin. 'Move on, Matthew.'

Margaret could walk here, true enough, if she could still stand once she felt some heat. And if she dared venture out again so soon.

A few hardy souls huddling beneath the eaves against the north wall of St Giles' called out their wares as the four travellers passed, but otherwise the street was deserted.

Though it was mid-afternoon, none of the shopfront counters had been unhooked from the houses to display goods. From the looks of them, Margaret guessed the shopfronts had not been opened for a while. A shutter off one of its hinges hung down over one of the shopfronts, on another house a cracked counter hung askew. A pile of refuse rose too high to allow the neighbouring shopfront to open. None of the doors stood ajar to invite custom.

In Perth and Dunfermline the shops had stayed closed for a time after the English had come through, but within a month or so trade had resumed, albeit modestly. Margaret had not considered how much worse it would be here, with the garrison in the castle above the town. She had not considered whether her uncle would have food for two more.

Andrew brought them to a halt just before the arch of Netherbow. Two tall, weather-beaten houses leaned slightly towards one another across an alley. A pole decorated with leaves projected above the ground-floor door of the house nearest Netherbow, letting passers-by know they could find wine and ale within.

'Will there be soldiers in there?' Celia asked.

'No, they have been ordered to keep well away from this lot,' said Andrew. He handed the reins of all four horses to Matthew. 'I'll ask Murdoch to have his groom help you down to Holyrood with the horses.'

The young man's shoulders slumped.

'Surely Matthew deserves a cup of ale first,' Margaret said.

'A tavern is no place for a cloistered lad,' Andrew said.

'Still, he needn't go thirsty. I'll ask Uncle to bring ale to the stable,' Margaret said, and entered the tavern.

At first she welcomed its warmth, the still air, the roof shielding her from the incessant rain. But two or three deep breaths later, her body rejected the air and she began to cough. Smoke was thick in the air. The room reeked of stale ale, sweat, rancid fat, vomit, urine – Margaret stopped herself from identifying any more. Andrew guided her farther into the room. The rushes were piled so deep on the floor that her footing was unsteady, her shifting feet stirring the odours. There were two shuttered windows that seemed to do little to vent the smoke and provided no light, a weak glow from the brazier and four oil lamps, one on each of the four trestle tables that lined the walls.

A half dozen men sitting on benches surrounding a small brazier in the centre of the room turned towards the newcomers. Their expressions were difficult to make out in the dim light, but their sudden silence felt hostile.

Celia stepped closer to Margaret. 'Mistress, we cannot stay in such a place.'

Thinking much the same, Margaret's instinct was to turn and run. But she had nowhere to go. 'This is but the tavern,' she said, 'the inn rooms must be cleaner or surely my uncle would have no custom.'

'Men do not care about such things,' Celia persisted.

Margaret could not allow herself to lose heart now. 'We are not so fine we cannot clean a room to suit us.'

A man moved towards them from the far end of the tavern, wiping his hands on his tunic. Margaret's heart lifted as she recognised her uncle's rolling sailor's gait – from a career of smuggling. Murdoch Kerr was the fourth son, youngest brother to Margaret's father. He was broad-shouldered, bow-legged, with a barrel of a stomach. His nose hugged his face unevenly, the result of many a drunken brawl, and his thick brows parted not over his nose but rather over his right eye, where a scar prevented new growth. He wore a felt cap – Margaret guessed that his pale red hair was thinning, or gone. Not a handsome man, but as a girl Margaret had prayed her husband might be just like Uncle Murdoch. He always had a smile and a tale for her, and though he thought Christiana's visions were the dreams of a madwoman he was one of the few people who could make her mother laugh. He was strong and quick. And Margaret had always felt safe in his company – for which she was particularly grateful at the moment, as the others in the tavern continued to stare. She smiled and held out her arms to her uncle.

He ignored them. 'Nephew, God help me, you're a fool to bring Maggie here in this storm. You did not cross the firth in this?' Murdoch was not smiling.

'We did, but it was not my choice to bring her, Uncle.'

'He is not to blame,' Margaret said, searching Murdoch's face – it was familiar in feature but alien in mood. His scowl frightened her. 'Will you not greet me, Uncle?'

Grudgingly, Murdoch came forward and hugged her. 'You are soaked through, Maggie,' he said as he stepped back. Glancing from Andrew to Margaret, he gestured to a doorway towards the rear of the large room. 'Come away in. If it is weighty enough to bring you all this way, it is not to be discussed in a public room. Though none other is so warm as this. Sim,' he called to a man wiping one spot on a table as he stared at them. He was tall and skinny, with fair hair thinning early. 'Bring peat for the brazier above, and some ale.'

Murdoch led them out the unlatched door and up an outside flight of stairs to the first floor. Celia stayed close to Margaret as if fearful of being left behind. Murdoch hustled all three through an outer wooden door and into a vestibule with a hide-covered doorway to each side and a wooden door ahead. He lifted the hide to the right and Margaret and the others stepped into a bedchamber, the bed a solid structure heaped with soiled linens. If her uncle had servants, whatever he paid them was too much. But, sweet heaven, it would be good to rest her head.

'It is filthy,' Celia whined.

Murdoch growled. 'I have lost my maidservant. It is difficult to find the time to come up here to sort things out.'

Margaret signalled to Celia to hold her tongue. She felt suddenly very unsure of their welcome and thought it unwise to fuss. She hung her wet cloak on a peg by the door, pushed the soiled bedding to the floor and sat down on the mattress – which had little stuffing, and none of it sweet. She gestured to Celia to do likewise. Andrew perched on the edge of a table.

Murdoch folded his arms across his chest, leaned against the wall near the hide-covered doorway. 'Now what is this all about?'

'I must find Roger, Uncle,' said Margaret. 'I fear for him after Jack Sinclair's murder. I must warn him.'

'You call it murder, eh? What says murder and not a fight lost?'

Margaret could glean nothing from her uncle's expression. Feeling as if she were edging out onto thin ice, she tested it with, 'What can you tell me of his death?'

'Naught, but I've seen worse wounds from a brawl.'

'I never knew Jack to brawl,' she said softly, but firmly.

Murdoch snorted. 'All men like a fight.'

That was nothing Margaret was ready to judge, but she did not believe Jack had been brawling on the occasion of his death. 'I saw his body. His throat and his belly were slashed, Uncle. He was murdered.'

'How did you see?' Andrew asked, horrified.

She did not meet his eyes. 'I had to be certain it was him.'

Murdoch shook his head, pushed himself away from the wall. 'A fine job of consoling and reassuring her you did, Andrew.' He lowered his voice. 'You cannot poke about in these times, Maggie. You'll get yourself and me in trouble.' His voice at last held a flicker of warmth, which encouraged Margaret.

'I must find my husband,' she insisted.

'For all you know he found passage to Bruges and is with your father.' Malcolm Kerr had settled his affairs and fled to Bruges after the slaughter at Berwick the past spring, worried that Perth might be next.

'Roger thought Father's flight cowardly. He would not follow.'

Murdoch raised his uneven brows in doubt.

'When did you last see Roger?' Margaret asked.

Murdoch frowned down at the floor. 'I don't recall. Jack came here asking about him too. Why did you think Roger would be here?'

Margaret told him about the letter sent from Edinburgh.

'He sent only the one message?'

Margaret cursed herself for blushing as she nodded.

Murdoch grunted. 'You think to bide here while you look for a man who has no reason to be here and hasn't seen fit to send word to you since before Christmas?'

Margaret had expected resistance, but not unkindness. She tried to keep her voice steady, confident. 'I hoped my maid and I might be welcome.'

'And why should I welcome you? You'll be naught but trouble.'

Don't drop your head, she thought. *Don't let him know how you doubt yourself*. 'Kin are always welcome in the house of a Kerr.'

'In a house, mayhap. This is an inn. I depend on paying customers here. You two cannot bed with men – you need a chamber to yourselves. Two paying customers you lose me, or more.'

'I shall pay you,' Margaret said. She had thought he would not have much custom at present and could therefore spare the room. She felt very naïve.

Murdoch growled. 'I cannot take your siller, Maggie.'

For that she was grateful, for she had little, but it was not the time to inform her uncle of her penury.

Murdoch's voice softened. 'You should not be in Edinburgh. What would your father say if he sailed into Perth and heard you were down here among the English soldiers? They will come sniffing about. They can think of only one reason women might come to the town – to service them. Oh, Maggie, you must be gone. Back to Perth with you. And your fancy maid.'

Had her father cared he would not have left Perth. As for the soldiers, she had not thought of them as a danger to her unless she threatened them. She must have a care. But it did not sway her. 'I've sat at home since Martinmas, worrying. Imagining all the worst. That Roger is injured and has no one caring for him. Taken prisoner. That he has left me and begun another life.'

'He will come home, I am sure of it,' Murdoch said absently, turning his attention to Andrew. 'Could you not find Maggie fit lodgings in Canongate?'

Andrew threw up his hands. 'I did not know she meant to come until last night. I have not had time to make arrangements for her, but I shall do so.'

Risking irritating her uncle, but recalling how he had encouraged decisiveness in her, Margaret said, 'I will bide here, Uncle.'

She watched for Murdoch's reaction to her determination as Sim shuffled in with a flagon of wine and four cups. 'I'll bring a pie by and by,' the man muttered as he withdrew. A lad carried in some peat, began to fuss with the brazier. Celia told him she could manage and quickly set to it.

Murdoch did not outwardly react to her comment. When the servants departed, he nodded towards the wine. 'Drink up, Father Andrew. You will have little good wine at the abbey. Your abbot has no doubt sent it to King Edward's captains at Soutra Hospital, and what is left will be rationed among their wounded troops.' Edward had taken over the great Hospital of the Trinity on Soutra Hill, which straddled the highest point on the King's Highway between the border and Edinburgh.

'There is precious little good wine left this side of the Forth,' said Andrew. 'Where do you find yours – on Edward Longshanks' ships?'

Murdoch growled.

Margaret had had enough of their contention. 'What say you, Uncle? Will you turn us out, Celia and me?'

Murdoch dropped his eyes to hers, touched her chin with his rough hand. 'I have not convinced you to go home, lass? What do you need to hear?'

'News of my husband.'

A shadow flickered across Murdoch's face. 'We shall talk in the morn. You are a woman in need of bed.'

'Do you have clean linen?' Celia demanded.

The woman did not seem aware of how precarious their situation was. Margaret told her to be still.

Murdoch snorted. 'Find me a laundress and I will. Women are fearful to go down to the water with all the soldiers about.'

'Dry clothes, that is what I need,' Margaret said. 'And to warm myself down in the tavern for a while.'

The men withdrew so she might change. But when the hide fell in place over the doorway behind them, Margaret did not move. She had expected to fall back on the bed, exhausted. Instead she just sat there, benumbed by the horrible turn life had taken since she had last seen her uncle. Her husband was missing, Jack was dead, she had travelled a long way, with a difficult crossing, with little plan but to resolve Roger's disappearance, the town was so changed, so broken and subdued, and her uncle, whom she had not seen since her wedding, plainly wished her anywhere but here. She could not remember a worse time in her life.

'Mistress, you wished to change?' Celia said.

Margaret shook herself. She unhooked her scrip from her girdle, drew out the few coins she carried and the weight she had found in Jack's shroud. The coins she poured back in – she would keep the scrip hidden beneath her kirtle at all times, or beneath her pillow at night. Every penny was precious to her.

'Pay my uncle no heed, Celia. He will come round to understanding why I came.' She studied the weight. It might be a fishnet weight, though it was small and far too clean, unless it was new. It was also too small for a thatching weight. She was almost certain it was a loom weight. A weaver would tie the end of the warp to this to keep it close to the floor, the thread taut. It was not something she would expect Jack to clutch as he died, nor was it something he was likely to have clasped in a fight.

'Your hands are so cold,' Celia said, rubbing them, knocking the stone to the floor.

Slowly, stiff from the saddle, Margaret stooped to retrieve the weight. The movement made her dizzy.

'You have not eaten in hours.' Celia helped her to her feet, untied the laces at Margaret's back and wrists, let the gown slip to the floor. 'Step out of it,' she said softly.

Margaret moved because she was told. 'You have not eaten either.'

'I am not eager to taste the food down below.' Celia straightened with a wince.

Of course. It had been a long ride for anyone, let alone one who had apparently never sat astride a horse before. 'I'll send up ale and food – you won't wish to climb stairs tonight,' said Margaret.

'I have a salve for saddle sores.'

Margaret shook her head at the proud woman. 'The sores are the least of it.'

The tavern was welcomingly warm and busier, now it was early evening. A rowdy dice game attracted a crowd around the table by the door. Margaret was glad to see two other women in the room. At one table an elderly woman wrapped in a much-mended plaid quietly reasoned with a bald man who pounded the table to emphasise his argument. Another woman sat nodding by the brazier, leaning against a man who was listening intently to the other men sitting there. At the third table a man sat hunched over an ale, listening to the diatribe of the man across from him. Both were well dressed, and both occasionally stole glances at Andrew.

Her brother was the only solitary figure in the tavern, sitting at the table nearest the back door, through which Margaret had just come.

Nodding in greeting, he poured her a cup of wine from a flagon.

'I must be off to the abbey as soon as Murdoch returns,' he said brusquely. 'He is fetching food for you and Celia.'

'If you must be off, be off.' Though grateful to him for escorting her, Margaret wearied of his stern manner. 'There are other women here, I can' – a hush fell over the room as the street door opened –

'manage.' A few heads turned as her last word rang out in the sudden silence.

The newcomer smiled into the anxious faces as he drew a fiddle from beneath his cloak. It broke the spell – a few people called out greetings. Others merely returned to what they had been doing or saying. The fiddler leaned against the table shared by the elderly couple, resting one foot on a stool, tested the strings, adjusted one, and then began to play a jig.

'You'll not sleep up above till these folk go home,' Andrew said. 'I'll find more suitable lodgings for you. It won't be easy, mind you. Strangers are unwelcome. Anyone could be a spy.'

The fiddler's entrance had made that clear. But Margaret saw no need for Andrew to make the effort – a tavern full of gossip suited her. 'I am biding here.'

'You saw how he is – Murdoch is not the one to help you if you get into trouble or fall ill.'

The wine, the warmth, the comforting background patter and now the music cheered Margaret. She took her brother's hands in hers. 'All this worry about me. What of you? Is it so what Uncle Murdoch said of your abbot? Is he King Edward's man?'

Andrew squeezed her hands, then withdrew his. 'Our uncle blethers about what he does not know.' He glanced over at the men who had been watching him, looked away as he caught one staring.

'Do you know them?' Margaret asked.

'Aye, of course. Edinburgh is smaller than Perth – and do you not know everyone there?'

That did not need an answer – he knew she did. 'They do not appear friendly.'

Andrew snorted. 'Men are ever uneasy near their confessors. I shall ask about Canongate for lodgings that would suit you.'

'I shall bide here until I either find Roger or learn where he is and what he is doing.'

'Our uncle might disagree.'

'Then I must persuade him.'

Andrew sighed one of his annoying sighs. She did not think he had even attempted to understand her need to know what had become of Roger.

Her attention was caught by a drunk who had walked into their table, then muttered, 'Longshanks' canons, all of you,' before lurching on to the back door. Murdoch was just entering. The drunk gave a cry of surprise as the innkeeper grabbed him by the arm and, with his other hand in the small of the man's back, pushed him out the back door.

'Pay him no heed, Maggie,' Andrew said sharply, his face red.

'It would seem the clergy are the scapegoats for the town,' Margaret said.

'I told him he was better off at home,' Murdoch grumbled as he sat down beside Margaret. 'Keep the peace, that is the duty of a taverner. I won't abide such talk. It starts brawls. I'll not have it.'

Andrew had already risen and was fumbling with his cloak. 'Watch over Maggie, Uncle,' he said. It seemed to Margaret that he was trying to avoid looking anyone in the eye. He blessed them both, then with bowed head made his way through the crowd to the street door and departed.

Sim placed a trencher, the hollowed centre filled with a milky oat and broth paste, before Margaret. 'I took one up to your maid,' he said.

'That was kind,' said Margaret.

She had not known whether she could eat. But once she inhaled the steam rising off the oats, she could not help but break off a piece of the hard crust of bread and scoop up a mouthful. Her stomach received the hot food gladly.

'I thought you'd have an appetite after that journey,' Murdoch said. 'It is the sort of thing your mother would do – making that journey in a storm.'

Margaret ignored him and ate.

Murdoch was quiet, tapping his feet to the music for a time.

'Are all the canons blamed for their abbot's support of Longshanks?' she asked him after a while.

Murdoch grunted. 'If you would be wise, keep to yourself and trust none in this town, Maggie.'

Not comforting advice. But at least he seemed resigned to her staying. For the moment.

⇜§ 4 §⇝

NOT A GOOD BEGINNING

Murdoch had given Margaret and Celia his chamber. It was far cleaner than the room beside it, in which they had talked earlier, and boasted a shuttered window and a wooden door.

Celia stood ready to help Margaret undress. 'Let me help you with your boots, mistress.'

Margaret's boots had tightened as they dried. Now her feet hurt, though she had not noticed the pain until Celia mentioned the boots. She sat down on the one high-backed chair in the room – it squeaked when she leaned against the back. But her head felt so heavy she thought she would topple if she did not sit back. The chair held, but Celia was now ready for Margaret to stand to be unlaced from her kirtle.

At last Celia stood beside the curtained bed, a sheepskin in hand with which to crown the blankets and linens. As Margaret slipped her cold feet between the covers, she found Celia had warmed the bed with a hot stone and left it down at the foot. Margaret was grateful for the cosseting.

Lying there, feeling her tired body ease into the mattress, she prayed she would fall asleep at once. But the bed, though comfortable, was unfamiliar, the sounds from the tavern below intrusive and now and again jarring. All in all, conducive not to sleep but to worry. Her chest tightened and she had to will herself to breathe. With breath came tears. Useless, embarrassing tears. She tugged the curtains closed so Celia did not witness her weakness.

In a little while Celia crawled into the bed from the other side, but she said nothing.

Church bells woke Margaret. For a moment she lay still beneath the piled coverlets getting her bearings. Her eyes were swollen from weeping and burned when she blinked. Her head pounded. She must do better than this. Her time here might be brief if Murdoch did not soften towards her presence. She must put her fears aside and plan her search for Roger.

A full bladder sent her sliding out of the warm bed down to the cold floor, where she fumbled about for the chamber pot.

'I put the chamber pot outside the door,' Celia said in a drowsy voice. 'I shall fetch it.'

'I can fetch my own chamber pot. I mean to go to Mass at St Giles' if I can dress quickly enough.' Margaret hoped it might comfort her, give her strength.

'Widow Sinclair would not want her gooddaughter handling a chamber pot.' Celia groaned as she sat up. 'I must dress you. You must make a good impression.'

'There is no need. None will mark me.'

'I need to move about.' Celia rose with much effort, lit another lamp from the brazier.

The light gave Margaret a better view of the wooden bolt that secured the door from within. The wood was worn smooth where it slid across the braces. To protect her uncle as he slept? She unbolted the door, peered without and found that the full pot had been exchanged for an empty one. The servants at least understood that basic service.

Celia groped at her cap, stuffing her hair inside, tugging at her dress to smooth it. It had fallen from its hook in the night and dried wrinkled. 'This evening I shall take more care with my gown.' She looked dishevelled and sleepy. She winced as she moved about.

'You need not accompany me,' Margaret said, feeling her own stiffness from the saddle.

But Celia insisted, and fussed with Margaret's attire.

The wind caught their skirts on the stairs and tugged at Margaret's veil. A cat streaked across the yard, vanished. Old bean vines rattled over new growth. The two women slipped out to the alley between the two tall houses, emerging on the High Street. On the climb to St Giles' in the early morning grey the only living creatures they saw were rats and a well-bundled person sweeping the street outside a shop. It was too early for shops to be open or the market set up, but not too early for market carts to be arriving in the town, or for folk to be leading their livestock to graze, and there were none of those. It felt as if everyone in the town held their breath.

The Mass bell rang as they were halfway up the hill. Margaret gathered her skirts in her hands and walked faster. Celia tried to keep up, but eventually fell back, complaining that she was out of breath. Ignoring her, Margaret arrived at the kirk door, tidied herself, and slipped in. She hurried to join the worshippers standing towards the choir, where the rood screen separated them from the clergy. Celia limped to her side a moment later.

Her fellows numbered less than on a typical day in St John's, her kirk in Perth, and far fewer than in the abbey at Dunfermline. From the crowd in the tavern the previous evening, Margaret had expected more. Perhaps the folk who stayed in town preferred to get their courage from ale, not prayer.

The singing calmed her, as if the voices moved through her. She bowed her head, prayed for God's help for her mission, for Roger's safety and for Jack's soul. For Katherine, her goodmother, who must be feeling quite alone with Margaret and Celia away. There were other servants in the house, but none with whom her goodmother might talk about her grieving for Jack. Fifteen years

Roger's junior, Jack had been a comfort to Katherine when her own son had gone out into the world. Though Jack had been living in Perth the past six years as Roger's factor, he had not forgotten the aunt who raised him, returning to Dunfermline for feast days several times a year.

Margaret fought past the memory of Jack's corpse, back to an evening a few months past. He had arrived at her house to dine, his cheeks bright from the cold, his blond hair glistening with melting snowflakes. When the maid left them to take Jack's cloak to the kitchen to dry, he had grabbed Margaret's hand, holding it for a long moment with his head bent to it. She remembered the feel of his breath tickling her. She had been in a reckless mood and had let him take his time kissing her hand. He had been so close she could smell wood shavings from the warehouse on his boots and wine on his breath.

'You opened a shipment of wine and brought none for me?' she had teased when he at last let go of her hand.

When Roger was away Jack dined with Margaret on Saturdays and told her how the business was going. What merchandise had arrived from Germany or the Lowlands – wine, finished wool cloth, pottery, how much wool and leather goods they were shipping out. She enjoyed the dinners, feeling more a part of Roger's business than when he was at home.

It was after Martinmas that she had begun to notice how often she thought of Jack, and how she looked forward to Saturdays, fussing over her dress, helping the cook make Jack's favourite dishes. He was a handsome man with a cheerful humour who appreciated her intelligence. And yet he could be an exasperating tease; he enjoyed the effect he had on her as he did all women. She should not have encouraged his attentions. But it was difficult to separate all her feelings for him into proper and improper. She had not wished to offend him; she valued him too much as a good and loyal friend. And truth be told, she had enjoyed being appreciated as a desirable woman.

She fought the vision of his bloated body in the shroud, the horrible wounds. *Holy Mother of God, Roger must be alive*. They must be given a chance to have children, to have joy of one another. They had been separated so often she felt she had only begun to know Roger, only just stopped being tongue-tied and in awe of him.

Margaret did not know what would become of her if her search led to a corpse. Her father was in Bruges, her mother at Elcho Nunnery, Andrew in the Kirk, Fergus so young. Her heart lurched as a new fear arose. If Jack's murder had any connection with Roger's trading, Fergus might be in danger, all alone in Perth. *Sweet Jesus, watch over Fergus. Help him know his enemies.*

But none was safe with Edward Longshanks set on claiming the kingdom of Scotland. All knew how the Welsh had suffered. Many Scots had fought on Longshanks' side in that slaughter. She had heard it whispered that it was God's retribution for which they were now slaughtered in turn. But the dead of Berwick had been traders, merchants, not soldiers. And the English went unpunished. Folk said Longshanks was old now, and bitter with disappointment in his heir, which made him cruel. *Dear Lord, let him die and his weak son turn his eyes inwards, give up this battering of Lothian, the humiliation of our king, John Balliol.*

And bring Roger home. Her greatest fear was of being left alone, penniless and with an overwhelming grief, of use to no one and without even the means to withdraw into a nunnery. *I am too young for this, Lord, I've had no life yet.* Foolish prayer. Babies died every day. And young mothers. Who was she to expect any different treatment from God?

She glanced round at her fellow worshippers. The English lived in their midst now. She wondered what their thoughts were this morning. The man with the scab on his bald pate, was he mourning someone killed in the fighting, praying for deliverance from the English, or merely trying to keep himself from scratching the tender spot? What of the woman in the fine mantle beside her? She kept her eyes down, but her hands moved as if she were examining them. They looked swollen, much like Margaret's did after laundry day. The mantle must be her finest. Such delicate wool, woven loosely. Not warm, but lovely. The gown beneath the mantle was difficult to make out in the dim light.

Someone behind Margaret stank of urine, no doubt a cure for boils or foot ulcers. A woman muttered her prayers accompanied by gentle clicking sounds – she must have Pater Noster beads. That is what Margaret should have done to keep her mind on her prayers. She reached into the scrip she wore on her girdle; her fingers touched the loom weight among the beads. Such a light weight might be used to add to a weight that did not quite balance with its opposite. It might also be used for fine work. Like the mantle she had been admiring.

As people began to take their leave, Margaret turned to look at the woman beside her. Her profile and her walk pricked a memory, but Margaret could not place her.

'I could not help but notice your mantle,' said Margaret.

Never meeting her gaze, the woman turned and hastened away.

'And why would anyone talk to a stranger with things as they are in the town?' Celia said.

Indeed. But if someone had spoken thus to Margaret she would have been too curious to resist a glance in their direction.

Outside St Giles' a fog had moved in from the firth, rounding the corners of buildings, foreshortening the street. Margaret paused to get her bearings. Gradually the worshippers disappeared and the two women were alone but for the sweeper they had passed earlier, who had covered much distance since they had climbed the hill.

'Does he sweep all the town?' Margaret wondered aloud.

'I believe he is watching us,' Celia said as she looked the other way.

'Let us disappoint him with a brisk walk back to the inn.'

Margaret's spine tingled as they neared the man. She could not resist a 'God bless you' as she passed him.

'Bless 'e,' the man muttered.

The exchange calmed her. He might be precisely what he seemed, a street sweeper. She must not let the atmosphere in the town frighten her.

'St Columba!' Celia cried as she tripped, pitching forward into a puddle.

Margaret reached out to help her up, but Celia waved her away. 'You will muddy your sleeves.'

The woman was mad worrying about another's clothing when she was on her hands and knees in a puddle. Margaret grabbed Celia by the waist and supported her as she rose.

'I stumbled on a rock,' Celia muttered.

Margaret guessed that the maid's stiffness from the previous day's ride had caused her to stumble over her own skirt.

'Holy Mother,' Celia cried as she shook out her skirts, 'look at the mud.' A patch of her plaid mantle and the skirt of her russet gown were the same dark grey-brown. She brushed her hands together and muttered a curse.

'Are you injured?' Margaret took Celia's hands, turning them palms up. A few pebbles were lodged in the sticky mud, but though the skin at the edges looked red there was no blood. 'No cuts, that's a blessing. Let's get you back to our chamber.'

They continued slowly, Celia pausing several times to brush her hands as the mud dried.

Behind Murdoch's inn was a garden patch with the brown, slimy remains of the past harvest, and beyond it a low building whence came smoke and enticing smells. The kitchen, Margaret guessed.

'Go up, take off those wet clothes, and warm yourself,' she told Celia. 'I shall follow soon.'

Margaret headed for the small building. This was not where she had thought to find her uncle, but there he stood stirring something in a large pot. And watching the door with a black look.

'Where have you been?' he demanded.

'At St Giles'. Celia and I went to Mass.'

'Mass? After such a journey, and without an escort? Did I not tell you the women of Edinburgh cannot safely go about without an escort? Do you not know what soldiers are like? Half of them are felons pardoned by Longshanks to serve in his army.'

'You mentioned the laundresses yesterday. But there were other women at Mass.'

He shrugged his shoulders, shook his head. 'The trouble with your being here is I'll spend all my time worrying.'

'I am a married woman and run my own household. I do not need tending.'

'This place is nothing like your household.' Murdoch grabbed two bowls from a shelf, a ladle from a hook. His motions were not hesitant – he knew where everything was. 'Had you the patience I would have brought some of this up to you myself. A soup with winter roots, a bit of coney and even some beef.'

'God bless you. I am starving.'

'Sit down.' He ladled some soup into a bowl.

'Celia should have some of this,' Margaret said.

'In good time. You are the mistress.'

'She fell in the High Street. She's wet and muddy.'

'Is she injured?'

'Only her gown, I think.'

'Thank the Lord you women are protected by all your skirts and mantles. Now sit. She will still be peeling off the layers.'

Margaret sat down on a bench, put the bowl on a window sill and wondered at the amount of meat she stirred up with her spoon. The English would have it if they knew it was here.

'Do you cook for the tavern?' she asked after several spoonfuls.

'I cook for myself, no others. I have a cook for the tavern.'

'This is not the tavern kitchen?'

'That is farther in the backland.'

It was a large kitchen for one man. 'Might I dry Celia's wet clothing in here?'

Murdoch's short eyebrow twitched. 'I'll not have it. There's a brazier in your chamber.'

'It will be for ever drying. A good cook fire's what's needed.'

'Ask my tavern cook – Roy's his name. His kitchen's behind the next cottage – where the chambermaid bides when we have one.'

Not wanting to outstay her welcome, Margaret took her leave as soon as she was finished and carried a bowl of the fine soup and a chunk of dark bread up to Celia. The maid ate hastily, then gathered her wet clothes and set out for the tavern kitchen, hoping to wash out the mud before the stains set in.

Margaret felt weary to the bone, but when she lay down and closed her eyes, she felt them fluttering behind the lids as if trying to catch passing ghosts, and every creak set her heart racing. She thought it might help to get her bearings, that she might rest more easily once she had seen more of the inn, the backland, the town, and understood the sounds.

The rain had stopped, though the stiff breeze carried its scent. The backland stretched out behind Murdoch's kitchen. The chambermaid's lodging was a shed half the size of his kitchen, wattle and daub with a thatch roof. Margaret pushed at the door. Inside it was dusty and smelled of damp. There was a platform for a bed, a shelf for a candle, and a stool. A shuttered window faced back to Murdoch's kitchen. Water puddled in a corner of the packed-earth floor. It was a simple room, but with a brazier, a good oil lamp, and a wattle screen by the bed to block the draught from the window it would be as comfortable as many simple homes. With the leak that had caused the puddle fixed it could be the best home a servant had ever had. Margaret must ask her uncle what had happened to the maid.

Stepping out, she shut the door behind her and turned the corner to continue down the backland to the tavern kitchen. She thought she might come to Celia's aid if necessary.

The tavern kitchen was twice the size of the chambermaid's lodging, with a tile roof, smoke coming from the smoke hole in the centre, benches lining the outside wall either side of the door. Raised voices, Celia's and a man's, came from within.

A young man appeared in the doorway, a bowl cradled in one arm. He stirred the contents with the opposite hand. He was the one who had brought the peat for the brazier the previous day. Dark hair, dark eyes, solemn. His clothes were shabby, but clean. The cook's helper, she guessed.

He withdrew into the kitchen, but the argument did not falter.

'Surely it is Master Murdoch's kitchen,' Celia was saying quite steadily, in the tone of the righteous.

Margaret stepped across the threshold. The wild-haired man waving floury hands at Celia must be Roy, the cook.

'How can I work with your clothes flapping about?' He matched Celia's righteous tone.

The room was indeed crowded, with several small tables, a large fire circle, a wall of shelving, several benches, and the two men moving about their work. Murdoch must not have considered that when he suggested Celia do her laundry here.

'I see the problem,' Margaret said from the doorway. 'Send a basin of warm water, some soap and a cloth to our chamber and we'll manage there. Come, Celia.' And before the imperious pair could continue their argument Margaret grabbed her maid by the elbow.

'Send a basin of warm water?' Roy exclaimed in disbelief.

As Margaret shoved Celia through the door she said, 'As soon as the water is warm.'

Celia trembled with rage. Margaret did not let go of her until they gained the stairs. 'Now go up and wait, Celia.'

Two spots of colour and eyes that seemed to be generating heat dominated Celia's thin face. 'That man.'

'He is the cook, not a servant under you. Do not make me regret bringing you here.' It was too late for that, but Celia might not yet realise it.

Her eyes widened, but she said nothing, just turned and gathered her skirts, mounted the stairs.

Margaret peered into the tavern. Murdoch was bent over

someone lying on a bench by the cold brazier.

'Murdoch wastes his time,' a woman spoke softly behind her. 'There's no waking Old Will till he's sober.'

By the speaker's breath, she was not sober either. Margaret turned in the little space the woman allowed.

A piece of dirty plaid kept most of the woman's dark hair in check, though a long greasy strand hung down over her left eye. 'You don't look like a Kerr.'

'Do you have business with my uncle?'

The woman lifted dirty, large-knuckled hands. 'These make the finest ale in Edinburgh. Ask your uncle about Mary's ale.' She looked Margaret up and down, grinning. 'Roger Sinclair's wife, eh?'

Margaret felt a shiver down her back. 'Do you know my husband?'

'I ken all who come to the tavern.'

'So there you are, Mary,' Murdoch interrupted. 'What have you got for me?'

'When did you last see him?' Margaret asked, willing to risk irritating her uncle for news of Roger.

'Save your gossip for later,' Murdoch growled.

Margaret murmured a farewell, vowing to seek out the brewster another time, and left the tavern.

Out back once more, she noticed a stable off to the left, beside Murdoch's kitchen. Moving closer, she saw that it was conveniently at the edge of Netherbow. It had a large yard, but as she stepped within she saw that the stable itself was small, with room for no more than six horses. The air was heavy with the dust of hay. A young man sat beneath a hole in the roof that let in light. He hummed as he combed the mane of a large-eyed ass. Sensing someone approaching, he shook his head to clear his hair from his eyes, glanced up at Margaret, then dropped his gaze back to the ass. He had stopped humming.

A horse snorted in the opposite corner. Margaret approached the ass, holding out her hand. The animal sniffed it with interest, then dropped her muzzle so that she might be scratched between the ears. Margaret obliged. The ass was a gentle, lovely animal, well cared for.

'Are you Murdoch's groom?' Margaret asked the lad.

He had stopped combing and watched her through the unruly fair hair.

'Who is asking?'

'Dame Margaret Kerr, Master Murdoch's niece.'

'God bless.' He gathered his long legs and stood up to make a little bow, keeping his gaze towards the packed-mud floor. 'I am Hal, mistress.'

Margaret still scratched the ass's head. 'She is well cared for.'

'Bonny. She is the master's, and proud of her he is. She likes you.'

She was the first in Edinburgh to do so. 'Does my husband ride her when he's here?'

'Master Murdoch keeps Bonny to himself.'

'Have you met Roger Sinclair?'

'I meet only the folk who come in to see to their beasts themselves, mistress.'

A sly response.

'I am not spying on you. I have come to Edinburgh searching for my husband. Any word of him, any memory of his time here might help.'

Hal raked a hand through his hair, peered at her intently before his eyes were hidden once more. 'I didn't hear he was missing. I don't ken much about him, Dame Kerr. He's never been sharp with me, that I can say.' His mouth twitched into a smile, and Margaret realised she still stroked Bonny's soft muzzle. 'You've a gentle touch with animals.'

'I like them. They're often kinder than people.'

'Och, aye.'

Margaret heard Mary the brewster call out a farewell as she cut through the backland towards Cowgate. 'Can I trust her, Hal?'

'Mary? Most times.'

Margaret took her leave of Hal and Bonny, returning to the tavern.

Murdoch now had the bench overturned. He was cursing under his breath as he tightened a leg with a bit of straw.

An elderly man sat on the fetid floor watching a slow drip from the ceiling near the street door. Margaret guessed from his age and his drink- and sleep-flushed face that this was Old Will.

'She's a splasher, that one,' he said.

Murdoch muttered a curse.

'Such language afore your niece, Murdoch?' Old Will gathered himself and rose with a grunt and a moan.

Murdoch glanced up at Margaret. 'Tell that maid of yours to keep the water in the basin.'

The old man tottered over to Margaret. 'The young weaver might ken where your Roger is. She had an eye on his cousin.'

'Will!' Murdoch shouted. 'I told you to be off.'

It rang true, a woman attracted to Jack. 'What is the weaver's name?' Margaret asked.

Old Will licked his lips, shook his head to help his memory. 'Bess, is it? Aye, Bess.' He shuffled on out the back door.

Murdoch shook his head as Old Will stumbled on his way to the alley. 'That was his wife's name, Maggie. He calls most women "Bess". See to your maid. She'll be the ruin of me.'

'Was his wife a weaver?'

'She might have been. It's long ago.'

'But he said she had her eye on Jack.'

'Old Will dreams in his tankard, and he likes a pretty face – he wanted to keep you talking.' Murdoch shook his head at the wet spot on the ceiling and moved towards the stairs.

'I'll see to her.' Margaret pushed past him and hastened up to her chamber.

Celia knelt over a basin kneading her gown and splashing water as she cursed.

Margaret walked over to where the maid could see her. Celia looked up, her eyes flashing.

'Your wash water is dripping through the floorboards,' Margaret said.

Celia yanked her hands out of the basin and sat back on her heels. 'That filthy cook told Master Murdoch he should order me to do all the laundry.'

'It is not my uncle's place to give you orders. He knows that.'

'He agreed that I should.' She lifted her red hands to Margaret. 'How can I handle fine fabrics with rough hands?'

'Stop your fretting and hang your gown to dry. It is surely clean by now.'

It was not a good beginning.

On the following morning the rain poured down in sheets, soaking Margaret in the short walk between the house and Murdoch's kitchen. She shook herself as she stepped across the stone threshold. The room was unoccupied, but a pot of broth simmered over the fire circle in the middle of the room and from the oven near it came a welcome warmth and an equally welcome aroma of fresh bread. Margaret walked slowly around the room, looking for a sense of her uncle in it. The wattle and daub walls had been much repaired, with patchwork plaster from which radiated hairline cracks, and water marks where the walls met the slate roof. A boarded-up window on the wall opposite the oven hosted a vine that twisted in through the slats and disappeared into the roof. The remaining window was on the wall with the door, looking out on the chambermaid's cottage and the tavern kitchen, not towards the tavern. Dried herbs hung from the rafters. Roots were stored in a shallow pit beneath a trapdoor far from the fires. This had not been fixed up by the same hand as Murdoch's bedchamber. There was no feel of a woman here.

'Bring that lopsided pot over for these, would you?' Murdoch stood in the doorway with an apron full of dried apples.

Margaret found the pot, held it for the tumble of fruit.

Murdoch took the full pot from her, carried it to a trestle table. 'Is your curiosity about my kitchen satisfied?' He picked up a knife, turned his back to Margaret and began to core.

'You wield that knife so well. I cannot recall Father ever picking up a knife in the kitchen.'

'Nor did your mother, I would wager. Too busy with her prophecies.' He sounded angry.

Margaret thought he still fumed about Celia's washing. 'I'll not allow Celia to wash up above again.'

'It was my fault,' he said, surprising her. 'I had forgotten Roy would likely be unfriendly.'

'You could predict he would not like Celia?'

Murdoch shook his head. 'Women. He was unfortunate in loving Belle, the chambermaid. She went off with a man who offered her safety to the north.'

'And Roy blames all women?'

'He'll mend in time.'

'You've been unable to find another chambermaid?'

'Aye. You have complaints about the bedchamber?'

'No. I thought that if you or someone else would show me the guest chambers, and where you keep mops, rags, brooms, and buckets, I could be of use to you.'

'As you can see, I am busy.'

They were dried apples and could keep. Unless he meant to toss them in the pot. But what was in there did not smell like it would mix with apples.

'Then let me help you with the apples.'

'Sweet Jesus.' He threw down the coring knife. 'Can a man have no peace?' His eyes glared beneath the uneven brows.

'I would like to help.'

Murdoch stirred the pot, took off his apron. 'Come on, then. I see you must not be idle.'

He hurried her through the rain to a lean-to on the corner of the tall house across the alley from the tavern. Opening a poorly fitted plank door, he stepped aside to reveal a collection of sorry-looking brooms, buckets, rags (she was certain they were home to a nest of rats or mice) and a ladder.

'Roy keeps the soap.'

Murdoch closed the lean-to, slogged through a puddle to a short stairway leading up to a door that opened onto the first floor.

'This house is part of the inn?'

'Aye.'

'What is down below?'

'A storeroom.'

The landing above the stairs was broader than in the other house.

'Three rooms up here,' Murdoch said, opening the first door. It was larger than either of the guest chambers next door, with two beds and a shuttered window facing the backlands. A wall of wattle hurdles separated one room from the next so that the shape of the room could easily be changed. The second room was also configured to be large, with many pallets and a tiny window high up, shuttered also. The third was a smaller room with a window towards the back and a fair-sized bed that took up most of the space.

'I am sleeping here at present,' Murdoch said.

'You could plant a garden in the dirt and dust.'

'I would not mind some tidying.' He caught her eye. 'I would be a fool to turn down your offer, eh?' He did not smile, but his anger had cooled.

'What of the storeroom?'

'We shift things often enough it needs no cleaning. Tend to what is suitable, the guest rooms. While they are empty!'

They descended to the backlands and bowed their heads against the rain that pelted them on their way to the stairway that led to her chamber. The stairway was roofed, praise God. Margaret already felt the damp soaking through her clothes and shoes. On the floor on which she was staying, Murdoch showed her the room to the right, which was the chamber in which they had talked on their arrival. The bed had been tidied, a man's tunic lay on an ancient chest, a pack lay on the floor. It was a wide enough bed to sleep two or three. The room opposite was much larger, with several pallets and one substantial bed without bed hangings. A man snored beneath a tattered hide. Two cloaks hung on hooks on the wall, some clothes were strewn on one of the pallets. The air in the room was stale – surprising with the draught from the doorway. Both doorways were covered by hides, not wooden doors. How cold it must be to lie on the floor in the draught.

'You will not interfere with the business of the tavern, Maggie.'

'This will be sufficient. I have a husband to find.'

'If it's too much work, find a good replacement for me, eh?' At last Murdoch smiled. 'Now I have work to do. And so do you.' He bowed to her and headed down the stairs.

She thanked God her uncle had accepted her offer. It would buy her time.

5

A Face in the Rain

Margaret tucked her hair up in a cap and the front hem of her gown up in her girdle, wrapped cloths round her forearms to protect her sleeves, and set to cleaning Murdoch's temporary chamber. Celia daintily dusted the doorway, the furniture.

'For pity's sake, clean the rest of the room before cleaning the furniture,' Margaret said, losing patience. 'The ceilings and the wattle walls are full of dust that will just settle again on the furnishings.'

'I was sent here to be your maid, not a chambermaid.' Celia flicked dust off her shoulders.

Margaret fought the urge to slap her. 'Neither am I a chambermaid, eh? But as my uncle was good enough to give us his room, this is the least we can do for him.'

'I would as lief stay in a less favoured room at such a price.' Celia regarded the rafters with a grimace and a shudder.

'You would speak to me in such a manner?' Who did she think she was? 'I am done with making apologies for you. You're of no use to me and you never will be. I don't know what my goodmother sees in you. You do nothing for your keep.'

Celia had dropped her gaze to the floor.

'Get yourself off to the chambermaid's cot. You will sleep there

56

until I arrange an escort for you back to Widow Sinclair, where the work is more to your liking. I'll ask my brother to make arrangements.'

Celia glanced up at that, her jaw dropping unbecomingly.

'Get you gone,' Margaret repeated, waving the maid on with a dusty cloth that produced a cloud she thought certain to disgust the dainty woman.

Celia tossed her cloth to the floor. 'Look at my hands.' She held them out, palms down. The nails were even and clean, the skin unbroken.

'A lady's hands,' Margaret said. 'I am not surprised.'

Celia turned her palms up. 'It took a long while to soften and smooth them so my mistress would let me touch her silk gowns.'

'So be off in search of your lady.'

'I thought as Master Roger's wife you would at least live as well as my mistress.'

The comment brought Margaret up short of a retort. It was in truth a reasonable expectation – in other times, with another husband. 'So did I.' Caught off her guard, Margaret spoke more from the heart than she had intended.

Celia dropped her hands, looking confused.

'Go now.'

Bobbing an awkward curtsy, Celia hurried out.

Climbing up onto a stool, Margaret snapped her cloth at a cobweb, angry that she had lost her temper and revealed her pain to the woman. She swung at another web. The dust caught in her throat, made her eyes teary. Two years of marriage had brought her to this. It was Roger's fault that she had half fallen in love with Jack, Roger's fault that Jack was dead, Roger's fault that she was childless. In what way was she a wife? She shoved the cloth along the rafter.

Blood bloomed on the cloth as a sharp pain reached her consciousness. She dropped from the stool, sank down on it, examined her hand. A large splinter lay beneath the fleshy base of her thumb inside her palm. She held her breath as she drew it out. Sweet Jesus. It was worse in the coming out than in the sinking in. She sank her hand into a bowl of rainwater that had collected beneath a drip and said several Hail Marys, then tore a strip from the cleanest side of the cloth protecting her left sleeve and wrapped her hand.

It throbbed, and her mind was unquiet. She needed air. A walk was what she wanted, but the rain dripped steadily into the now bloodstained water and drummed on the roof above her. No matter, it would wash away her thoughts, her irritation, cool her hot hand.

Donning her old plaid mantle she slipped down the stairs, through the alley and on to the High Street.

The rain slanted down, making her blink. She pulled the edge of the mantle forward on her head and splashed up the street through puddles. Her toes were soon wet and cold, then her heels, then her ankles. New boots had been out of the question last autumn when money dwindled. She wished she had thought to bring pattens; but the idea of sitting idle in her chamber was too dreary.

So she moved on. Beneath the tron in the marketplace she could not help but pause. Here was where Andrew heard Jack had lain, somewhere beneath this weigh beam, nine days ago. Discovered early in the morning, he must have been murdered during the night. Someone who lived within sight of the tron might have seen something, at least heard a cry. Jack would not be struck down without a struggle, without a shout of anger or terror. Surely someone remembered that night, such a violent attack. She backed beneath the eaves of the nearest house and considered the houses that clustered round. Light shone through the shutters of one just opposite her, directly across from the tron. She should ask her uncle who lived there.

She moved farther beneath the eaves as a half dozen men approached the market area, voices low. There was a stealth in their movements. When they were almost past her, she felt her eyes drawn to one of them. It was difficult to pick out features with the veil of rain and gloom, but the man's stride, the way he leaned forward with his upper body as he walked was familiar – dear God, Roger held himself so. The man moved out from the shadow of the overhangs. 'Roger,' she whispered, taking a step forward. He could not have heard her, but he glanced her way, then turned more fully towards her, walking backwards a few steps. She reached out towards him. Sweet Jesu, the left side of his face was striped with wounds. 'Roger!' Margaret called out and ran towards him. He hesitated, but two of the other men grabbed him and pulled him with them. They ran across the street and disappeared down a close.

Margaret pursued, increasing her speed until her lungs hurt.

'Halt!' a man cried behind her.

She heard more than one set of boots chasing her, but she kept running. A piece of cloak fluttered behind one of the men ahead as he turned into a wynd. She slipped, caught herself, hurried round the corner. Empty. She wept, kept running, sobbing, 'Roger!'

A hand grabbed her arm, jerking her to a halt. She turned and blindly struck out with her fists not caring who it was. Damn him for stopping her. Damn him!

'That was my husband,' she cried. Her blows made contact with a fleshy face before her arms were pulled behind her, causing her mantle to fall away. She screamed with pain. The man in front of her shook her by the shoulders until she stopped struggling and quieted.

'Why were you chasing those men?' Water dripped down the soldier's forehead. He shook it away.

'One of them was my husband. I have not seen him for months. I did not even know whether he was alive. You made me lose him.'

'In this gloom how can you be certain it was him?'

'A woman kens her husband,' she said through chattering teeth.

Her arms were released.

'They cannot be far,' one of the soldiers said.

Margaret rubbed her upper arms as both men took off in the direction in which Roger had disappeared. She closed her eyes, trying to remember every detail of what she had seen. Four gashes on his face, perhaps more. He had stopped, looked at her. It was the others who pulled him away. Was he a prisoner? Had the men with him wounded him? But he had not seemed a prisoner when they approached, only when he hesitated as if meaning to turn back to her. Why? Damn those soldiers for stopping her. She might even now be with Roger. Would he embrace her? He had not seemed indifferent, he had stopped, had not tried to ignore her.

Sweet Jesus, he was alive. She choked back a sob as she began to run again, then stopped, realising too much time had passed, she had no hope of finding him now. It was not such a large town, but big enough for a man who did not wish to be followed.

And then she realised: Murdoch must have known Roger was in Edinburgh. He heard all the gossip in the tavern. Yet he had not told her. She did not know what to make of that, but it frightened her. Everyone was turning on her. No one was as they had seemed. It was as Murdoch had said, she should trust no one.

Slowly, in a daze, she bent to pick up her sodden mantle, then headed down the High Street, shivering in her wet clothes. From behind she heard the soldiers returning, but she did not bother to look up.

'We found no traces of them,' one of the soldiers said as he fell into step beside her.

'What did you expect? You wasted the time stopping me.'

'It is our duty to question all those who disturb the king's peace.'

Whose king? she wondered, but she was beginning to know better than to speak in such wise. 'Why did you chase me? Why not them?'

'They ran only when you shouted to them.'

Not true. Or was it? 'My husband was wounded. Stripes of blood down the left side of his face, deep enough for me to see in the rain. Have you seen such a man?'

'I do not recall a man with such wounds.'

Margaret did not even know whether Roger was their king's prisoner or supporter. She knew so little about him.

The soldier asked pardon for hurting her, more kindness than she had expected.

'My pain is in losing sight of him.'

The soldier declared he would escort her home, and insisted on giving her his mantle. 'I am sorry about your husband.'

She walked in silence, wondering frantically about Roger's wounds, the men accompanying him. In front of the alley between the inn buildings she paused, lifting the mantle from her shoulders and holding it out to the soldier with thanks.

'If I see a man with a wounded cheek I shall direct him here,' the soldier said, and with a bow he headed back the way they had come.

Margaret took the alley to the back.

Murdoch caught up with her. 'God's blood, escorted to my tavern by a man wearing the badge of an English soldier. Do you want me cursed by all my customers?'

'I saw Roger.'

'What? Is he now fighting in Edward Longshanks' army?' Murdoch touched the bandage on her hand. 'Did they injure you?'

She glanced down, having forgotten why she had ventured out into the rain. 'I cut myself earlier.' But everything had changed since then. 'Roger is alive, Uncle. I saw him.' She did not know whether to rejoice or weep.

'You are shivering. Come.' Murdoch put his arm round her and led her to his kitchen. She sank down on a bench he drew close to the fire circle.

'What is this about seeing Roger?'

Haltingly, she began the story, but when Murdoch handed her a cup of mulled wine she stopped to drink.

'Clouds, rain, the smoke from fires – how close did he come to you that you recognised him?'

'I might have touched him in three strides.'

'Fairly close, then. But are you certain it was him?'

'He is my husband. I know him.'

'It would not be the first time the heart betrayed the eyes, Maggie.' He did not believe her – his gaze was soft with sympathy. 'I pray you are right.' He frowned down at her a moment. 'Were they headed towards the castle or away?'

Perhaps he did not doubt her. Buoyed by the question, she stumbled over her words. 'They were walking up the High Street, towards the kirk, the castle, how can I know? But when they ran it was towards Cowgate.'

Murdoch took her mantle, hung it over a bench by the fire. 'Your bandage is bloody.' He crouched down, began to unwind it.

Margaret embarrassed herself by beginning to weep afresh.

'Och lassie,' Murdoch gathered her in his arms. 'He does not know how to be a husband.'

With a stern act of will she gradually stopped the tears, remembering her uncle might have known of Roger's presence. 'Did you know Roger was here?' she asked.

Murdoch drew back from her, eyeing her with puzzlement. 'Why would I keep that from you? I'd be free of you. I'll fetch your maid to see to your wound.'

The earlier scene with Celia came flooding back. 'I banished her to the chambermaid's cot.'

'What?'

'She is of no use to me. She wishes to be a lady's maid, handling silk, sewing pearls on scarlett. So I said I'd find an escort to take her back to Dunfermline.'

Murdoch snorted. 'No wonder she has been searching for you. But she can at least see to your hand.'

He withdrew, leaving Margaret in a nauseating swirl of emotion. Might she have imagined it was Roger? But he had hesitated, turned towards her. A stranger would not do that. *Holy Mother, help me find him.*

*

Celia had apologised. Margaret had forgiven her and invited her back to the chamber. But Celia chose to stay the night in the chambermaid's cot 'in case your husband should come to you'. Margaret tried not to hope that would happen.

At the moment she was trying to distract herself by examining her bedchamber. Except for a draught that ran across the floor, it was very comfortable. Not the sort of room Margaret imagined Murdoch in. The walls were plastered and had painted borders. Though creaky, the high-backed chair was a luxury. The bed hangings were fine twill. The pillows were down-filled and the linen covers were embroidered at one edge. The mattress had been aired recently. She wondered who the woman was who fussed with this room and no others that Margaret had seen.

With a pin Margaret worked at the lock on a chest in the corner, hoping to find some evidence of the woman in Murdoch's life. Picking locks was a skill her uncle had taught her when she was small. Her mother would lock trunks of stores and lose the keys. He had given her tools for more complicated locks. When she opened the chest she was disappointed – inside were only her uncle's clothes, more covers and an extra pillow. He must have already removed whatever had been valuable or revealing.

Or perhaps she was wrong about a woman. Perhaps her uncle was as alone as she was. And more fastidious than she had thought.

She had begun to doubt she had seen her husband. She cursed herself for calling out Roger's name. She should have quietly followed the men. But she had been so astonished to see him, and she had not expected him to run from her. Perhaps the man had realised at that moment that he did not know her.

Restless, she paced from one end of the room to the other, from one corner to the opposite. A tread on the floor without her door made her heart race, but the footsteps continued into one of the other chambers. A shout down below pulled her to the window, but it was one man calling out to another. She cursed Celia for planting the hope in her head. Roger had run from her. He had been running from her ever since the day they had wed. Perhaps he had watched her enter Edinburgh, knew very well where she was. She must quit this foolish vigil and go to sleep. Her legs ached too much for such pacing.

At last she lay down on the bed, drew the curtains, but she lay awake listening to the sounds from the tavern below. She was still awake when Murdoch called the curfew. Soon all she heard was the rattle of empty tankards, the faint noise of tidying, Murdoch calling to someone, the front-door bolt clanging into place. In the young silence she heard a rat somewhere in the roof, the lonely wail of a cat defending its hunting ground.

Something scratched at the door. Margaret scurried to her feet. 'Roger?'

A cat mewed.

A much more likely visitor than Roger. She threw on her mantle, slipped her feet into her shoes. She shoved the bolt aside, opened the door slowly. The cat's eyes glowed. Margaret bent to pet it, but it led her across the vestibule to the opposite door, scratched to be let out. Men talked quietly in the guest chamber to the right.

She opened the door to the outside stairs. The yard was dark, quiet except for some skittering near the tavern's back door. The cat rubbed against her leg, then slinked off down the stairs.

As she turned to go in, Margaret heard footsteps below. But she could see no one when she looked down. It sounded like several people. A knock on the ground-floor door of the other inn building startled her. A dim light appeared as the door to what Murdoch had called his storeroom opened. A man stepped aside, three men entered. The door shut.

Margaret returned to her room, closed the door and bolted it behind her.

She gave up trying to sleep before the bell chimed for Mass. Her aching hand and her confused feelings about Roger had given her a restless night. At one point she had stoked the brazier embers for enough light to check that her hand was not twice its normal size, but it was not as swollen as it felt. She was glad, for she had much work to do.

The bandage made her clumsy. Her clothes fought her. But she managed to dress warmly for morning Mass and took a lantern for the pre-dawn walk to St Giles'.

Past the other rooms she slipped, out the wooden door to the stair landing. Down below, the first step creaked. Margaret shuttered her lantern and backed against the door.

'It is Hal, from the stable, Dame Kerr.'

She let out her held breath, opened the shutter and went down to him.

Hal watched her descent, but the moment she reached his level he dropped his head.

'What do you want, frightening me like that?' she asked.

He said something, but it was necessary to ask him to repeat it. He raised his chin just enough to be better heard.

'I am to go with you wherever you wish to go, Dame Kerr.'

'This is a turn. My uncle's orders?' She had not thought he would go to such efforts to protect her – or to know her movements.

'Aye.'

'How do you come to be here now?'

'He said you might slip out for Mass.'

So her uncle did not wish her to be escorted by a soldier again. But she wondered how was this young man to prevent that. She opened her mouth to protest, then thought better of burdening him with her lack of faith.

'Then I welcome your company to St Giles',' she said.

As they walked she enquired whether he could find some fresh straw for the tavern floor.

'Difficult, mistress. The English soldiers have many beds to make and horses to stable.'

'But not impossible.'

'No.' He did not sound happy.

'Do you know of any weavers in the town?' She had spent much of the night wondering about a connection between the loom weight and the young weaver Old Will had mentioned.

'Goodwife Janet by Blackfriars.'

'Another called Bess?'

'Goodwife Janet would know.'

'Then you must take me there later.'

⊰ 6 ⊱

HE MIGHT HAVE WARNED HER

Celia had tidied the chamber and brought up food and drink for Margaret as soon as she returned from Mass. Margaret saw the question in the maid's eyes but did not enlighten her about whether Roger had come in the night. No doubt she already knew he had not – servants had their ways of kenning.

The ale was just beginning to warm Margaret's toes when Murdoch knocked on the door and told Celia he wished to speak to her mistress alone. As Celia slipped away, Murdoch settled himself across the table from Margaret, his chair set sideways.

'Hal has asked permission to escort you to Janet Webster's this morning. Why?'

'You said he was to go with me where I wished.'

'But why the weaver? Because of what Old Will said? He was drunk, Maggie, thinking of his dead wife.'

'I have my reasons.'

Murdoch was not looking at her, but the floor, or perhaps his worn shoes from which one of his small toes stuck out. His sock was dirty.

'You need a laundress,' Margaret noted.

'That is not news to me. Why would you speak with Janet?'

'You know why I am here, Uncle. Is there something you should tell me before someone else does it for you?'

'What do you know of your husband, lass?' Now he looked her in the eye.

His look, his tone made her lose her appetite. 'It is plain from your face that whatever I know, it is not enough.'

'How often has he been at home for any time?' Murdoch pressed.

Her heart pounded. 'He is a merchant. He—'

Murdoch banged his fist on the table, his breath coming in angry bursts. 'A merchant. An excuse for long absences and no one the wiser to his other life.'

'What are you saying?'

'He has used you ill, that is what I am saying. He has the prize of Perth, of all Scotland, and he stays away. Fie on him.'

'Tell me what you know, Uncle.' Margaret reached for her cup, but she did not trust herself to hold it steadily. She sat on her hands. 'I must hear it. I must know what I face.'

Murdoch, elbows on knees, dropped his head to his hands for a moment. Then with a great sigh he straightened. 'Just afore the summons to Berwick last summer, Roger brought a woman here, asked if she could bide at the inn until she found a more permanent home. She had fled Berwick.'

Margaret felt the heat rise to her face. She took a great, long drink. 'Go on,' she said.

'I tell you this only because you will eventually hear of Mistress Grey.'

'Is she here now? In Edinburgh?'

Murdoch shook his head. 'She left the town after Christmas.'

'Have you seen Roger since?'

'Once. He did not speak of her.' Murdoch rose to fetch the pitcher, filled her cup.

Beautiful, she thought. *Younger even than me.* 'Tell me about her.'

'She is his age, I would guess. Two score, I would say. Handsome of manner and dress, and speech, aye, she has a noble way of speaking. Not bonny. Dark hair. The gossips thought her a lady in disguise or a lord's mistress. Mistress Grey she calls herself. No

Christian name that she admits to.'

A lady in disguise or a lord's mistress? 'Is this how he spends our siller?' Margaret would kill Roger if ever she saw him again.

'She is not his mistress, if that's what you're thinking, and of course you are. Roger could not have dressed the woman in such finery, Maggie. Nor could he have paid for the food and drink she demanded.'

The costly curtains and bedding. 'She stayed here, in your chamber,' Margaret said dully. 'It was she who had the bed curtains made, painted the walls.'

'Aye.'

Margaret rose. 'I cannot stay here another night. I must move my things.'

'Sit down, Maggie. I thought of telling you last night, when it seemed Andrew had not yet told you, hoping you would turn round and flee to safety across the Forth.'

'Did Jack know about her?'

'I don't know, Maggie. I saw Jack Sinclair but once this winter. He asked for Roger, stayed long enough to tell me how you fared, then was gone.'

'Near the time he died?'

Murdoch shook his head. 'More than a fortnight ere he was found.'

'Where did Roger stay?'

'Sometimes in the room I have now, when he was in the town. He never stayed a long, unbroken stretch. He'd be weeks away, then return for a few days. Mistress Grey never behaved as if she missed him. It was as if she knew where he was and how long he would be gone.'

It would be difficult enough to learn this of her husband, but harder yet to realise how public was her shame. No wonder Mary the brewster had been curious. 'Celia can help me move my things.'

'Stay, Maggie. It is the safest room in the inn. I tell you again,

Mistress Grey was not Roger's mistress. She was above his station.'

Margaret turned away from him. 'Then what were they – are they – to each other? Why does he spend more time with her than with me?'

'They worked together in some way, so I believe. Informants or messengers, or both.'

'For John Balliol or Edward Longshanks?'

'I pray they were not involved in anything of such import.' Murdoch shook his head. 'I was gey happy when she left.'

Margaret sank back down on the chair. 'Why did you permit her to stay?'

'I was not quick to realise she could bring me trouble.'

'You did not ask her business? Nor did you ask Roger?'

'You must learn, Maggie. These days you ask no man or woman their business. You will not get the truth, and you may reap trouble.'

'Roger told me nothing of this, Uncle, nothing.'

'He might have meant to protect you.'

'He betrays my love with every step. What am I to do?'

Murdoch moved towards her.

She shook her head. Silence was what she needed, a moment to catch her breath. All these months she had expected to comfort Roger when he returned, to bury her anger at his absence once she knew the cause. She had ached so for him. But at the moment she felt only anger and a frightening loneliness. When she felt steadier, she said in what she hoped was a stronger voice, 'I still mean to find him. And to find Jack's murderer.'

Murdoch's expression changed from sympathetic to curious. 'You seem equally upset about Roger and Jack Sinclair.'

'Jack was Roger's cousin and factor.'

'Maggie,' Murdoch said softly, 'did you—?'

'Roger is my husband, Uncle, though he does not act it. I keep my vows. As for Jack, I feel responsible. It was my brooding over Roger that committed him to come here to search.'

'I thought he'd come on Alan Fletcher's business.'

'He grabbed the chance.'

'But Fletcher sent him.'

'He would not have left me if he had not thought it a chance to find Roger.'

Murdoch shook his head at her. 'Jack is not the only person to die in this town of late, Maggie.'

'Roger?'

'I do not speak of him.'

'Who then?'

'Many. That is my point. Within days of Jack's death, a man's body was found on the bank of the River Tummel east of Holyrood Abbey. And a week ago a woman was raped in the close by her own home, then her husband was executed for threatening the life of the guilty English soldier. The widow has disappeared.'

'Is she dead?'

'Who knows? Listen to what I am saying, Maggie. Edinburgh is a dangerous place, especially for someone asking questions that might bring them to the notice of the English.'

'Is that why you set Hal to watch me?'

'Damn it, I set him to protect you, Maggie, don't twist my actions. But it's not enough. You should return to Perth.'

Margaret did not answer. Celia knocked on the door, opened it at Margaret's invitation.

'We are finished?' Murdoch asked.

'For now. I need to think.'

Uncle and niece regarded Celia silently. She looked from one to the other, smiled uncertainly. 'Forgive me if I intrude.'

'Do I have Hal as escort to Janet Webster's?' Margaret asked.

Murdoch shook his head, but said, 'Aye.' Mumbling some complaint, he departed.

Margaret considered the bedchamber while Celia took the uneaten food away. The sprigs of heather and broom painted on the walls sickened her now that she knew they had livened the room for Mistress Grey. It was not difficult to imagine that the mysterious woman knew Roger better than Margaret did. Perhaps he thought that compared with Mistress Grey his wife lacked wits.

Damn him. How many nights when she lay awake worrying about Roger had he sat in this comfortable room with Mistress Grey? Or down in the tavern? Nothing had prevented him sending more messages to Margaret. He had not chosen to. Neither had her uncle.

And as for her brother Andrew, he must have heard about Mistress Grey – the canons of Holyrood were not likely immune to gossip. He might have warned her long ago, saved her the shock of hearing it now, after she had slept three nights in the woman's chamber. Margaret grabbed her cloak. She did not believe in wasting anger. She went to the stable, hoping to find Bonny unattended. But Hal was there, raking out a stall.

'You look busy,' she said. It was a long walk to Holyrood Abbey, through Netherbow and all the way down the hill, as far again as from here to the castle. She eyed Bonny.

Hal pushed back his hair, but kept his chin down, eyes averted. 'You would go to the weaver now?' He mumbled his words.

'Not yet. I have business at the abbey. How difficult is it to get past the guards at Netherbow?'

The hair flowed back over his eyes. 'We are free to come and go. They will ask you some questions, but they will not fuss.'

'It is a goodly walk.'

Hal nodded. 'A hard climb back.'

'Might I borrow Bonny?'

'You must ask Master Murdoch.'

'I would rather not.'

The young man studied his hands for a moment. They were large hands for a lad, and encrusted with dirt. Then he actually raised his eyes to Margaret's. 'Are you plotting trouble?'

She wondered whether he sensed her agitation. 'No. Visiting my brother.'

'But you don't want Master Murdoch to ken?'

This required a small lie. 'He does not agree that I might be better lodged elsewhere.'

Hal wrinkled his brow, considering.

'You must go with me, either way.'

'Aye,' he said to Margaret's feet. 'I'll lead you on Bonny.'

Margaret slipped out of the stable, went to wait in the alley. The ass sniffed the air as she approached Margaret. Hal stopped, steadied Bonny while Margaret mounted.

The afternoon was dry, with a brisk wind and scudding clouds. The guards at the archway were busy examining a laden cart and waved them on. Behind Margaret, Edinburgh Castle rose on its rock high above the lower cluster of buildings. The spires of St Giles' were lost against the crag. Below her, houses lined the street leading to the Abbey of Holyrood, which dominated the hollow below. Beyond the abbey complex rose a steep, rocky crag known as Arthur's Seat that was even higher than that on which sat Edinburgh Castle.

'Up here many houses were burned by King Edward's army.' Hal nodded to several burned shells. 'Down farther most of the houses were spared.'

Canongate seemed a lovely, open place after Edinburgh. The plots were larger, the houses more sprawling than stacked. 'Who lives here besides canons?'

'Some folk with shops in Edinburgh. Some landowners have town houses here.'

Father Andrew sat at prayer in the cloister blowing on his hands frequently. Though the sun shone, the wind was still chilly. He did not know why he stayed – his mind was too full to pray. A servant approached, settling his gaze on Andrew as he spotted him. Perhaps Goodwife Logan had changed her mind about lodging Margaret. Andrew nodded to the servant.

'Dame Kerr has come to see you, Father Andrew. She awaits you in the parlour.'

Crossing himself and dusting off his habit, Andrew made his way to the parlour. How annoying. No doubt she came alone and he would need to find someone to escort her back.

Margaret looked agitated. He could tell by how she tucked her hands beneath her mantle, as if they could not be trusted. Her eyelids were swollen. Heaven knew what Murdoch had seen fit to tell her.

'*Benedicte*, Maggie. I did not think to see you here.'

'*Benedicte*, Andrew.'

'Did you come without escort?'

'No. A young man led me into Canongate on an ass. Like the Blessed Virgin entering Bethlehem.' She smiled, but it was a cold twist of her mouth. Already Edinburgh poisoned her.

'You are not as content at uncle's inn as you thought to be?'

'Why didn't you tell me of Mistress Grey?'

St Columba, Murdoch had told her of the woman so soon? 'All merchants have mistresses, Maggie.'

'Do they?' she snapped, then her eyes widened. 'So she *was* his mistress.'

The mysterious Mistress Grey was not someone he wished to discuss with Margaret. 'Who told you about her?'

'What does it matter?'

'Uncle Murdoch?'

'He assured me she was too grand to be Roger's mistress.'

Andrew would like to know what Murdoch thought Mistress Grey was to Sinclair if not a mistress. 'I am sorry you heard of her all the same, Maggie.'

'She stayed in the room I slept in the past three nights.'

Here was safe ground. He told Margaret he had already discussed her lodging with one of the women of the parish. She was unable to accommodate Margaret, but there were others to ask.

'It is a steep climb from here to Edinburgh,' Margaret said, biting the inside of her cheek, an unbecoming habit. 'And with a body found in the Tummel nearby, not a safe one, perhaps.' She nodded to herself. 'All the more reason to stay in Edinburgh rather than risk walking through both Canongate and Edinburgh every day.'

'You are better off at home than in either of them, Maggie. In Perth. Once King Edward departed the men grew coarser. And you in a tavern. By all that is holy—'

'I have had no trouble, brother. Not here. It was not so at home when Edward came through with his men. Roger could tell you.' Her voice broke. She looked away. 'Edward Longshanks thinks we are beasts, and would treat us so.'

'Maggie.' Andrew reached for her.

She put on a brave face. 'I'll bide at Uncle Murdoch's for now. Celia, however, is to return to Dunfermline. If you hear of a company in which she might travel, I pray you send me word.'

'Idle journeys are not common these days.'

'Idle maids are ever common. I need a laundress and a chambermaid. I have too much work and Celia will be useless.'

'You cannot work there.'

'I have no wish to live in filth.'

'You should have better lodgings.'

'I do not need them. I shall make the inn better lodgings.'

'Promise me you will not be seen in the tavern.'

'This is not a time for the manners of a fine lady, Andrew. I am strong and capable, and I cannot think that any man would risk Murdoch's anger by laying hands on me. But I do need a laundress and a chambermaid.'

'Is that why you came? To tell me that? All that way?' She was impossible.

Margaret drew herself up, her sharp chin thrust out, the hazel eyes beneath the pale red brows hot with anger. 'Why did I come? I hoped to find solace in my brother. Why, I cannot say. You have never comforted me. You did not even tell me what you knew of Roger.'

Perhaps Andrew had been wrong not to tell her. He could think of nothing to say that would calm her. He lamely asked, 'What would Roger say about your being here?' He knew it was a mistake the moment he said it.

She caught her breath. Her fine eyes glistened. How like their mother Margaret was. *Does she know my secrets?*

Softly she said, 'It is because of my husband that I am here.' Catching her skirts, she swept out the door. Her footsteps echoed down the corridor.

Such a knot of feelings washed over Andrew as she departed. Their mother had predicted trouble for him, but she had not said it would touch every part of his life.

He had gone to Elcho Nunnery to see their mother on his way from St Andrews, just before Jack's death.

'You have betrayed your people,' she had said. 'I knew this would come, but not why.'

'He is my abbot. I had no choice.'

Christiana had touched his face. 'You are angry and frightened.'

'Tell me what is to come, Mother.'

Sadly, she stroked his cheek. 'You will pass through fire, Andrew.' She would tell him no more.

He did not know what to do about Margaret. So proud, so fine, so reckless. He could not expect any woman to understand the complex dangers here, but he should be able to guide her. He must think how.

A servant announced that Andrew was summoned to Abbot Adam.

Andrew must put Margaret from his mind for the moment. Conversations with his abbot took all his concentration. It was difficult to hide all he felt. He prayed for calm as he walked.

'*Benedicte*, Father Andrew.' Abbot Adam's smile was broad, his voice friendly. He motioned to Andrew to sit across from him at the table strewn with documents trying to curl closed. 'I did not realise you had a sister in Edinburgh.'

'She travelled with me from Dunfermline.'

'In the midst of war?'

'Is it a war, My Lord Abbot?'

The abbot threw up his hands in mock confusion. Strangers sometimes thought him a gentle fool. 'You have not been yourself since you returned from St Andrews. What is troubling you, my son?'

'Today it is my sister who troubles me. She has learned her husband was unfaithful and now demands more information from me. But I am not so cruel as my uncle.'

'Murdoch Kerr. How much did he charge her for the information?' Adam attempted a joke.

Andrew could not force a smile.

The abbot shook his head. 'I have offended you, though all say he is a conniver. Still, it is good you have such feeling for your uncle. I like that.' Adam settled his elbows on a small, cleared space and leaned towards Andrew. 'But I remind you of your vow of silence.'

'If you think I am such a fool as to tell anyone what I know, you chose unwisely.'

'Still angry. That is what all this is about. There will come a day when you will be proud of what you have done for the king.'

Shame was all Andrew felt. And hatred, for the abbot and himself. 'I am ever your obedient servant, My Lord Abbot.' And will be for ever damned for that.

'We are travellers well met, Dame Kerr.' A man Margaret faintly recognised bowed to her and Hal as they passed through the abbey gateway onto Canongate. 'James Comyn. I saw you with Father Andrew in the tavern the other evening.'

Margaret remembered – he had been one of the well-dressed men sitting near her brother. So he was a Comyn – they were one of the most powerful families in Scotland, and kin to John Balliol, the king Longshanks had betrayed. He was dressed in more sombre clothes today.

'Good day to you, Master Comyn.'

'You were visiting your brother?'

'I was.' She was not in a mood to gossip or while away the time discussing the weather. Let him be useful if he wished to chatter. 'Forgive me, you will think this a strange question, but do you know of a good laundress for my uncle's inn?'

He had a pleasant smile, and expressive brows. 'An unusual conversational ploy, but I am equal to it. I fear that I do not, milady. Might you recommend a good bowyer?'

She could not help but laugh. 'I am Murdoch's niece.'

'I know.'

Quietly, suiting Margaret's mood, Comyn walked with them to the crossroad with the Leith Road, where he said, 'I must bid you farewell for now.' He bowed to them and continued north.

Margaret and Hal crossed into Netherbow.

'He is a pleasant man,' she said as she dismounted in front of the stable.

'Pleasant enough, mistress, though I have seen him lose his temper.'

'Over what?'

'I should not gossip,' Hal said as he unfastened Bonny's harness.

'Is he often at the inn?'

'Oh aye, mistress. All the time.'

'Then it would be a kindness to warn me of his temper.'

'He would not lose it with you. It is the master he argues with. And more than that I cannot say.'

Margaret did not press him. In any case, James Comyn had provided a much-needed laugh. But as she faced the inn, all that she had learned today came rushing back. What a fool she was, and everyone in Edinburgh knew. She rushed to her chamber, not wanting anyone to hear the sobs that she could choke down no longer.

Andrew could not sit still. He kept remembering the time Roger Sinclair had surprised him in Edinburgh. He should have told Maggie of that at the time, but he had prayed it was still possible they might be happy.

Within a fortnight of the wedding, in late April two years ago, Roger had departed Perth, for Bruges, he had said, an important merchant to see. He had left Margaret alone in the partly furnished town house in Perth, and Jack Sinclair in charge of the business. Jack was a good factor. He could have made the trip for the newly wed man. Andrew had thought Roger just an overzealous merchant until he saw him in Edinburgh a week after he had supposedly sailed. Unfortunately, Roger had seen Andrew as well, concocted a plausible story and hurried home to a delighted Margaret. But Andrew had lately learned that by June of that year Roger had again departed Perth, staying away until Michaelmas. Andrew saw that as indifference on Roger's side. Margaret brought connections and a large dowry, and would decorate any gathering, being a lovely woman. Such reasons for marriage were not uncommon, but she deserved better. He must do something for her.

Her Marriage's Great Chance

Margaret shooed Celia from her chamber. Her stomach burned, her breath came in gasps, she did not know whether to cry or scream. Damn the men in her life. Roger had abandoned her, Murdoch and Andrew had kept information from her, Jack had dallied with her, and none of them trusted that she had any wits.

No doubt Jack had also known of Mistress Grey. She feared all of Edinburgh knew; perhaps all of Perth had known. Margaret's face was hot. She pounded her thighs with her fists. Damn them.

Roger had not been wounded, nor had he been dying somewhere without aid, but he had been helping a stranger flee Berwick before the summons to sign the Ragman Rolls. Perhaps not a stranger. Whether Andrew was right that Roger and Mistress Grey were lovers, or Murdoch that they worked together in some political scheme, the woman seemed of more concern to Roger than his own wife.

How foolish Margaret felt for hoping that she and Roger would grow closer, that her husband would come to value her opinion, her companionship. When Longshanks had arrived in Perth with his army in June she had been so afraid. Her father had already fled the country, her mother had retired to Elcho, Fergus threatened to join a group of young men who were hiding food and goods in the

80

countryside, Jack had ridden to Dunfermline to see how his aunt fared. On the second evening Roger had returned, unexpectedly. He said he had ridden hard to be there to protect her. And when a few mornings later a soldier grabbed her as she walked to the kirk and demanded a kiss, Roger, departing the house a moment behind her, had fallen on the man with a fury that was frightening to behold. The town's calamity had seemed her marriage's great chance.

But at the beginning of August, when Longshanks had moved on, Roger had departed again.

Margaret slowed her pacing. In March Edward Longshanks had moved on Berwick with a large army and slaughtered a great number of the townsfolk. Yet this Mistress Grey had not fled then, she had waited months. Until August – until Roger went for her? Margaret did not like all that implied.

Murdoch had asked what she knew of Roger. So little, she realised now. But she had not felt the lack until after they were wed. When he had approached her father about a possible match Roger already owned his house and had established his business in Perth. She had often wondered at his settling in Perth when it was Berwick that was vital to Roger's trade. His explanation was that many merchants sold the same wares on the east coast, but Perth reached a needier market to the north. She had known from the beginning that there were parts of his life he did not mean to share with her. He had assured her that his mother had never bothered herself with much knowledge of the family business. Margaret had used Jack's willingness to explain the importing and exporting, the shipping agreements, to learn more. But it had not occurred to her to question others about Roger.

Mistress Grey might be the wife of a merchant of importance to Roger, even a friend. Margaret would not know.

She sank down at the table. She might confront Roger, but she could not force him to confide in her. She tried to think of an instance in which he had expressed a need of her beyond her housewifely skills.

Though she had had glimpses of Roger when he consulted with her father on trade, greeting him at the door, offering refreshment, bringing his mantle, Margaret had known nothing of Roger's temperament until the afternoon he settled in a chair near hers and asked how her mother fared. A frightening vision had sent her mother to bed for several days. All Perth knew of the incident.

'She rests comfortably.' Margaret had been particularly exasperated by the incident, which left her to manage the household at the busy time of airing before Easter.

'As you are the only daughter in this household, much falls to you at a time like this, I should think.'

An intuitive comment that had surprised her enough to lift her eyes from her needlework. 'Who has told you that?'

'I see it with my own eyes.'

'Needlework is not my complaint.'

'I know. But you have just this moment sat down after rushing about seeing to the servants.'

'It is a daughter's duty, nothing more.' But she liked him for noticing.

After that day it became his custom to stop and talk to her before he left the house. She was flattered by the attention. And yet he did not speak of undying affection, made no claims that he could not go on without her, urged no assignations. Her friends thought perhaps such things could not be expected from a man of his age and stature – he was twenty years her senior and well placed in the community. But despite his reticence they all envied her. In time he spoke with her father, and then he kissed her when she acknowledged that she was willing. It was a long, sweet kiss, and she had loved the scent of him, his warmth. Thereafter until their wedding they stole many kisses, and once she had come unlaced as they tumbled on the lawn of her mother's walled garden. She looked forward to more of that once they were wed.

But after their wedding he was so often away. And his presence meant long days without him as he saw to his business and entertained in the evenings – she was seldom included. *I am not accustomed to having a wife*, he had explained. *You must give me time.* At night he was often quite tender, but he said little, and was soon asleep. Her mother counselled patience. Margaret wondered how often he thought of her when she was not lying beside him. From recent events she guessed not at all, damn him.

Roger knew she was here, that she had chased him proved he was not mistaken in thinking it was her, and he knew Murdoch Kerr's inn full well, and that she would be here. Just as she had faithfully waited for him for two years in Perth.

Perhaps Roger believed Mistress Grey had greater need of him. Margaret tasted bile in her throat. What of *her* needs? It was not fair, her present lot, a married woman without a husband, without children, yet without the freedom to remedy her loneliness.

She almost laughed. As if there were a man with whom she might remedy her solitude. As if she were likely to find another attentive companion like Jack. All the men were now too caught up in their hatred of Longshanks or Balliol.

But the real barrier to her freedom was that she loved Roger, and prayed that it was him she had seen, that they would be reunited.

Margaret slept poorly, but Saturday was market day in town and she might hear some gossip at the stalls. Collecting Hal, she headed up the High Street. With the English troops buying most of the goods at their own prices, if they paid at all, it was not a bustling market. But some desperate farmers were there, as well as fishmongers, fleshers and artisans. Margaret saw only sickly live-stock. Wherever Murdoch was finding the supplies for the tavern it was not here. Near the market cross the street was far livelier than she had yet seen it, with women moving about with baskets, children clinging to their skirts, some clerics. She searched the crowd for Roger with both hope and dread, though he had not behaved like a man who would risk such a public place. So far she saw no knowing smirks, no folk whispering behind their hands as she passed. She was much relieved.

She considered who might know of weavers and laundresses. She noted two women haggling with a man over a length of cloth. It was undyed wool, poorly woven. Margaret waited until the women departed, then stepped forward to ask the merchant if he knew of a laundress in the town. It was a good opening, she thought.

'The soldiers, curse them, have the best of all.' He had few teeth, wore a russet tunic.

Not a wool merchant but a weaver, perhaps. And from the countryside not the town by the looks of him.

'Do you know a young weaver called Bess?' she asked.

'If you don't want my cloth, be off with you, goodwife. I have mouths to feed. My daughter was widowed in the slaughter in Berwick and she and the children must eat. You've a nice blue gown and your face is full, you're not wanting.' He turned sideways on his bench signalling he wished her gone.

'God bless you for taking them in,' Margaret said. 'How much is the cloth?' It would make scratchy but warm bedding.

Hal tapped her arm, motioned her aside. 'The old man makes much of other folks' misfortune.' As usual, Hal addressed his feet. 'He collects their stories. He lives on mead and he bides alone.'

The gummy grin of the old man was only what she deserved for being so gullible.

Margaret moved over to the cobblestones where a woman was arguing with a flesher about the price of his pork.

Just beyond them she caught sight of the woman in the delicately woven mantle with whom she had tried to speak at Mass that first morning. She had paused in front of a trinket seller who huddled beneath a makeshift tent. Margaret approached them.

'God be with you this fine morn, goodwife,' said the trinket seller.

The gaunt woman in the mantle glanced up at Margaret, then

looked quickly away.

Suddenly Margaret placed her. Besseta Fletcher. They had played together as children, during a brief period when their fathers had entered into some shipping contracts together. It was her father, Alan Fletcher, on whose business Jack had come to Edinburgh. Margaret did not know the woman well any more. Their fathers had fallen out over the loss of a valuable shipment and the families had severed contact. It had been a long time since the two women had spoken more than civil greetings, but Margaret remembered her fondly. 'Besseta! I'm gey glad to see a face from Perth.'

Besseta turned slightly towards Margaret, but she barely raised her eyes from the table of pins and combs. 'Good day, Margaret.' She was no older than Margaret but she looked unwell – shadowed eyes, a sharply gaunt face, trembling hands.

'Have you come to Edinburgh to see about the business Jack was transacting for your father?' Margaret asked – perhaps too bluntly, but she feared Besseta would bolt before she could approach the subject tactfully.

Besseta met Margaret's gaze momentarily, with a puzzled squint. 'Father's business?'

'Then what brings you—?'

'My sister Agnes is unwell and I am here to care for her.' Margaret had not known Besseta's sister well. A few years ago she had left Perth to be married, but Margaret had not known she had come to Edinburgh. 'In faith,' Besseta continued, 'I have left her alone too long. God go with you.' She bobbed her head to Margaret and hurried away.

'No trinkets?' the merchant called after Besseta. She shook her head at Margaret. 'A nice bauble for you, mistress?'

Margaret fingered an ivory comb.

'Lovely comb,' the woman crooned. She beckoned Margaret closer. 'You seek news of Jack Sinclair, eh?'

From so little the woman had guessed that. Margaret's first

impulse was to deny it, but the damage had been done. 'Do you know something?'

'Aye. Name of the lad who found him. For a price.'

'Tuppence for the comb and the name.' As she dug in her scrip Margaret hoped it was accurate information, worth her precious pence.

The woman flicked her tongue across her lips as she grabbed the money out of Margaret's hand. 'Will Harcar, the lad who fetches for Guy the fishmonger. Over yon.' She nodded towards a young man talking to another his age.

Margaret picked up the comb, headed towards the young man.

Will Harcar glanced at her, said something to his companion, who nodded and scooted away. When Harcar lowered the foot he'd had propped on a sack of roots, that hip dropped a hand's breadth beneath the opposite. A porter with a short leg. What his back must suffer. His arms looked strong, however, and the expression on his face menacing.

Hal fell into step beside her. 'Dame Kerr, this is not wise.'

The same thought had pricked Margaret's mind. It was not advisable to question the man in public. It might pose a danger to both of them. She put a hand on Hal's arm to stop him.

'Aye, you have the right of it. Take me to Janet Webster.' Perhaps the weaver might recognise the weight. Margaret's tuppence would not be wasted – she could seek out Harcar later, without an audience.

Hal led her down a narrow wynd between two houses and their assorted buildings and plantings in the backlands. This was the way Roger and the men had run the other day. But it was a large area and Margaret could not guess where they might have gone once she lost them. After the noise of the market the backlands seemed quiet. Too quiet. She found herself straining to hear footsteps following. She was glad of Hal's company.

They came out on Cowgate, the well-trodden lane along which

livestock were led out to pasture. Across the way were smaller houses than those off the High Street. Hal turned left and stopped at the corner of Potter Row, across from the enclosure of Blackfriars.

It was a smiddie, with a mud and wattle house behind.

'Janet Webster is wife to Davy the smith, who is missing,' Hal said.

'What do you mean, missing?'

'Just that. For a fortnight, more or less.'

The house was whitewashed, thatch-roofed, and boasted a wooden door. Hal knocked, greeted a portly, white-wimpled good-wife and introduced Margaret. Deep-set, sad eyes looked her up and down, then the woman nodded and stood aside, inviting her in.

'I'll wait without,' said Hal.

The one room was dominated by several looms. A fire pit smoked in the centre. Two box beds took up the far corners. A bench was drawn up to the largest loom. Janet had attached the beginning hem to the cloth rod, one end of which sat atop a support rod. The other end rested on one of the supports for the heddle rod.

'I must settle the rod.' Janet turned back to the loom. Lifting the rod off the support, she stretched awkwardly. She was a head shorter than Margaret.

'Let me help.' Margaret mounted the bench, slipped the right end of the cloth rod onto the support beam.

'Your height is useful. I thank you.' Janet slipped off the bench and perched on the edge of a stool, watching Margaret. 'Murdoch has a large spot in his heart set aside for you.'

The comment certainly surprised Margaret. Murdoch might have told her he knew the woman so well.

Janet sighed. 'I mind when I was so young.'

She did not seem old, though there was a weariness in her movements. The wimple hid her hair, but the fine down on her chin and cheeks looked blonde. Margaret wondered what their relationship was that Murdoch had not mentioned it.

'It is not a new mantle you've come for. That is fine work. Good cloth and dye.'

Margaret had not planned her speech. She moved towards the smaller loom, studying the weights that kept the warp taut. None seemed quite like the one in her scrip, but then they varied a great deal, some with centre holes, some bone-shaped, with the thread wrapped round the waist.

Margaret had a thought. 'My uncle has new bed curtains in his chamber, made of fine twill. Is that your work?'

'It is.' Janet dropped her gaze to her hands.

'For Mistress Grey?'

Janet looked up, searching Margaret's face. She nodded once.

'Did my uncle order them?'

Janet shook her head. 'Mistress Grey ordered the curtains.'

'She must have paid a bit of siller.'

'Aye. And she had no need to ask the cost, just wanted the finest and the warmest, but of cloth, not skins, and light enough to pull aside.'

'She sounds a grand lady.'

'This I tell you, young Margaret, should you be wondering, she is not one who would dally with a merchant from Perth.'

Margaret sank down on the edge of one of the beds. If the weaver understood so much, it was pointless pretending indifference. 'What is she like?'

'A queen should carry herself so.' The weaver rolled her eyes. 'Half again your age – my age, more like. Fine wool clothes.' She twitched her skirts. 'A red underskirt.' Lifted a foot. 'Well-made shoes of leather to walk in the countryside.' Janet's were simple leather shoes, soft soled, tied with strips of hide. 'Plucks her dark hair to broaden her forehead. She might be handsome but for her skin. Pox pitted. She uses a paste to smooth it. It gives her an unhealthy pallor. She does not go to such trouble for the likes of your husband.'

But he is good enough for me, Margaret thought. 'He brought her to Edinburgh.'

Janet sniffed. 'I say *she* brought *him*.' She eased back in her chair, arms folded across her ample chest, nodded at Margaret's surprise. 'That is how I see it.' A draught blew the peat smoke into her eyes. Janet coughed and changed seats. 'You don't seem a woman to make unnecessary journeys. You must have believed you would find your husband here.'

'I wearied of sitting and waiting. Forgive me – I understand that you, too, wait for your husband.'

'Davy, aye.' Janet sniffed as if impatient with her emotion. 'Tell me your story. Murdoch has given it to me in pieces.'

The request, so frankly and simply made, reached into Margaret's loneliness. With so little encouragement, she blurted out her whole sorry tale, even to her mother's prediction.

'And what was that?'

Margaret told her.

'A daughter in your arms and the King of Scots in Edinburgh. It sounds a fine future to me.'

'It does not seem likely at present.'

Janet fussed with the fire in the centre of the room. 'Your mother has the Sight?' she asked as she poked.

'She does.' Margaret shifted uneasily on the bed, drew the loom weight from her scrip. 'I have another question. A friend was clasping this in his hand when he died.' She placed it in the woman's outstretched hand.

Janet fingered it, held it up to the light from a high window, shook her head. 'Not one of mine. Too new.' She dropped it into Margaret's palm, pressed her hand with both of hers. Her expression was unreadable. 'Jack Sinclair, your husband's factor?'

'Yes. Did you know him?'

'You hope I ken whose this is, and why Jack carried it.' Janet shook her head. 'I cannot say. He might have found it lying in the gate.'

'Old Will said a weaver named Bess might know something.'
'Poor old man.' Janet rose. 'I'll see what I can find out for you.'
'I am grateful.' Margaret rose also, seeing she was meant to go.
'I have much work to do.'
'Would you know of a good laundress?'
Janet smiled. 'Life must go on, eh? I might think of someone.'
'God go with you, Goodwife Janet.'
'And you, young Margaret.'

When Margaret returned to the inn she found Celia pacing at the bottom of the stairway to her chamber. Her face was flushed.

'Master Comyn went up to your chamber looking for Master Murdoch. He walked in without knocking.'

'What were you doing?'

'Applying salve to my saddle sores.'

'You with your skirts hitched up?'

'I'd not thought to bolt the door.' Celia was about to cry.

Margaret was alarmed. 'Did he touch you?'

Celia shook her head. 'He begged forgiveness.'

'I hope you chastised him for his discourtesy?'

'I did.'

Margaret did not know how to comfort the prickly woman. 'We must remember to bolt the door,' she said.

Now here was a puzzle – James Comyn such a good friend he walked in like that, yet not so good a friend he knew who currently occupied Murdoch's bedchamber. 'Why was he looking for my uncle?'

Celia pressed her sleeve to her eyes. Sniffed. Composed herself. 'Folk were asking for drink, the cook said he could do nothing without the key to your uncle's kitchen where the ale is stored, and the master has not been seen since yesterday midday.'

'James Comyn takes much on himself. Where is he now?'

'I did not follow.'

Margaret tried the door of Murdoch's kitchen, found it locked.

In the tavern kitchen she found Roy stirring something in a pot, Geordie the kitchen lad standing on a bench searching the shelves.

Roy's brows were pulled together in a ferocious frown. 'The master cannot go off like that without telling me. I needed a new barrel of ale.'

'Where is Master Comyn?' Margaret asked.

Roy nodded towards the tavern. 'As we are serving his ale, he thought he would have some.'

'He provided the ale?'

'Aye. From his own store.'

Comyn's behaviour mystified her. 'Is he often here?'

'Aye, for the ale and the gossip.'

In the tavern, a crowd had formed around two men throwing dice. James Comyn sat alone at another table, observing the activity. Margaret considered his face, his thick, arched eyebrows, the strong lines of his bones, a straight but broad nose. He turned towards her, as if sensing her eyes upon him. His cool regard after barging into her chamber sparked her irritation and made her bold.

She perched on the bench beside him, facing out from the table. 'It was good of you to provide the ale.'

'My pleasure. I must apologise to you as well as your maid for trespassing in your chamber.'

That he volunteered the apology spoke well of him. Her irritation mellowed to curiosity. 'Do you often enter my uncle's bedchamber uninvited?'

'I thought to find him lying across his bed drunk.'

'Does that happen often?'

'It is not his custom to be away from the tavern on market day.'

'Surely he deserves time away now and again.'

'But on market day?' Comyn shook his head. 'I saw you walking with an English soldier the other day. You looked wet and upset.' He phrased it as if concerned, but she saw by his expression that he was suspicious.

As she might be if their situations were reversed. 'How did you come to see me?'

'I bide across the street.' He nodded at her bandage. 'Did they hurt you?'

'This was a splinter.'

'Ah. Good. Well now you are here, perhaps you might tell me where Murdoch is.'

'I don't know. He has not been gone long – we spoke yesterday. Why are you so concerned?'

'Forgive me. I make much of nothing.'

'Thank you again for the barrel of ale,' she said, rising. 'We shall send a barrel to your house as soon as may be.' Thinking she sounded too pleasant, she added, 'My maid is much disturbed, Master Comyn.'

'I regret my thoughtlessness.'

Back in the tavern kitchen, Roy was forming oatcakes, getting ready to bake. Flakes of chaff sprinkled his dark hair. His arms were floury to the elbows, where his pushed-up sleeves began.

'Is it so unusual for Master Murdoch to be away a night?' Margaret asked.

'Without word. And not returning for market day. It is a busy day. Too much for Sim alone.'

Margaret was growing concerned. 'Let Geordie help Sim.'

Roy straightened, brushed some hair from his eyes, making it now a pasty lock, and glared at her. 'I cannot spare him.'

'You will until Master Murdoch returns.'

Roy opened his mouth to protest, but Margaret turned and left before he could make a sound.

Weary and yearning for a moment of quiet in which to sort all she had heard today, she climbed up to her bedchamber. Celia stood by the small window, staring out.

'When did you last see my uncle?'

'Midday yesterday. I was cleaning his chamber. He ordered me out.' Celia turned round, patting her cap. 'I should see to your hand, mistress.'

Margaret sat down. 'Was he long in his chamber?'

'I didn't notice.'

Celia removed the bandage and a piece of splinter that had worked its way out of the wound. A dab of thyme ointment felt soothing, a new bandage refreshing. Flexing her hand, Margaret thanked Celia.

'You looked distressed when I walked in. Because of James Comyn?'

Celia looked down at her hands, shook her head.

'How did you occupy your morning?'

'I shook out the bedding in the empty chambers and wiped down the floors and walls. We should hang some dried herbs in the corners or tuck them into the wattle hurdles.'

'You've done a good day's work.'

'Aye.'

'I am grateful, Celia. And glad you've moved back in here.'

'There are rats in the roof of that cottage.'

'And in the walls of this house.'

'It is a wretched place.'

'You've a roof o'er your head and a full belly. But I know you dream of more.'

'I am trying to be content with it, mistress.'

And Margaret was trying to be more patient. 'I spoke to Comyn.'

'I'll bolt the door, no matter,' Celia said as she did it.

Margaret dropped down onto the bed and closed her eyes. Her feet and her head ached, her eyes burned from wind and smoke. But she could not rest. Behind her eyes lurked James Comyn, Besseta Fletcher, Roger, Murdoch, Janet Webster, Mistress Grey.

She rose, reached beneath the bed for her card weaving. She pulled out the bag. Her hands felt chaos where there should be thirty threaded wooden cards in a neat stack, the warp ends tied in an overhand knot, and all secured with cord. She held the bag up to the lamp beside the bed. The knot and the cord had come undone.

The cards were jumbled in the bag, the thread twisted every which way.

Celia shook her head at the confusion. 'You need someone good with card weaving to sort that.'

With her hand still bandaged, Margaret did need help. She thought of Janet Webster.

⋙ 8 ⋘

THIS IS NO LIFE

Over the alley that stretched along the inn's backlands the glow of sunset was fast fading into peat smoke-thickened evening. Still stiff from the journey and limping slightly from her fall a few days before, Celia made the lantern light lurch as she negotiated the infrequently used alley. But when Margaret offered to carry the light she was rebuffed.

Stepping out onto Cowgate, Margaret noticed someone standing in the smiddie yard across the way. She wondered whether Davy the smith had returned. But the fire was not lit, and the person stood unmoving. As they drew closer she recognised Janet Webster's bulk. The woman cradled something in her arms.

'That is a queer object of affection,' Celia whispered when they drew close enough to see it was a large hammer.

'Her husband the smith is missing.'

'She is gey worried.'

The weaver looked up at the light and the murmur of voices, then hurriedly put the hammer on the anvil. 'Who is it?'

Margaret identified herself, introduced Celia. 'I hoped you might help me untangle a quantity of thread.'

Janet led the way into the house. It was cold and dark but for the central fire, which had clearly been untended for a while, perhaps since Margaret had departed in the afternoon. Celia held the lantern steady as the weaver stirred the fire to life. When it was burning well she invited them to sit near it.

'Now. Show me what you brought,' Janet said, easing herself down beside Margaret.

'It is to be a border for bed curtains,' Margaret explained. She described the intricate diamond pattern, and the colours. There was no question of cutting the thread and beginning again – the goods were too precious.

'Best not to look for the pattern in this, but follow the threads,' Janet said. She told Celia to fetch the light from the far corner. Then the three sat at the small table, Janet and Margaret unwinding the threaded cards, Celia lending a hand when directed.

While they worked at untwisting the cards the three women spoke in bursts about patterns, thread, some of the fine cards they had seen. The silences were comfortable, until Margaret said, 'My uncle has been gone since yesterday. The cook and James Comyn are worried about his absence on market day. Is it such an odd thing?'

Janet leaned closer to the work, said nothing for a long while. But she grew clumsy, and finally, as she paused to wipe her eyes, she whispered, 'God help us.'

'What is it?' Margaret asked.

'A man is gone for a night and a day and we fear him dead. This is no life.'

'They are right to worry?'

'Your uncle never did bide by the laws of others. In such times as these that is dangerous. He could be taken for a spy.'

'How long has your husband been gone?'

'Not two weeks. It feels a long while.' Janet, her head down to hide emotion, gathered the cards already unwound, knotted their warps. 'We need daylight for this.' She shoved the work into the bag, handed it to Margaret. 'Come back tomorrow.'

Shaken by Janet's reaction, Margaret appreciated Celia's silence as they walked back to the inn. She tried to calm herself, reasoning that her presence was the cause of her uncle's unusual behaviour, that he had felt he could leave the inn and tavern in her hands, but it was a futile effort, she did not believe it.

As she and Celia were passing the tavern kitchen, Roy came hurrying out the door.

'You must go to the tavern.' His hair stood on end. His beard was crusted with oat flour. 'You must decide where tonight's boarders will stay.'

'Murdoch has not returned?'

'No.'

Margaret considered the choices. 'The chamber to the left of mine. Two will be comfortable in there.'

Roy shook his shaggy head as he started back to the kitchen. 'They won't share a roof much less the same room,' he called over his shoulder. 'One is an Englishman, so the other says.' He turned as he reached the doorway, hands on his hips. 'Each wants the other sent away.'

'*Is* the one an Englishman?'

'I cook here, that is all.'

'Yes. I see. I'll talk to them.'

At the tavern doorway, Margaret handed the bag of weaving to Celia. 'Go on up to our chamber.'

Margaret stood a moment in the tavern doorway, blinking. Her eyes had already been tired before the close work on the cards.

Sim had sidled over to her. 'The leather-clad man and the barelegged redbeard,' he said, 'they are the troublesome ones.'

It was no chore to pick out the Englishman. He was clad all in leather, his clothes well made but caked with mud, grey hair trimmed about his forehead and ears, and short behind. The other, wrapped in a plaid, his rough beard redder than the hair atop his head, sat glowering at a table with some of the regular patrons.

'We will put the Englishman in the chamber beside me.

Redbeard will stay in the other house. I shall ready the chambers for them. Tell them they are both welcome, and there is no need they stay under the same roof.'

Sim was not happy with the assignment, but said only, 'Aye, mistress.'

Margaret went to find Celia and prepare the rooms.

When they were finished, Margaret sent Celia to the kitchen for food, and she stepped into the tavern for a pitcher of ale.

She noticed that James Comyn was talking to Redbeard.

He glanced up, met her gaze.

She sat down at the edge of the table near the door, waiting for Sim. Comyn said something to Redbeard, who nodded into his tankard, then joined her.

'Your uncle would not like you here unescorted.'

Margaret had not noticed the deep dimple in his chin before.

'You take uncommon interest in my uncle's business.'

'Your presence worries him. As for the business, it is partly mine.' At her exclamation he frowned. 'He did not tell you?'

'No. A Comyn owning part interest in a tavern? The world turns strangely these days.'

Comyn lifted his tankard, nodded to Margaret and drank.

'How did you come to be partners?'

After some silence Comyn said, 'It was not your uncle's choice. It is for him to tell you how it came to be. If he has a mind to do so.'

'You thought the English soldier might have hurt me yesterday. Why?'

'We all worry about our women with the garrison perched above us.'

'You thought my uncle had gone to defend my honour?'

Sim set the pitcher on the table.

Comyn began to rise.

If Comyn and Murdoch were partners, Margaret thought perhaps she might trust him with her growing concern about her uncle's absence. 'My uncle disappeared after telling me of Mistress Grey. Could that be cause to worry?'

Comyn sat back down, searching her face.

She would be damned if she would lower her gaze in discomfort. In a while Comyn closed his eyes, freeing hers.

She took that to mean he suspected a closeness between Roger and Mistress Grey. She glanced round the tavern, looking for something to rest her eyes on. She watched Sim balance four tankards on a tray.

'I saw my husband the other day,' she said.

'Here?' Comyn asked. 'In the town?'

Sim made it through the door. Feeling calmer, Margaret faced Comyn. He stared at her with urgency now.

'Yes. Near the tron.'

'Are you certain? Did you speak to him?'

'No. I was not close enough, and the men he was with pulled him away from me. They ran and I could not follow.'

Her heart pounded, Comyn's look was so dark as he rose from his stool, downing his drink.

'Should I be worried for my uncle? Or for Roger?'

'For us all.' Comyn strode out of the tavern.

Most of the others paid no heed to the man's abrupt departure. But Redbeard watched the door for a moment, then rose and followed.

Margaret was surprised her hands did not tremble as she lifted the pitcher and departed.

'The pie is now cold,' Celia said.

A pie. Margaret cared nothing for the pie. She poured herself a cup of ale.

'I ate my portion while it was yet warm,' Celia said. 'But I had no ale.'

Margaret pushed the pitcher over to her.

'You should eat.'

Margaret tasted the pie – pastry stuffed with cooked roots and a bit of salted beef. It might as well have been ashes in her mouth.

'You've said not a word since you returned.'

'I am frightened, Celia.'

'About Master Murdoch's being away?'

Margaret nodded. 'Pray he returns safely. And soon.'

'Aye. What would you do now?'

'Go to bed. What else can I do but wait?'

Celia had begun to unlace Margaret's shoes when a commotion began beneath them in the tavern. Voices raised in argument.

'I must see what it is,' Margaret said.

'Should you go down there, mistress?' Celia's eyes were on the bolted door.

'Yes.'

'Then I'll attend you.'

'Stay here. Bolt the door behind me.' Margaret slipped out before fear clutched her, made her way down the stairs expecting at any moment to see someone come sprawling out of the back door of the tavern. But now that she could better hear individual voices, it seemed excited chatter, not an argument. And many exclamations of distress. She prayed it had nothing to do with Murdoch's disappearance.

Roy, Sim and Geordie stood just within the doorway.

'What is it?' Margaret asked.

'Davy the smith,' said Roy. 'They have found his body. In the bog where the Tummel streams meet. Right north of the abbey.'

'Not Janet Webster's husband?' Standing in the smiddie yard, holding his hammer . . .

'Aye,' said Sim. 'What went on there, I ask you? First Harry, now Davy.'

'Who is Harry?'

'He was a cobbler, a friend of Davy's. Found floating in the Tummel a week ago,' said Sim.

'He and Davy went missing the same time,' said Geordie.

'Both were stripped naked,' Sim added.

'Quiet,' Roy muttered.

Margaret remembered hearing that a body had been found in the Tummel a few days after Jack's death.

'They say he looks like he's been in the water all this time,' said Sim. He seemed to enjoy relating the more unpleasant details.

Margaret remembered Jack's bloated body after only four days. She did not want to imagine what the smith would look like after having been exposed to the waters of the bog and the creatures that fed in it for a fortnight. 'All that time,' she whispered. 'How did they know him?'

'The men who found him knew him well,' said Sim.

'Where has he been taken?'

'The canons have him at the abbey,' said Roy. 'His wife is on her way down.'

Poor Janet. 'How did you hear of this?'

'Men of the town have been watching that place ever since Harry was found downstream of it,' said Sim. 'It's the abbot, they say. Edward Longshanks' man. None of the English king's men have been found murdered.'

With a spreading chill she remembered the hostility Andrew had suffered in the tavern. So all the brethren at the abbey were under suspicion. She could not believe her brother would have any part in such an act. 'Why would Longshanks' men murder a cobbler and a smith?'

'You may as well ask why they murdered all the men of Berwick and left them in the streets to be eaten by the gulls and ravens,' said Roy.

Some of the drinkers sat sallow-faced and shocked, others drew heads together, talking earnestly. An argument had broken out near the door. 'Will you close up when it's time, Roy?' Margaret asked.

'Aye, mistress. This is no place for you.'

⤚ 9 ⤙

THERE WON'T BE MANY MOURN HIM

The dark, silent backlands swallowed Margaret as she stepped out of the tavern. Anything, anyone, could hide behind a building, in the shadows beneath the stairs, against the houses. But that was not what she feared. To be alone, abandoned by all her kin – that was what she feared. And she feared Edward Longshanks. He had betrayed the trust of her countrymen, humiliated their king and stolen his crown, butchered the citizens of Berwick, and now his poison was seeping into all their lives. She would not believe that Andrew supported him. No matter what else he might lack, Andrew had a conscience. His abbot might be a traitor to this country, but not Andrew. If she was right, she feared for him.

But what of Murdoch? All the other taverns in Edinburgh had been taken over by the English or closed because of trouble. Only Murdoch's remained open to the folk. Might the same moral lack that drove him to smuggling and thieving lure him to treason against his people? No. She could not believe that of him.

She shivered and thought to go up to bed, but her eyes were drawn to the lantern that hung over the doorway of the next house, the house in which Murdoch would rest his head if he were here tonight. Margaret headed for it. With the lantern in hand, she mounted the steps to her uncle's temporary bedchamber. Slipping

102

through the hide door she set the lantern on a small chest, considered the sparse furnishings: a bed, a shelf beside it with an oil lamp, a stool, the chest on which she had set the lantern. That was padlocked. Kneeling, she examined the lock. It looked like the sort opened with a slide key. Simple to open with the proper tool. She had a slide key and a notched post up in her room – they had served her well when her mother lost household keys and she carried them with her out of habit.

Margaret stepped onto the landing and froze, sensing someone there.

'Uncle?'

Redbeard stepped into the light. 'Murdoch's not returned?'

Seeing who it was did not ease her fear, even though his chamber was just behind him so he had cause to be here. Something in his manner frightened her, and she did not like that he knew Murdoch was away. 'You made your way up without the light?'

'A man who cannot pick his way in the dark is worthless, lass.'

He seemed huge in this low, narrow space, and his calling her 'lass' meant to her that he knew the effect he had. He had approached so silently up a dark, unfamiliar stair. His stealth added to her uneasiness.

Margaret shone the light towards his chamber. 'You will find a cruisie in there with a twig for lighting from my lantern.' She watched him use it.

When he had lit the rush wick of his lamp he said, 'God keep you,' and bowed to her.

Sweating with fear, Margaret hastened back to her own chamber.

Celia opened the door before Margaret knocked.

'You have been so long. Was it a fight?'

'The body of Janet Webster's husband was found in the bog.'

'Holy Mother of God!' Celia's eyes were dark beads in the lamplight. 'That poor woman.'

'Aye. I cannot think how a wife looks on such a sight.'

'Will you go to her?'

'She has gone to the abbey.'

They finished the pitcher of ale before retiring to the great bed.

Margaret lay down only for the warmth – she would not sleep. Redbeard's appearance without her uncle's chamber had been the finishing touch for her. He might have snapped her neck without anyone knowing. She tried to push down such thoughts. She had no proof he meant her harm. He might simply have been headed for his chamber. But she had felt such a darkness in his presence, such a burning anger.

She sat up in alarm each time one of the boarders mounted the steps. If Murdoch did not return, if his body was found somewhere . . . She tried not to think of that. And in truth, what need she fear, for Andrew would come to her aid. But if his abbot was a murderer . . . Celia moaned in her sleep.

The Englishman came up quite late, just as Roy was shouting that all must leave. Margaret wondered why the men had tolerated him in their midst. Listen to her – she grew like the men in the tavern. Not all the English were like their king. Surely not. Still, any peaceable Englishman with sense was long gone from this place. She held her breath, listening for sounds from the man's room, wishing she had put him in the next house. But then she would have had Redbeard next door to her. *Come home, Uncle. Dear God, watch over Murdoch and bring him home safely.* Andrew and Murdoch were right. This was no place for her.

In the early morning Margaret bucked up her courage and resolved to examine her uncle's kitchen and the chest in his chamber. He must have cause to lock them, and that cause might shed light on his disappearance. What she would do with the knowledge she had yet to figure. First she must have it.

Celia woke at the noise Margaret made rummaging for the tools. She sat up, asked sleepily, 'What is it?'

'I am going to see if Uncle is in his bed,' Margaret lied.

She unbolted the door. But as she opened it, she heard the floorboards creak unevenly in the room she had given the Englishman.

She heard voices, a pair. They quieted.

'What—?' Celia began, but stopped as Margaret shook her head at her.

Halting footsteps approached the other doorway. Margaret shuttered her lantern, blew out the lamp beside the bed, kept the door open a crack.

At the edges of the hide in the guest chamber she saw a light approaching, and prayed it did not illuminate her door.

The hide lifted. The crooked torso explained the halting walk. Harcar, the fishmonger's lad, the one who had discovered Jack's body. His eyes swept over her doorway, then the doorway across the way, and lastly the doorway to the outside stairs. With a nod to the person holding the hide – Margaret could not see him – Harcar crossed in his awkward gait to the outside door and exited with caution. The hide curtain fell back in place over the Englishman's doorway.

It was a suspicious time for a visitor. All the fears of the night washed over Margaret. She shut her door and waited until her heartbeat slowed and she was calm enough to move quietly. She could hear Celia's frightened breathing. The Englishman might be listening too. Margaret could not move past his chamber without some noise betraying her. So she must not steal past his door, but walk past as if nothing were amiss.

'I am going to make some noise in leaving,' she whispered to Celia.

'You should come back to bed.'

And lie there soaked in fear? She had borne enough of that for one night. 'Bolt the door behind me when I go.' Margaret pulled the bed curtains aside noisily, making one of the posts knock the wall. She relit the cruisie, carelessly drew the bolt on the door and cursed when she did not find a clean chamber pot. Shut the door. Opened the chest and let the lid drop.

Noisy enough, she hoped. Now she left the room. Someone grunted in the room to her right, but the Englishman's room was silent. When she slipped through the outer door she resumed her earlier stealth, glad for the quiet stairs as she descended, and the thick fog that had rolled in as dawn approached.

At the bottom of the steps she paused, listening. She did not want to be surprised while working on the lock. A rat scuttled across her foot, followed closely by the dark cat, which growled deep in its throat as it narrowed in on its prey. She crossed to the kitchen in their wake, waited yet again, then crept round to the door at the back.

She shone the lantern on the lock. It was a padlock much like the one on which Murdoch had trained her. But she had no need for her tools – the lock hung open.

She caught her breath, gently tried the latch. The door swung inwards. It was dark inside. She took another step forward, reaching out to feel for the window sill where she could set the tools and free a hand.

Someone grabbed her from behind, twisting her left arm behind her. Margaret pressed back into him as she felt steel against her throat. She tried to move her right arm to shove the lantern back into his groin, but his arm pinned hers down.

'Mother of God!' she gasped, letting go of the lantern.

'Maggie!'

It was her uncle, not a murdering Englishman, not Redbeard. Murdoch let her go. She sank to her knees, weak and gasping for breath. The lantern. It would start a fire. She groped for it, praying that it had hit bare ground.

'God's blood, you'll be the death of me.'

Margaret found the lantern and opened the shutter.

'No light, Maggie,' Murdoch hissed.

'Why such stealth in your own kitchen?'

He was wearing a plaid, his legs and feet bare. His shirt was darkly stained, his eyes wild. He grabbed the lantern, shuttered it. 'Get out.' His voice was hoarse and shaky.

'Where have you been? Do you ken how worried I've been?'

'Get out.' He pushed her towards the door, thrust the lantern at her. 'I almost killed you, you foolish woman.'

She reached out for him.

'Uncle—'

'For God's sake, Maggie, go.'

She backed out; he shut the door, sliding the bolt into place. She sank down on the bench outside to catch her breath. Her neck stung. She gently probed with her fingertips, found the spot sticky. Queasy at the discovery of how close she had come to being seriously injured, if not killed, she dropped her head into her hands. Murdoch was back, he was alive, praise God. But his presence did not mean safety for her. She had been mad to step within after discovering the door unlocked, the kitchen dark.

The fog settled on her, and eventually dampened her clothes sufficiently to rouse her with the chill. Picking up the lantern, she opened the shutter enough to light the path just before her feet. Halfway to the house she heard a woman scream and nearly dropped the lantern. The fog played with the sound, but a second scream was closer. She shuttered the lantern, stood very still, trying to hear over her own terror. Uncertain footsteps approached from the direction of the alley, someone breathing quickly and moaning prayers. Margaret opened the shutter a little.

Celia's eyes were huge in a pinched white face. 'Mistress, thank God it is you.'

'What are you doing here? Why did you scream? Are you injured?'

'There is a dead man lying in the alley.'

Margaret heard someone behind her. She turned to blind them with the lantern. The light wobbled in her trembling hands.

Hal shaded his eyes. 'What has happened?'

Murdoch was right behind him, his plaid arranged to hide the dirty shirt.

'Come, Celia,' Margaret said, managing to sound far steadier than she felt. 'Show us the body.'

'It is in the alley.'

'Show us,' Murdoch said.

Celia led them to the alley between the inn buildings, slowly, for the fog was even thicker now and the pale lantern beam fell just beyond their feet. Halfway down the alley Margaret saw a man sprawled on the ground, face down, blood from his head mixing with the mud. It looked as if one leg was drawn up beneath him. But as Margaret let the lantern play over his legs she saw that one was shorter than the other.

'Harcar,' Margaret whispered.

Murdoch had crouched down. 'Aye. There won't be many mourn him.' He looked up at the sound of footsteps out on the High Street.

Margaret shuttered the lantern and tried not to breathe.

As soon as the footsteps faded, Murdoch headed back down the alley. All three stumbled after him in the dark. Once in the yard, Murdoch slumped against the stable wall, burying his face in one arm.

Celia began to sob. Margaret held her and prayed – for them, not the dead man. Hal hovered next to his master as if waiting for a sign of what he was to do.

At last Murdoch straightened, turned towards them.

'This will go ill for us if discovered.' He nodded to Hal. 'We'll move the body to one of the sheds behind the kitchens. Then you'll fetch Father Francis from St Giles'. Tell him we found Harcar and took him in to shelter, but he was already dead. Tell Father Francis, mind you, no other.'

'It would be better to fetch Andrew from Holyrood,' Margaret said. She wanted to see her brother.

'No!' Murdoch said vehemently. 'Not the abbey. St Giles'. Father Francis will not tell the English we found him. Abbot Adam would be only too happy to do so.'

'What has this to do with the English?' Margaret asked.

'They will see his murder as a threat to them. He spied for them.'

Celia whimpered.

'Andrew would say nothing,' Margaret said.

'Nothing need be said. Abbot Adam knows all that passes in the abbey. You two women, go to your chamber, bar the door.'

Margaret gave Celia the lantern, told her to go on.

Murdoch shook his head, muttering to himself.

'Uncle,' Margaret said quietly.

'Well, what?'

'Harcar left the Englishman's room next to my chamber just before I came out to your kitchen.'

'You saw him up in the room?'

'I saw him leave it.'

Murdoch crossed himself. 'Get yourself up to your chamber, bar the door as I said. I'll send for you.'

Upstairs, Celia stood in the middle of the room clutching her elbows and whimpering like an injured pup.

'Why were you in the alley?' Margaret asked.

Celia hiccuped as she tried to still herself, held her breath.

Margaret poked at the embers in the brazier.

'The Englishman left his chamber,' Celia said at last, her voice rough. 'I thought you'd wish to know where he'd gone.'

'Are you mad?'

'That is all you can say?' Celia took a step towards Margaret. 'What is that on your throat?'

Margaret touched the scratch. The blood was dry. 'I cut myself. Where did he go? Did he see the body?'

'He stopped by it, then walked on by. Like it was a sleeping dog. I bent to it, not expecting— Oh, dear Lord.' She pressed her hands to her face.

'Did you scream while he was yet in the alley?'

Celia dropped her hands, shook her head. 'Not at once. No. I stood over the body and prayed for us.' She took a deep breath. 'I must lie down.'

The Englishman was not the murderer, then. But Murdoch might be. It might be Harcar's blood she had seen on her uncle's clothes. How she wished she had stayed in Dunfermline or returned to Perth. She felt as if she had walked off a precipice and had yet to stop falling.

Murdoch sat by the fire, feet on a stool to warm, drinking ale. He had cleaned himself up, changed clothes. An empty tub was turned over near the fire. He glanced up, nodded to her, returned to his study of the fire.

Margaret was about to sit down beside him, but changed her mind and sat where she might see his face. The fire played on his ruddy features, the pale brows that drew together in the middle, parted at the scar over his right eye, the often broken nose. She had never seen him so clean.

'I did not think you a man overfond of a bath,' she said.

'You meant to break into my kitchen.'

'You might tell me where you've been.'

'I didn't give you those tools to pick my locks.'

'I didn't know how long you'd be away. Yesterday James Comyn supplied the ale from his own stock because Roy could not fetch any from here.'

'So what if he did? Comyn can spare it.'

Margaret rose and poked at the fire, added a block of peat.

'Damn you, woman, let it be!' Murdoch dropped his cup, cursed her for making him spill his ale too.

Margaret refilled his cup, and poured one for herself. In silence, she handed his cup to him. She lifted her own and drained it. The peat fire had begun to smoke. As she bent to see to it, Murdoch shifted in his seat. She prepared herself for another outburst.

'I didn't mean to hurt you,' he said gruffly.

'I was a fool to walk into a dark place. But I was gey worried. I couldn't sleep. Davy the smith is dead, did you hear?'

'Aye.'

'Does Harcar's murder have to do with Davy's?'

'Do you have lugs? I've told you not to ask such questions.'

Murdoch rubbed his forehead. He did look weary. 'This is no place for you, Maggie. Go home.'

'When Edward Longshanks moves north to Perth, where do you suggest I go then? To Elcho Nunnery with Mother?'

Murdoch stared at her silently for several heartbeats. 'If the English hear where Harcar was found, we'll have no peace, Maggie. Better you were in Perth.'

'I thought you had a pact with the sheriff.'

'Why would you think that?'

'They closed the taverns in Perth when Longshanks was there. Why do the English allow this tavern to stay open?'

'If Longshanks were at the castle they would close it.' He sat back, frowning, tapping his fingers on the cup in an uneven rhythm. Suddenly he stopped. 'You think I killed Harcar.'

At last it was out. 'You were here in the dark, hiding.'

'By God!' Murdoch shouted. 'Oh, Maggie, you ken me not a whit if you think so.' He shook his head at her. 'But I tell you this, if I was wont to murder someone I would not hesitate over the likes of Harcar.' He gulped down his ale, sprang up and went for more.

'If you hadn't just come from Harcar, why did you fly at me like that? You thought you were followed.'

'I'm always followed, woman. You asked about my pact with the English. My pact is my innocence. They can accuse me of nothing. I keep the peace in my inn and tavern, and when evil is done I always have proof of where I have been.'

'Harcar spied for the English,' Margaret whispered.

'Did you not wonder how he came to find Jack in the middle of the night? Course not. You pitied him, aye, that's a woman for you. Cripples are saints.'

'He killed Jack?'

'Not with his hands. You ask *me* about pacts with the English? Harcar spied on us all for the captain of the garrison.'

'So that is why he was in the Englishman's chamber.'

'You're daft. A man in the pay of Longshanks would not stay here.'

'But Redbeard refused to sleep under the same roof.'

'Who?'

Margaret described the man.

Murdoch dropped his chin, shook his head. 'I see.'

'What do you see?'

'Leave it be, Maggie.'

'You say you always have proof of where you've been when trouble occurs. Then what would you say if asked where you were yesterday and last night?'

'Leave it be, Maggie.'

'I saw the stains on your clothes.'

'You see too much. But they were not his blood.' He rose. 'I've wasted time. I should speak to the Englishman.'

'He's well away. Celia followed him as he departed – that is how she came to find the body.'

'She witnessed the murder?'

'No. But she said the Englishman was not surprised when he came upon the body.'

Murdoch grunted and went out the door, leaving Margaret with more unanswered questions than when she had arrived.

She searched the kitchen for his soiled clothes. They must be either in here or in Murdoch's room. Nothing came to light.

Outside the kitchen Margaret found Hal sitting by the door, bent over a harness, working oil into the leather in brief, even strokes over a small area.

'Did you hear anything last night?' she asked.

Hal pushed his hair back with an oily hand. It stayed put for once. He addressed Margaret's hem rather than her face. 'Not until Celia cried out.' He met Margaret's eyes for a moment, allowing her to see how troubled he was. 'It is a terrible thing, the murder of a man, no matter if he was a spy.' Then he dropped his gaze to his work, moved farther down the length of leather, scooped up more of the oily mixture from a bowl, began to rub and knead.

She guessed he was of an age with the dead lad. 'Did you know Will Harcar?'

'Not well.'

Murdoch came round the side of the kitchen, muttering an oath. 'The guest who sounded like an Englishman – where's his horse?' he asked Hal.

'Don't know who you're talking about. I don't often meet the riders.'

'Show me the horses that have been stabled here since yesterday.'

Hal picked up the bowl, rose with harness in hand, followed Murdoch to the stable. Margaret followed them at a little distance, stayed out of sight, listening.

'This belongs to a red-bearded MacLaren,' Hal said. 'From the Trossachs, a day's ride from Stirling Castle. He came with it to see it was stabled well.'

So that was Redbeard's name – MacLaren. And he was still here. She remembered him following Comyn out of the tavern the previous night. Nervous, she glanced behind her.

'This belongs to someone who does not come far to Edinburgh and comes through often.'

'Ian Brewster,' said Murdoch.

Margaret had put him in the room opposite the Englishman last night.

'No other?' Murdoch demanded.

'Not last night.'

Margaret withdrew before they came out.

WE HAVE NOT BEGUN TO SEE

Margaret had the card weaving spread out on the table, trying to unravel more of the thread. Her hand had healed to the point where she no longer needed a bandage. The work was a good use of her hands while trying to quiet her mind enough to search for connections between what was going on around her. She saw Roger's presence in town, his running from her, and Comyn's reaction to the news that she had seen him as a set. But she did not know what to make of it. For it had not been clear whether Comyn saw Roger's presence as dangerous or as a sign of danger. Harcar's murder the night of the discovery of Davy's body might mean that someone blamed Harcar for Davy's death. She feared that someone had seen her begin to approach Harcar and killed him before he could tell her about finding Jack's body, which would mean she was being watched, and that someone did not want her to learn anything about Jack's murder. She did not know how to interpret MacLaren's antagonism towards the Englishman, his following Comyn out of the tavern, his stealth outside Murdoch's room last night. Then there was Murdoch's absence just as all this took place, and Comyn's concern about it. If only she knew where her uncle had been. Yet even that might tell her little. There were too many pieces, and she did not know whether they were all connected. Certainly James Comyn figured largely. She wished she knew more about him. He was like an object in the night, seeming clear when seen from the corner of her eye, but insubstantial straight on, impossible to focus on. That made her very uneasy.

Celia sat across from Margaret darning some bedding. A knock on the door brought her quickly to her feet. She crossed herself before she asked who was there.

'Father Andrew.'

Celia unbolted the door.

Shaking his cloak, Andrew asked if he might come in.

Margaret knotted the warps together and tied a cord around the cards, sorted at last. She would begin again on the border when she could pay it her full attention.

'Celia, take your work to my uncle's kitchen. It will be warm in there.' She could not speak plainly with Andrew if the maid were in the room, and she had a favour to ask of him.

'Master Murdoch will not be pleased,' Celia said.

'Tell him I sent you.'

Celia took her mantle and her sewing and departed, slamming the door behind her.

Andrew had gone straight for the brazier. He stood there rubbing his hands together close to the heat. His curly hair clung damply to his temples, his beaked nose was red.

'You have had a cold walk up here.' Margaret took his mantle – such heavy wool it always surprised her – hung it on a peg near the brazier to dry.

Andrew's forced smile did not distract Margaret's attention from his eyes, which looked desperate. She prayed Abbot Adam had not already heard about Harcar, that Andrew had not been sent as his emissary. She tried to hide her anxiety as she offered him the high-backed chair.

He dropped into it with his hands folded, his elbows close to his side, like a lad awaiting a lecture. 'I have been with Janet Webster.'

A weariness in his voice seemed at odds with the tension in his body.

So it was that business, not Harcar. Almost gasping with relief, Margaret sat on a stool, took out her spindle to keep her hands busy. 'How is she?'

'Widow Smith is strong. She did not collapse with grief though it's plain she feels it.' Andrew had unclenched his hands, shifted in the chair. He looked calmer. 'She wished Davy's body brought to the smiddie this morning. While she stood watching the servants shift him from the cart to the house she asked at last what our infirmarian had said about the body.'

Widow Smith. That is how people would know Janet now, until she remarried. If Margaret were widowed, she would be Widow Sinclair, just like her goodmother. 'What had he noted?'

'He saw no marks on the body but a head wound.'

'And poor Davy ended in the Tummel naked like Harry the cobbler.'

'Perhaps they fell into an argument beside the river.'

'Naked?'

Andrew threw up his hands. 'I don't claim to ken how they came to be there.'

Margaret ignored him. 'Was Davy wounded in the front or the back of his head?'

'Why? What does it matter?'

Margaret tugged at the wool, said nothing.

'Davy's injury was to the back of his head, at the base of the skull.'

'So he was hit from behind.' Margaret thought about that. 'How did Harry die?'

'His neck had been broken. But not simply snapped. Crushed. A strong man like Davy could murder a man so.'

'And then Davy hit himself in the base of his skull? Or perhaps Harry was yet so strong after a fatal wound?'

Andrew's full, handsome face looked grey, despite his recent travels, which would normally put colour in a man's cheeks. 'Perhaps there was a third man.'

'Forgive me. I should not argue with you as if you had cause to lie. I am only trying to make sense of all this. You look weary. It is good you are through with your travels for a while.'

Andrew ran a hand through his tonsured hair. 'Our people are stirring all round us, Maggie. Raids on English ships, attacks on the king's messengers, the barns burned in which they stable their horses.' He dropped his head to his hands and was quiet a moment. 'We have not begun to see the bloodshed. When I was at Elcho I heard the rumours. I prayed I would reach Holyrood before the uprising began.'

There had been many rumours of skirmishes, particularly up north, around Aberdeen – she worried about Fergus – but the tales were of individuals fighting to keep their provisions, cattle, horses – that was a far cry from a rising. 'You believe the people will fight for John Balliol?'

Andrew said, 'I do,' without hesitation. 'Our countrymen may fight among themselves, but they will not support a soulless murderer like Edward Longshanks. They will be loyal to their king.'

'And you think this uprising could happen any time?'

'Andrew Murray in the north, William Wallace down here.'

'Sir Andrew Murray? But he was sent to England with King John.' He was of one of the noblest Scots families, with lordships north of the Forth.

'No, his son.' Who had also been imprisoned in England. 'He has fled Chester Castle and headed home with a will to oust the English.'

'You ken far more about this than I imagined. But of course – you were in St Andrews. Was it for the meeting you spoke of, between Bishop Wishart and the Steward?' From what he had said at the ferry crossing, the bishop and the steward had consulted William Wallace.

The question seemed to make Andrew uneasy. He waited so

long to respond that Margaret had just opened her mouth to apologise if she pried when he spoke.

'I was – I happened to be there at the time. But I was not privy to their discussions.'

She did not like that answer if it meant he had been there spying for Abbot Adam and had been discovered. But she had not intended to make Andrew uneasy. 'When you returned to Dunfermline with Jack's corpse you were taking a greater risk than I knew.'

'It was the right thing to do.'

'Brave, nonetheless.'

They were quiet a moment, each lost in a place the other could only guess at.

'Do you think Jack's death had anything to do with the deaths of Harry and Davy?' she asked in a while.

'I see nothing to connect them.' Andrew seemed distracted, studying his hands, gazing round at the room.

'I have blethered on without asking your news. Did you find lodgings for me? Did you come to argue me away from biding here at the inn?'

'No. Everyone is frightened. I do not think anyone will come forward to accept a stranger, despite your being my sister.'

'Because of the murders on the River Tummel?'

'No!' It was almost a shout. Even Andrew seemed taken aback by the vehemence of his denial. 'Because of the trouble all round us,' he said softly. 'Might I have some ale?'

'I'll fetch it.'

Margaret pondered Andrew's mood as she went down to the tavern kitchen. It was not his usual bristly irritation, but something much deeper, and not aimed at her. She wondered how she seemed to him, weighing her words as she was, fearful of mentioning the corpse in the alley that was so much on her mind.

Andrew was pacing the length of the room when she returned with cups, followed by Geordie with a heavy pitcher.

'A nice, large chamber,' Andrew said when Geordie had gone.

'Well fitted. This was Mistress Grey's?'

'Yes. She fixed it up to suit her.'

'I am sorry about her.'

'Let's not talk of it. There are those who say she was *not* Roger's paramour.' She poured the ale. 'You have said little about your time with Mother before Easter. Has she embraced a more purely Roman worship?'

Andrew thought Christiana's second sight was a pagan thing, not a gift from God as the sisters thought.

'We did not discuss it. She looked well.' His eyes roamed the room again. 'Did you find an escort to Dunfermline for your maid?'

'Not yet.' She saw no need to admit she had not tried. 'You have not heard of anyone travelling north?'

Andrew shook his head. 'I doubt I shall find someone suitable.'

This banter was irritating. Margaret had a favour to ask. 'Andrew, as a priest you have freedom to move about the town, to mingle with your countrymen and the English.' She shook her head as he opened his mouth to speak. It was time to tell him about Roger. 'Hear me out. I saw Roger on Thursday.'

'Here? In Edinburgh?'

She told him what had happened. 'He had such wounds on his face. I can't bear not knowing whether he is still in the town, whether someone is seeing to his injuries. I hoped you might ask at the castle.'

Andrew frowned at her as if she had suddenly begun to talk in tongues.

'He is your sister's husband,' she said. 'It would not be unseemly for you to enquire about him. And Jack's death. If you could just ask whether he had been in trouble with the soldiers.'

Andrew had begun to shake his head as if trying to dislodge the words from his ears.

'It cannot be such an impossible request,' she cried. 'He is my husband. Jack was his factor. You are—'

'I am a canon of Holyrood, Maggie. Not one of the priests the

English brought with them. I can go to the castle, yes, and I might mention Roger, but both of them? Surely you see how that would look?'

'How would it look?'

'At the abbey we strive to favour neither Edward's nor John Balliol's rule.'

'But all that you said about our countrymen supporting King John. What you called Longshanks—'

'My own beliefs do not count. I am God's instrument. I cannot show favour.'

'Concern about your family shows favour to one of them?' His courage was selective. 'What of the foot soldiers? What harm would it be to speak to one of them? All hear the gossip, surely.'

'I am obedient to my abbot.'

'I am not asking you to disobey! He cannot have ordered you to put your family aside.'

'All Christianity is my family now, Maggie.'

'Words. Just words.'

'It is a vow I took.'

'Other priests care for their families.' Damn him. He could so easily do this without declaring a side.

'Maggie, do you realise the English don't even use us as confessors? They bring their own priests on campaign. Do you know why? Because they fear what a confessor might hear and divulge to others. Oh, yes, we take vows not to speak of anyone's confession, but in time of war men are wise to have doubts.'

'That has nothing to do with what I ask of you.'

'You do not listen!'

'I am an excellent listener, Andrew. I had to be, with Mother and her vague pronouncements. What you have lost is your heart.'

'I brought your husband's factor to Dunfermline, remember? I'd not call that no heart.'

They drank their ale in hot silence. Margaret could not accept Andrew's excuses. If he loved her as she loved him, he would do this small thing for her. How was she to learn anything about Roger and Jack if even her brother would not risk himself to help? When Andrew had drained his cup, he rose, retrieved his cloak.

'I have heard one thing of use to you, Maggie.' He looked apologetic. 'A woman on Cowgate takes in laundry. Rosamund is her name. Her house is almost directly across from Davy's smiddie.'

'Let me walk you down,' she said, having cooled a little.

When they reached the end of the alley, Andrew put his hands on Margaret's shoulders, shook his head and sighed deeply. He kissed her forehead. 'I shall go to the castle for you, Maggie.'

'Oh, Andrew.' She hugged him tightly. 'God go with you.'

'And with you, Maggie.' Andrew called to his servant Matthew and started up the High Street with long, strong strides.

Margaret watched until she could no longer distinguish him from the others in the High Street. She wished she knew what had changed his mind. And what was on his mind. He was so full of contradictions. What he had said earlier had made it clear he had chosen a side, that he was for King John. Yet he had so adamantly denied his right to support his king when she asked her favour. And then agreed. Belatedly, she hoped she had not pushed him too far. He was such an unbending man – if ever he decided to take a stance, he would risk all for it. And being so high in Abbot Adam's favour, he could not easily hide his new allegiance. *Dear God, watch over him. For he is one of your most loyal servants.*

She walked back down the alley. Glancing in through the open tavern door, she saw Murdoch in there, talking sternly to Sim. Hoping that would keep her uncle occupied for a while, she retrieved her tools from his kitchen. Celia muttered a greeting from her seat by the fire, then bent to her work.

'You might go back if you like.'

'I'll bide here a while.'

Margaret mounted the steps quietly, stole past MacLaren's room. She needed to discover what Murdoch kept in his chest, but she would not welcome another encounter with Redbeard.

Entering Murdoch's chamber, she saw that the soiled clothes he had worn in the early morning were not lying on his bed, nor were they tossed on the floor or hanging on a hook. A leather pack on a bench beneath the window contained only a piece of iron apparently broken from something and a pair of gloves, so often worn they retained the shape of Murdoch's hands. Margaret moved the lamp from the plain chest beside the bed to the floor, took the slide key and slowly, holding the padlock in one hand, slid the key in, holding her breath as she strained to sense the second it touched the springs. After a few unsuccessful tries, she rose and walked back and forth, loosening her hands and her back – she was forced to kneel in a cramped position. When she returned to it, she at last managed to hook the key into the holes in both springs, compress them, and push them through, opening the latch.

In the chest she found unlaced leggings, soft shoes, a clean shift – who had washed that for him, she wondered – a length of plaid, muddy along part of one side. Murdoch had lived in the highlands for a time as a young man and had taken to wearing their long lengths of colourful wool, draped and belted, when doing physical work or travelling. She lifted it. Still damp. She wrinkled her nose at the smell of tidal mud. Something sticky matted the wool in another spot. She stepped over into the light from the window. Mud and slime with the distinct stench of low tide. Smuggling, she guessed. That is what he had been up to. It was a wonder there were ships with cargo worth stealing at present, unless he was boarding English ships. Murdoch might be so bold as that. Andrew had said something about thefts on English ships.

She unwound the plaid. A shirt fell to the floor. This is what she had noticed in the morning. The sleeves were caked with mud. Drying, the mud cracked and crumbled, littering the floor. The left sleeve was torn near the shoulder. There was blood above that, and on the chest. If the injury was Murdoch's, he hid it well.

Abbot Adam be damned. Sitting there with Margaret, seeing the yearning in her eyes, the strain in her voice, Andrew had felt something shift in his heart – or perhaps just right itself. His family came before all but God, that was the right way, that was the only way of honour. What he had said to Margaret about his countrymen – that had come from his heart, not the pit of his stomach, where the abbot held him. But no more – he would not cower before Abbot Adam again.

With Matthew trotting behind, Andrew walked with purpose up the High Street, past the tron, the market cross, St Giles', across the well-trodden mud of Lawnmarket, to the first guard post. It must have been a shock for Margaret to think she saw Roger after all this time only to lose him even before they spoke, before she could be certain it was him. Andrew doubted that she had seen him, but he would do what he could to help her find Roger. Because it was what she wanted and Andrew loved her, not because he thought the man good for her.

He explained to the guards who he was, that he knew Sir Walter Huntercombe, and that he wished to speak with the sheriff about a private matter.

Not so long ago Andrew knew the guards, two of them from Perthshire. Now they had been replaced by English guards, younger men, glowering, expecting trouble. Even so, Andrew and Matthew were passed through to Castle Hill.

Here those houses not burned in the fighting had been taken over by King Edward's army and those who fed it, clothed it, repaired weapons, stabled and cared for the horses. Tents and long, low buildings of hasty construction cluttered the area. A blast of heat smote them as they passed the castle smiddie. The track began to wind to the north, climbing gradually to the citadel. The Firth of Forth glistened in the pale sunshine of the afternoon. Ahead, due west, rose the faint outlines of the mountains.

'Father,' Matthew gasped. He held his side, his face red. 'I pray you, Father, I cannot walk so fast for so long.'

Andrew had been unaware of walking quickly. Until Matthew's

reminder, he had not felt his own state. His left heel ached, sending a pain up his leg. The wind chilled his damp temples. Despite the cold, his habit clung to his sweaty back.

'There is no need for such haste. We will stop a moment.'

At the inner gatehouse, Andrew requested a meeting with Sir Walter. A bench inside the gatehouse was offered for their wait. Matthew gladly slumped down on the end. Andrew settled beside him.

A servant came to lead them to the sheriff's lodgings in a half-timbered house on the slope above the chapel of St Margaret. The quarters were exceedingly modest compared to what Andrew remembered of Sir Walter's manor house near Oxford. A tapestry was drawn over the doorway to a small chamber. It would take more than that to protect one against the braw winds that howled without. Andrew ducked beneath the tapestry, Matthew after him.

Sir Walter rose from a leather slung chair, arms spread in welcome.

'Father Andrew, it is good to see a friendly face.'

After exchanging news of their families, Andrew returned to Margaret, whom he had mentioned in passing.

'It is about my sister that I have come. Her husband has been missing for a long while. She expected him in Perth at Christmas, but he did not come. She has not seen him since Martinmas.'

Sir Walter sat back in his chair, spread his arms. 'In time of war . . .' He shook his head.

'He is a merchant, not a soldier.'

'Is she certain of that?'

'She has no cause to believe otherwise.'

'Then it is a long absence.' Sir Walter looked sympathetic. 'But I do not see what I might do.'

'My sister believes she saw her husband three days ago – here in Edinburgh. The men who accompanied him pulled him away before he could speak to her. He was badly cut on the left side of his face. I hoped you might know something of this. Roger Sinclair is his name.'

'She expected him in Perth, you said. Your sister has come all the way from there?'

'From Dunfermline, where she has been staying with her goodmother.'

Sir Walter asked for Roger's name again. Andrew repeated it.

'Sinclair.' The sheriff pondered. 'The Sinclairs are friends of John Balliol, are they not?'

'The wealthier, more powerful members of the family are, yes. But Roger comes from a family of merchants from Fife, traders across the North Sea.'

'Traders. Sinclair knew folk from Berwick?'

'He shipped from Berwick.'

'Ah.'

'I pray that God has not changed His mind about saving him from that massacre.'

Sir Walter shook his head at mention of the slaughter. 'Though some might call it treason to say it, I cannot think other than that it was a terrible thing that King Edward allowed at Berwick. I have not known my liege to make such a misstep before.' The sheriff was quiet for a moment, lost in his own thoughts. 'Sinclair is a familiar name. It was a Sinclair who escorted Edwina of Carlisle to Murdoch Kerr's inn.'

'I do not know that name. Roger travelled with a Mistress Grey who lodged there . . .'

Though the sheriff studied his hands, Andrew could see the look of concern on his face.

'I shall return in a moment.' Sir Walter rose. His servant lifted the tapestry, opened the door. The sheriff nodded to Andrew and left the room.

The story Andrew had heard was that Roger had helped Mistress Grey escape from Berwick, her husband a victim of King Edward's slaughter, so she had claimed. That had bothered Andrew when he heard it. It felt wrong that she had taken five months to leave Berwick. Edwina of Carlisle. Andrew rose, fingered the carving on the back of his chair. Edwina was a Saxon name, common in the north of England.

A servant opened the door. Sir Walter entered the room, his face solemn. His chin tucked in, he avoided Andrew's eye as he resumed his seat. Another servant brought a tray, poured wine into cups, offered one to Andrew. Brandywine.

'Do you have news of Roger?' Andrew asked.

'Perhaps,' Sir Walter said, his head down, the cup untouched beside him. 'Mistress Grey *was* Edwina of Carlisle, a lady of noble birth who lived in Berwick until recently. The terrible massacre there forced her, finally, to decide to leave her home, but she feared her Cumbrian name would antagonise the people of Edinburgh while she awaited safe conduct across the border. She claimed that her husband, William Carlisle, a merchant of Berwick and landholder in Cumbria, had sent money north for her escort back to England. She came to Edinburgh under the mistaken belief that the money had arrived at the castle. It had not.'

'What became of her?'

'In the end she sold some jewellery to fund the expedition back to England. Three men, including Roger Sinclair, were in the escort. A week ago the bodies of Dame Edwina and one of the men were found near the border. I do not know which of the men was slain.'

'He was escorting a wealthy Englishwoman across the border?'

'I see that surprises you. Roger Sinclair is not loyal to King Edward?'

Andrew did not like the interest Sir Walter exhibited. 'In faith I do not know which way he turns. But having known so many in Berwick . . .'

'I understand.'

'Were they robbed?'

'Jewels, much of their clothing, horses . . .' Sir Walter studied the signet ring on his finger, as if noting what he might lose in such an attack.

'My sister will surely ask whether it was just theft or something more.'

'One never knows on the border. Robert Bruce has close ties to Carlisle, you know.'

First he had mentioned John Balliol, now the Bruce. It sounded to Andrew as if Sir Walter was not at all sure it was a simple theft. 'I thought Mistress – Dame Edwina was a widow.'

'Part of her guise as Mistress Grey, I should think.'

'Did you not wonder about her? Why she had stayed so long in Berwick after the siege of the town?'

'In such times I would be negligent of my duties not to wonder.' Sir Walter spread his hands. 'Her tale was that her husband had gone south to see to their property in Cumbria, while she had remained to see to their land up here. But of late he had felt it was no longer safe for her in Scotland. Both were rightfully fearful that she might be in danger, being English. And her husband is indeed in Carlisle – that much at least is certainly true. But I know no more.'

Andrew's stomach knotted. What a miserable tale to take back to Margaret. More uncertainty.

'It is a difficult time for all the people of this country,' said Sir Walter, his voice suddenly gentler. 'And the north of England. When people turn against their king, violence follows. King Edward has done well by us. Your country would enjoy peace and order under his rule. Being Abbot Adam's man, I doubt you would deny that.'

Any king who had to go to such lengths to subdue those he ruled was no good king, but Andrew had come to that opinion late. He had been naïve. He had not believed Edward Longshanks meant to depose their king. As for being Abbot Adam's man, he had been, to his shame, far longer than his conscience should have tolerated. Yet the abbot was his lord.

Even so, his mouth would not form the conciliatory words. 'We had a king who suited us well enough.'

Sir Walter seemed startled by the words, but merely pressed his hands together, shook his head. 'I wish I could give you more definite news.'

'My sister was so certain she had seen him on Thursday.'

The sheriff downed his wine. 'So you said, but I would expect to know of his presence, if that were true. She has come all this way seeking him. It is no surprise her eyes tricked her.'

'Are you certain it was them?'

'Dame Edwina carried letters identifying herself.'

'They left a letter identifying her?'

'It was sewn into her shift. They did not strip her completely.'

Both men bowed their heads.

Andrew said a prayer for the woman's soul – if the man were Roger he deserved no prayers, leaving his wife to go to the aid of an Englishwoman. 'Where is the man's body?'

'I was not informed. It was part of a larger report from Glasgow of risings in the west.'

'So you don't think it an ordinary theft?'

'The king's warden of Galloway and Ayr, Sir Henry Percy, does not. As for myself, I see no clear evidence.' And yet he had suggested Robert Bruce.

'Did you arrange the escort?'

'No. Sinclair did, but I do not know how he came to be associated with the lady. Apparently neither do you.'

Andrew shook his head. At least this was something, he could tell Margaret that Roger had been acting on his own will.

'We must talk about your journey to St Andrews,' said Sir Walter. 'Another time, of course. Can I offer you more brandywine?'

'I must go to my sister,' Andrew said, rising.

'Of course. It will be a difficult meeting.'

Andrew closed his eyes. *Holy Mother, guide me in telling Maggie*, he prayed. 'I thank you for seeing me. It will be some little comfort, to hear it from her brother rather than a stranger. God go with you, Sir Walter.'

'God go with you, Father Andrew.'

Andrew hastened down the hill, Matthew pounding along behind him.

☙ 11 ❧

It Is a Difficult Time

Margaret sat by the fire with her spindle, watching Murdoch prepare the meal.

'You will not tell me where you were for two nights?' she asked again.

'Are you my keeper?'

'James Comyn and Roy both thought it unlike you and worrisome.'

'Bothersome to Roy. But Comyn – what did he say?'

'He asked where you were, that is all. But I could see how it troubled him.'

'With my mistress.'

'You're a better liar than that.'

Murdoch snorted. 'It is the truth.'

'Who is she?'

'I'll not say. You'll not like that I was with her.'

'Even Janet Webster seemed worried for you.'

Murdoch splashed himself with an overhasty stir.

So that was the closeness she had sensed. 'I was with Janet twice yesterday. You were not there.'

'I did not say she was my mistress.'

'I saw mud on you, and blood, Uncle. You wore the plaid. You do not wear that clothing in the town.'

'I told you—'

She stared at him until he dropped his gaze.

'You are too curious, Maggie.'

'You do not appear injured. So whose blood was it, Uncle? Harcar's?'

'No! I've told you I had no part in that.'

'So?'

'I took too much of a risk boarding a ship. It is possible I killed someone – but he attacked me first. I'm not a murderer.'

Like Roger, he had his own moral code. Margaret understood that in times like these a certain ruthlessness might be necessary, but it still chilled her.

The cat rubbed against Murdoch's leg. He dropped a piece of fish for him.

'You spoil the cat, feeding him scraps of food. He'll never be a good mouser if so well fed.'

'Agrippa is good company,' said Murdoch. 'And a good mouser. If you were a cat, so would you be, I think.'

She was not sure she liked that. But cats had been much on her mind. 'Might it have been a cat that wounded Roger? No man's fingers could dig such wounds. Not four of them. But such great claws they must have been. A far larger paw than I have ever seen.'

Murdoch blew on a spoonful of stew, tasted it, tossed in a pinch of savoury. 'You are sure of what you saw, Maggie?'

'For a few breaths I was close enough. He must be in great pain.'

Murdoch shook his head as he sliced bread. 'No man would stand still for four swipes of a knife. You are certain of four?'

She was not certain about any of it any more. 'I might be mistaken about the number.'

'Four claws, that's what you were thinking, eh?'

'You don't believe me.'

'Believe you I do, Maggie. But to the counting of the wounds . . .' He shook his head.

She tugged at the wool spun out below the spindle.

'Maggie, have you ever had a vision, like one of Christiana's?'

The question surprised and annoyed her. 'You know that I'm not like my mother. I did see him.'

'How can you be certain it wasn't a vision?'

She wished she had moved more quickly. If she had touched Roger she would be more certain. 'The soldiers saw him.'

'Did they say they saw him? Or a group of men?'

Murdoch was confusing her. 'The men.' Margaret tried to recall her mother's descriptions of her visions. Outwardly, it was clear that Christiana was staring at something that was not there, or that did not warrant such an expression as she wore. She might move towards it, or reach out to it imploring, or behave as if someone had touched her. Once she had bled from the touch of steel in her vision. Andrew had borne witness. He had sworn that she had not moved, the blood had just appeared. She did not see Christ or the Blessed Virgin or the saints. She saw ordinary people in scenes from the past or the future. If that had happened to Margaret, it was possible that Roger's wounding was something yet to happen.

Murdoch grunted as he set a trencher with stew in the centre before her. 'It is something to think about on a full stomach.' He sat down, started to eat at once.

Margaret had no appetite. 'What will happen if the English hear you found Harcar? Father Francis might have been seen moving him to St Giles'.'

He frowned up at the ceiling. 'With Sim's tongue we'll soon ken. I caught him telling a stranger that Harcar was killed on his way from the tavern this morning. I do not ken what is stuffed betwixt his lugs, but it's not a brain.' Murdoch stuffed a piece of bread in his mouth, chewed energetically. 'But it's only to be expected of the son of a flyting fishwife,' he continued after swallowing. 'Thrice brought up before the magistrate for it.'

Margaret gave up trying to eat, put down her spoon.

Murdoch held out a rough hand.

She grasped it.

'They cannot prove a thing. We'll talk of other matters.' He frowned as he sought out a topic. 'Do you remember your aunt, lass?' He began a tale of romance that Margaret did not believe, but it distracted her enough that she finally picked up her spoon to eat.

A knock at the door brought both their heads up. Murdoch shook his. 'Eat, lass. I'll see who it is.' He crossed to the door, opened it. 'Andrew, good day to you. Or is it evening? Doesn't your abbot fret when you are not there at vespers?'

'I would see my sister, Uncle.' Andrew's voice was strained.

Margaret turned round in her chair. Andrew unwound his mantle, draped it over Murdoch's arm. Her uncle grunted, then handed the mantle to Matthew, who had entered behind his master, wiping his forehead. His face was red from exertion.

Not so Andrew. Dear God, if Andrew had looked pale before, he looked far worse now.

Murdoch muttered to Matthew to hang the mantles on the pegs and take a seat by the door, and he would have some ale to fortify him for the rest of his journey.

Margaret pushed back from the table and rose to take her brother's hands. They were dry and cold. He avoided looking her in the eye. 'Andrew, what is it?' She had to take a deep breath to manage more words, he frightened her so. 'Did you go to the castle?'

'I have just now spoken to Sir Walter Huntercombe.' Andrew shook his head at Murdoch's offer of ale, slumped down onto the bench farthest from the door, crossed his hands, stared down at them.

Margaret drew her chair over to him.

'It is possible Roger is slain, Maggie.'

The choking sensation was now almost overwhelming. She stood, hand on her ribs, and forced herself to remember how to breathe.

*

'Look what you've done!' Murdoch shouted, running to Margaret, who pushed him away.

'Do not silence Andrew now.' Her words came in gasps. 'Go sit.'

Andrew glared at Murdoch, hoping to push him back towards Matthew, but the stubborn man pulled up a chair near Margaret's.

Andrew drew Margaret down on the bench beside him. She smelled like peat fires and rosemary. Her hair was undone, tumbling down her back. She was so young, and not even her mother here to comfort her. He saw her pain in her shadowed eyes, the lines of fatigue in her face, a stiffness of posture as she fought for control. She was not so faint of heart as most women, but to lose a husband must be a terrible thing to bear. He told himself that she would recover, she would remarry, it was not the end of happiness for her. But it would take time before she could see that.

'What makes you think Roger is dead?' She spoke more easily now.

Andrew felt her breath on his cheek. He could not remember when he had last been so close to anyone. How could he say anything but the truth when she was so close? 'Roger accompanied Mistress Grey to the border.' It was not the time to explain the names. 'She and one of the men in the party have been slain. The man was not identified.'

Margaret crossed herself. 'Since Thursday?'

That cursed vision of her husband. Andrew moved away from her, to the end of the bench, so that he could turn to face her squarely. 'Perhaps a week ago, Maggie. On the border. You did not see him the other day.'

Her eyes narrowed. With distrust? Anger? 'I did see him. I am certain of it.'

Andrew took her hands in his. They were warm. Her grasp was strong.

'I did,' she insisted. 'It must have been another man in their company who was slain.'

Her eyes widened to contain tears. When they were young

134

Andrew knew her bad days by the colour of her eyes – the same deep green as today. But what could he do but tell her the truth, help her accept it? She could not be spared the pain.

'Maggie, the sheriff believes he would have heard if Roger was back in Edinburgh.'

Murdoch shifted on his seat. 'How many men were in Mistress Grey's company?' he asked, his crooked brows drawn down in challenge.

Why would he not go away? 'Three.'

Murdoch shook his head at Andrew. 'Then there is more than an even chance he is not dead.'

Such unfounded optimism would not help Margaret face her possible loss.

'Why was Roger escorting this woman?' Margaret asked.

Once again Murdoch interrupted. 'Indeed. The sheriff has nothing to tell you, so he tells a tale. Maggie—'

'The woman's real name is Edwina of Carlisle,' Andrew said loudly, to drown out Murdoch. 'Roger was escorting her to her husband in that town.'

'Carlisle? Why?' Margaret asked.

Andrew told her what the sheriff had told him, though not his mention of Robert Bruce. It did not seem as clear in the recounting as he had thought it when hearing it before. He still did not understand why the woman had remained in Lothian, why her husband was not with her.

Margaret withdrew her hands. 'I do not understand Roger's involvement. Does he think helping this English merchant's wife will gain him a port?'

Murdoch snorted through his oft-broken nose. 'Do you have a body to show for this story?'

'No.' God's blood, the man irritated Andrew. 'By now they will be buried.' He prayed that they were, that they had not been left where they lay.

Margaret studied her hands silently.

'I wanted you to know as soon as I heard,' Andrew explained, wondering why she said nothing. 'I did not want you to hear it from others. Not as you did about Mistress Grey – Edwina.'

Margaret clutched her elbows, tucked in her chin. She began to bite her cheek and tap one of her feet. Andrew moved to embrace her, but Murdoch's arm was already circling her. What right had their uncle to comfort her when Andrew was here?

She shook herself loose from Murdoch, turned to Andrew.

'How did the sheriff learn of their deaths? I want to talk to someone who saw them.'

'He received a report from Glasgow. I doubt the messenger had witnessed any of it.'

'How far is Glasgow?'

'Too far,' Murdoch said.

'What would you accomplish?' Andrew asked. 'They would never agree to your opening the grave, Maggie.'

'How am I to know whether to mourn him?' she cried.

Andrew could not look at the pain in her eyes. It seemed a day of widows. His journey up the hill with the lyke of Davy the smith seemed so long ago, but it had been just this morning. The morning of a long day. And he must get back to Holyrood. 'I must leave you now, Maggie. My lord abbot awaits word of my meeting with Widow Smith.'

'Pray for Roger,' Margaret said, still turned from him. 'Pray that I saw him on Thursday.' Her voice trembled.

Matthew jumped up to retrieve their mantles.

'Godspeed to you,' Murdoch said grudgingly.

'I will pray for you and Roger all the night, I swear,' Andrew said. Turning Margaret around, he kissed her on the forehead. She put her arms round him and held him tightly for a moment.

❦ 12 ❧

ALL THE DIFFERENCE

There had been a moment a year ago when Margaret sank into the abyss. Her flux had begun after two months – all that while she had happily believed she was with child. When she saw her blood, she fell into despair and walked in a colourless, silent land with an endless, bleak horizon. She walked there again now.

'Maggie?'

Margaret turned into Murdoch's arms.

He hugged her hard, then let her go. 'We must talk, Maggie.'

Closing her eyes, she remembered the warmth of the bed when Roger was there, the scent of wine and spices that never seemed to fade in his clothes, his hair.

'Maggie, are you taking a turn?'

She opened her eyes. 'I'll not faint here.'

'Have I not asked you what you ken of Roger?'

'Do you remember how it felt when you lost your wife?'

'I do, Maggie, that is why—'

'Edwina of Carlisle – did you know that was her name?'

'Maggie, if you will just be quiet I will tell you all—'

'Now. Oh, yes, now I've lost him you'll tell me all. Now I can't bear to speak of him you'll—'

'It was Roger you saw, Maggie,' Murdoch shouted, interrupting her. 'It cannot have been him killed at the border.'

Margaret felt her world revolve and re-form itself once again. 'What is this?'

Murdoch took off his cap, wiped his sweaty head with it. 'We have much to talk about.'

Margaret fled to the door, swung it wide, gulping the evening air.

Murdoch stood behind her. 'Come, Maggie,' he said gently. 'We must talk within.'

Gingerly, feeling she could not trust her own feet, she moved towards the table, sat down, poured herself more ale. Leaning her elbows on the table, she took a great drink.

Murdoch closed the door and eased down across from her. 'You might put that aside. I have much to tell you.'

In a foolish act of defiance she drained the cup before putting it aside. Still leaning on her elbows, she asked with a slight slur, 'Roger's wound? Is that real too?'

Murdoch looked up through his uneven brows. 'Are you going to remember a word I say?'

She was certain she was hearing quite clearly. Pulling herself up to her full height, she repeated the questions, this time without any trouble.

'Aye,' Murdoch said. 'I have heard of it.'

'From whom? Who saw him?'

'Janet Webster.'

'Ye gods!' It felt good to shout and hit the table with the side of her fist. And she had cause. Neither Murdoch nor Janet had deemed it a charitable thing to tell Margaret this news. 'Both of you. How could you be so cruel?' She was now fully sober.

'I have told you all along, Maggie, there is no trusting anyone. Even now I fear not for myself but for all those others who are fighting for the same thing. What you know you can be forced to tell.'

'You and Janet Webster can be trusted, but not me? Is it because you fight for something so awful I cannot possibly support it? Tell me. What are you fighting for?'

'Freedom.'

'John Balliol?'

Murdoch leaned back in his chair, crossed his arms, watched her closely as he said, 'I don't much care who it is as long as it is not Edward Longshanks. But John Balliol has been taken to the Tower of London and we need a new leader.'

'Who would that be?'

'Roger believes it is the grandson of the Competitor, Robert Bruce. I helped Roger because he believed it so firmly. And I will do so again.'

She made a connection. 'Robert Bruce's father was constable of Carlisle.'

'Aye. Edwina of Carlisle has known the Bruce for a long while. She believes he is the man who might rally the nobles.'

'You have lied to me, Uncle. All this you might have told me. I knew you were a thief, but I thought you had honour when it came to family.'

He jerked as if she had slapped him, and looked pained. She hoped he took notice.

'Maggie, listen to me.'

'I have been listening to you. Much good it did me.'

'I never chose to be a part of it and I have feared for my life, my tavern, my family ever since.'

'Such noble feelings. My husband does not appear to have had them.'

'They asked me for help stealing letters, any information we might find, from the English ships. I confess Roger spoke to my pride. I was honoured to be asked to use my skill for such a noble end.'

'All this time Roger has been out there working for Robert Bruce?'

'He takes great risks. With his silence, he hopes to protect you.'

Though Margaret wanted to believe her uncle, she found it difficult. Roger had not cared enough to make certain she understood that he loved her. 'Why did he not speak to me when I saw him?'

'I don't know. He might have been with someone who would use you.'

Implications flooded her mind. She bowed her head and her throat tightened. 'What sort of wife am I if I could not see his preoccupation, guess what it might be?'

'It was the slaughter in Berwick, Maggie. So many people he had known. He had stayed in their homes, shared meals with them, danced with their wives and daughters. You must have noticed a change in him after that?'

'Of course I did, but he said so little. I tried to talk about it, but he behaved as if I were merely curious, looking for gossip.' He had treated her as a child. She did not believe she had given him cause to consider her such. 'He left with the promise to return at Yuletide with no intent to do so.'

'He did not know when he left that he would be caught up in it. He left intending to honour his promise. But something happened on his way to Dundee. I do not know what.'

'It happened well before his journey to Dundee if he brought Edwina of Carlisle here before the summons to Berwick this past summer.'

'Aye. But he left her then for a long while.'

'He has left me for a long while.'

'It was after Yuletide he returned, already travel-worn, and ready to escort Dame Edwina to Ayr.'

'They were not on their way to Carlisle?'

Murdoch shook his head. 'No, they were headed to the Bruce, the Earl of Carrick.'

'I don't understand. Robert Bruce is Edward's man.' The Bruces did not accept John Balliol as King of Scotland. They claimed to be the rightful heirs to the throne, and after Longshanks chose John

Balliol as King of the Scots over the earl's grandfather the family had refused to pay fealty to him or to support him in his belated uprising against the English. As constable of Carlisle the earl's father had defended the English castle and town against King John Balliol's forces. Robert Bruce, Earl of Carrick, was much at Longshanks' court.

'Robert Bruce has turned against the English,' said Murdoch. 'He is raising the men of Ayr against Longshanks' warden in the west, Sir Henry Percy.'

'Why should anyone believe Bruce will be loyal?'

'He has everything to gain from supporting Longshanks, that is why.'

Perhaps Margaret had drunk too much. She did not understand the logic, nor did she care about Robert Bruce's allegiance at the moment. 'Do you think it was Edwina Carlisle's body they found at the border?'

'I doubt it was at the border. I doubt the sheriff told Andrew half what he kens about the killing.'

'Did you lie about her too? Were she and Roger lovers?'

'I never saw them together in such a way, Maggie. He did not spend the nights in her room.'

'Did he mention me?'

Murdoch hesitated. 'Not as often as I thought he should. But he had much on his mind.'

'Yes.' Margaret pushed herself up from the table, realised she was wobbly on her feet, and her stomach was queasy. 'And now to bed. It has been a long and tiring day.'

She wove towards the door. Murdoch caught her round the waist, helped her out to the yard, where she promptly lost what little food she had managed to swallow. Then, a supporting hand beneath her elbow, he helped her to her chamber. She accepted his kindness, though she did not yet forgive him. It was merely expedient in order to make it across the darkening backlands and up the stairs.

Murdoch growled at the bolted door.

Margaret called to Celia.

It seemed a long while before the maid opened the door. She was a blur as Margaret made her way to the bed, dropped down onto it.

'Mistress, what can I do for you?'

'Let me be.'

Her thoughts were fluttering butterflies trapped beneath her ribs and in her skull, all trying to find a way out. Murdoch's and Andrew's voices vied for possession of her ears. Murdoch had kept all this from her. She could think of no motive but distrust. She had been a fool to come to him, asking for his help, this man who believed she would betray him. She had remembered him from childhood as her hero, the one person who would always come to her aid. But he had lied to her from the moment she arrived.

As for Roger, she hated him. Yet she prayed that she had another chance with him, to convince him that she was as strong and admirable as Edwina of Carlisle. She had never had the chance to prove that. She had been a merchant's daughter, raised to quietly stay in the background and care for a household. Her life had been uneventful until now, except for her mother's Sight. She had had the charge of her father's household when she met Roger, and then she had charge of his. No one had ever asked more of her.

She did not believe Roger had kept her ignorant to protect her. It would have made all the difference to her these many months to have known what he was about and any man in love would know that.

Perhaps worst of all, if she had known Roger was working for the Bruce she would not have fretted so much in Jack's presence. She would have been frightened, but she would not have spoken of it. She would have put on a brave face. Jack would not have come to this cursed town. He would be alive.

❦ 13 ❧

THE MURDERER MIGHT BE ANYONE

Margaret lifted her head, then dropped it back down onto the pillow, rueing the quantity of ale she had drunk the previous evening. She smiled when she remembered that Roger was alive, that it had been him she saw in the town. Practical thoughts woke her more – perhaps she should return to Perth now, ready the house for him.

A vague feeling of dread insinuated, and then came memory. Roger was alive, yes, but her marriage was ashes. Her husband had not trusted her enough to explain to her what he was about, what he was willing to die for. She turned over onto her side, clutching her stomach.

She felt absolutely alone.

Four days ago her husband had been so near but made no effort to see her, speak to her. For two years she had shared her bed with a man about whom she had known nothing at all. Nothing. Yet she had worried so about him that his cousin had been moved to search for him – a kindness for which he had been rewarded by a violent death. A needless death. Roger's danger had at least been of his own choosing.

Murdoch thought it likely Harcar had been murdered because of his complicity with the English. Murdered in the alley next to this house in which she lay. The murderer might be as near as James Comyn. Or Roger. Neither supported Longshanks, for whom Harcar had spied. Yet each had cause to protect Murdoch – Comyn as his partner, Roger for the help Murdoch had given him. She did not think either would let the body lie in Murdoch's alley. But Celia had come upon it so soon after the deed – perhaps there had not been time to move Harcar. The murderer might be anyone.

Celia entered the chamber balancing in one hand a tray with bread and a pot of something steaming and smelling of mint. She must have walked fast, to keep it so hot.

Celia set the tray on the table, turned round, gave Margaret a good look. 'Your uncle says it's best you don't go with him to the smith's burial.'

'The burial.' Margaret had forgotten that was this morning. 'Why should I not?'

'For the same reason you're still abed.'

After what Margaret had learned last night she was loath to be in Janet Webster's company on such a day, when folk were meant to offer her comfort. Perhaps she should use the excuse to stay away.

'Come, mistress, sit up and drink this mint and honey before it gets cold.'

The sweet drink lured Margaret. It soothed her raw throat and warmed her. Celia knew much about the art of comfort. She had proved her mettle and her usefulness over the past days. It occurred to Margaret that Celia might be in danger – the Englishman's failure to raise the hue and cry upon finding the body might mean he had been involved, and he might have been aware she followed him.

The dark eyes regarded Margaret beneath the white cap. 'I have never seen my mistress in such a state as you were last night.'

Margaret could not imagine her goodmother Katherine imbibing so much. 'Nor will you see me in such a state again.' She pulled the small loaf apart, chewed on a piece. It was difficult to swallow. She washed it down with more of the sweet drink. There were still reasons to accompany Murdoch – it was a chance to meet the town folk who did not frequent the tavern. It would not do to stay cloistered for fear of danger – there was no place without danger now.

'Dress me, Celia. We shall join in the prayers for Davy Smith's soul.'

The morning mist was cool and refreshing on Margaret's face. She and Celia paused by the place in the alley where Harcar had lain. Both crossed themselves. He, too, would be buried today.

They both started at the sound of someone following them at a run. Margaret gathered her skirts to flee, grabbed Celia's hand, but it was Hal who came round the corner of the inn.

'The master is already gone,' he said, gulping air. 'I do not think he expects you there.'

'Then he'll be surprised.'

By the time they reached St Giles' kirkyard the priest was concluding his prayers over the coffin. Margaret joined Murdoch, who stood across the open grave from Davy's family.

'Did Celia not give you my message?' Murdoch hissed under his breath.

'Aye, but I disagreed.'

Across from them, Janet, head bowed beneath a hooded cloak glistening with the morning moisture, stood between a young woman wrapped well in a mantle and a young man who had fixed his gaze on two English soldiers standing at the edge of the small group of mourners. Other folk raised their eyes to the soldiers as the service ended.

To one side of Davy's family a woman sobbed into the shoulder of another woman. Margaret could not distinguish much about them.

Four men stepped forward to lower the coffin into the grave.

'The coffin is not just for the ceremony. He is being buried in it,' said a gruff voice beside Murdoch. 'James Comyn's generous gift, that coffin.' The speaker was Mary the brewster, wrapped in a coarse-woven mantle that seemed to exude peat smoke as she leaned towards Murdoch.

Margaret glanced round the crowd for Comyn. She did not find him.

'Belle has returned, did you hear?' the woman said to Murdoch. The chambermaid.

'I'll not have her back,' Murdoch growled. 'Roy be damned.'

'He went off to fight, her Perthshire farmer,' Mary said, then slipped away to join the mourners who had begun to move away from the soldiers.

'Go back to the inn, Maggie,' Murdoch said as she began to follow.

She ignored him and kept walking. He grabbed her elbow. She tried to shake him off. One of the soldiers moved towards them. It was the one who had walked her back to the inn.

'Is he hurting you?'

'God's blood,' Murdoch growled, 'reassure him.'

Margaret felt the eyes of all the mourners on her as she met the soldier halfway across the graveyard. 'My uncle fears I am not well, that is all.'

The soldier had gentle eyes, a kind smile. Margaret doubted he was much older than her. 'It must be a catarrh from your walk in the rain. Have you found your husband?'

She shook her head, wiser now to the danger of alerting the English. 'I must have been mistaken in thinking it was him. God go with you.' She fled across the kirkyard to where Hal, Celia and Murdoch awaited her. The rest of the crowd had departed.

'He behaves like he is your protector,' Murdoch said, casting an angry look towards the soldier who had now rejoined his partner.

'Why are they here?' Margaret asked.

'The garrison keeps the king's peace,' Murdoch said with a snort. 'They watch gatherings for signs of trouble. And they watch who attends. Many stayed away for that reason. And they'll not come to Janet's either.'

'Because Davy was murdered by soldiers? They know that?'

'It is most likely.'

'Will soldiers be in her house?'

Murdoch shook his head. 'But mark me, they will be watching without. You should return to the inn.'

The rain came down harder now. Margaret felt the damp entering her shoes. She doubted she would be welcome at Janet's after calling attention to herself in the kirkyard. But she must face the folk sometime.

'I'm going to Janet's.'

Murdoch grumbled, but said no more.

All heads turned when Margaret, Murdoch, Celia and Hal arrived at Janet's door.

'What is she doing here?' a woman cried, pointing an accusing finger at Margaret. 'You saw her in the kirkyard, the English ready to protect her. She's just like her husband's cousin.'

'Maud, Harry's widow,' Murdoch whispered. 'The weeper in the kirkyard.'

'What does she mean about Jack?'

'I told you no good would come of your being here.'

For the sake of Janet's family Margaret agreed, and turned to go. At the door Janet caught her. 'Come after vespers.' Her face was drawn, in her eyes Margaret noted a guardedness that had not been there before.

'What right had she to come here?' Maud's voice cried out.

Janet glanced over to the woman, then back at Margaret.

'I'll come,' Margaret said.

Janet hurried back to Maud. Margaret departed, Celia and Hal close behind.

At the alley to the inn, Margaret paused. 'What did she mean by that, Hal?'

He hunched his shoulders.

She could not believe Jack guilty of murder, nor that he wanted Longshanks for his king, but having lately learned how little she knew her own husband, Margaret did not doubt there were parts to Jack's character of which she was ignorant.

If there were rumours, Andrew would know them. She might send a messenger telling him that Roger was alive, and ask him what he knew about Jack. She asked Hal to take a message to Andrew.

Hal raked back his wet hair and glanced at the sky. 'Aye,' he said, without enthusiasm.

She gave him the message, telling him to describe what had happened at Janet's house as the cause for her need to know of any rumours about Jack.

'I am glad about your husband,' Hal said, then bobbed his head and departed on his mission.

'You show better sense today,' Celia said, 'sending him rather than going yourself.'

Hal returned by midday, his face red from the journey, his clothes soaked. Andrew had received her message, praised God for the news of Roger, promised to discover what he could about Jack.

In the early afternoon the rain had the inn roof leaking in all the bedchambers. Margaret and Celia used some of the cleaner straw from the stables to patch a few leaks that threatened to enlarge. For once, Celia worked without complaint.

As they headed from their building to the other, they saw Murdoch and Hal loading a barrel of ale onto a cart. There was much shouting and grunting. Murdoch's and Hal's wet hands slipped on the bent staves of the barrel, their feet lost purchase in the mud. Bonny waited patiently, head bowed, ignoring the two men and all the shoving and jolting going on behind her.

'For James Comyn,' Celia said. 'I heard them talking.'

Accompanying Hal might provide an opportunity to see Comyn's home. It was a brief walk – his house was just across the High Street and up a few doors. The cart was necessary only because the barrel must be taken from one backland to the other, a long way to balance it in the mud.

'Fetch my mantle.'

Celia withdrew, returned with the mantle, which she slipped over Margaret's shoulders.

'I'll go with you.'

'No. Stay here.'

Margaret descended the steps, waited until all was settled and Hal was leading Bonny to the alley. Then she lifted her skirts and made her way through the mud to join him.

'Where are you going?' Murdoch demanded.

When Margaret did not answer, Murdoch splashed through the mud, grabbed her by the elbow.

It was becoming a habit with him.

'What now, Uncle?'

'You'll not say a word about Harcar?'

'I hoped by now you would know I'm not a fool.'

'You might have saved yourself much trouble if you'd listened to my warnings this morning.' But Murdoch let her go. Raising his voice, he called to Hal, 'Tell Comyn it's a better ale than what we're replacing.'

Hal waved his hand, signalling he had heard.

When he and Margaret were out of range of Murdoch, Hal cleared his throat. 'You might wish to know before you speak with Master Comyn that he was prowling round the kitchen when you and Master Murdoch were talking last evening.'

Keeping up with Hal's long stride so that she avoided falling back to where the cartwheels churned up the mud took most of Margaret's concentration. 'You saw him?'

'I was sitting by the door,' he said, 'guarding it.'

She glanced over, saw that Hal's expression was grim beneath his hair.

'I thank you for that. Do you think he heard anything?'

'No. Nor did I.'

149

'I know that anything you might have heard will be safe with you.'

Margaret had noticed James's house before. It was half-timbered on a stone base. There were few houses of such sturdy construction in Edinburgh. It presented a modest whitewashed exterior to the street except for a glazed window on the first floor, another above the door in the alley. Two glazed windows meant wealth. Hal led Bonny down the alley past the main door, stopping along a wicket enclosure to the rear. A servant pulled aside two of the wattle wickets so that the cart could pull up to the back door. James Comyn called to Margaret from the doorway, welcoming her into his house. She hesitated but a moment.

It was a study into which she stepped from the back garden, with a long table, several cushioned chairs, silver candlesticks, a stone floor with a rush mat over it and a brazier in the corner by a small window. The man was wealthier than she had imagined. The inner walls were painted and outlined with flower borders. Margaret was conscious of her mantle dripping on the rush mat. Behind the study door there were pegs, she guessed, for she could see the edge of something black with a tattered hem.

Comyn invited her through to the main hall of the house, with a brazier near another long table, a few benches as well as one high-backed chair. Two tapestries graced the larger walls, one a hunting scene, the other of wine-making. Here, too, were candlesticks, some of a grey metal she did not recognise, some of silver. In a cupboard were handsome silver plates and two of the unusual metal, as well as a tankard.

Comyn must have followed her gaze. 'Pewter. It is made with both tin and copper or lead.' He handed one of the plates to her. 'I bought them in York.' It was a heavy plate, but the metal had a satiny finish and feel. 'These were made in Paris. In York they make only items for the kirk. No one makes pewter in our country.'

'Have you often travelled to York?' It seemed as far away as Bruges.

'I have property outside York, so I have lived there from time to time.'

Margaret noted a fine carved wood screen to one side of the brazier. This was the way she had dreamed her home in Perth would look in a few years, filled with treasures from Roger's travels. She wondered in what coin Robert Bruce rewarded Roger's service.

On one of the benches lay a fiddle and bow.

'Do you play the fiddle?' she asked, glad she was now on stone with scattered rushes, as she was still dripping.

'Rather well. And you?'

'No. Mother took our harp to the convent. But I played very little.'

'Your mother withdrew to a convent?' He sounded genuinely curious.

She reprimanded herself for mentioning Christiana.

'It is not uncommon after a woman's children are grown.'

'But your father is in Bruges, I think?'

If he knew that, he most likely knew of her mother also. She was glad of the reminder to watch her tongue. Comyn changed his expression at will, and she had been fooled by his apparent interest. 'Father agreed to her retirement before he departed. Uncle says to tell you this is a finer ale than the one that put him in your debt.'

Comyn laughed. 'His always is, even if brewed the same day in the same house. I pray you, sit and we shall test it.'

She shook her head. 'I have much to do.' And no stomach for ale this morning.

'Have you heard anything of your husband since the day you saw him?'

She tensed at the question. 'No. Have you?'

'Why should I hear anything? I asked because you look weary.'

She did not believe him. His attempt to eavesdrop the previous evening was just one more item on a fast growing list of things about which he was suspiciously curious. 'There is much to do at the tavern.'

'Ah.'

Her repetition certainly signalled her discomfort. He said no more.

Even that made her uneasy, his easy acquiescence. He enquired, but he never pressed. She took her leave with much relief, exiting through the study so she might collect Hal.

Abbot Adam had not asked about the rest of Andrew's day the previous evening, but it was clear he meant to now. He had summoned Andrew to take a letter, but he had no documents spread before him, there was no sign he had been at work. Instead, he was kneeling at a *prie-dieu* in his parlour when Andrew arrived. Abbot Adam often put on a display of piety when he was about to impart bad news or make unpleasant demands.

Now he rose slowly, clutching at the *prie-dieu* for support, bowed slightly to Andrew with his hands still folded in prayer, sat down on a leather-seated, backless chair, tucked his hands up his sleeves, blinked his eyes several times as if bringing himself back to the mundane world.

'Ah, Father Andrew. Sit, I pray you.' He expounded on the rewards of prayer for a while.

Andrew patiently listened, nodding in the correct places, all the while tensed for the assault.

'Indeed,' Adam said, 'I imagined you yesterday kneeling in prayer with the widow of the smith. All the day I pictured you there, through vespers, through the evening meal, enjoining her to pray for the soul of her departed husband. What a comfort Father Andrew must be to the bereaved woman, I thought.'

Andrew squirmed. 'As I mentioned last evening, My Lord Abbot, I saw my sister afterwards and went to the castle on her behalf.'

A long, dramatic sigh. 'So you did.' The abbot touched his head. 'I become forgetful. I pray you, tell me again whom you saw and what you discussed.'

Judging it unwise to argue that the abbot's memory was excellent, that last night Andrew had told him only that he had made the journey, not what he had discussed, he launched into an account of his meeting with Sir Walter Huntercombe. He took care with his choice of words, his emphasis.

Adam listened with eyes closed, his head tilted slightly as if making an effort to hear clearly in his best ear. There was nothing wrong with the abbot's hearing. He nodded now and then, clearing his throat delicately.

When Andrew was finished, Adam allowed a long silence. Then he said, 'Interesting. Sir Walter did not mention what happened at Lanark yesterday?'

'Something happened?'

'William Wallace slit the throat of William Heselrig, the sheriff of Lanark.'

Andrew crossed himself. 'Had he been provoked?'

The abbot looked at Andrew askance. 'You know that Wallace needs no provocation. He believes he is John Balliol's champion, and hopes to return him to the Scottish throne.'

'Was he alone?'

'No. And Heselrig was not the only one to die. The garrison marches from Edinburgh Castle today, to hunt down the murderer.'

And so the bloodshed began. Wallace and his men had moved against the English. The garrison had at last been set loose to pursue the quarry. Andrew prayed Wallace escaped. 'You mentioned a letter. It is of this you will write?'

The abbot touched his temple as if thinking, then shook his head. 'I have thought better of it. I shall speak to the brethren at Mass in the morning. I am commanding all the brethren to confine themselves to the abbey grounds. With the garrison's protection gone, we must have a care.'

Andrew knew too well the townspeople's hostility towards the abbey. It might indeed be dangerous for the brethren to go abroad without the garrison keeping the peace in the town. Yet he must talk to Margaret. 'But My Lord Abbot—'

The abbot swept to his feet.

Andrew clamped his mouth shut and bowed his head.

'If your sister is concerned about her husband's factor, she must pursue the information herself.'

The hairs rose on the back of Andrew's neck. Someone must have been close enough to hear the message Hal had brought.

'She will find her factor's murderer among the Scots who drink their lives away at her uncle's tavern, I have no doubt of it,' Adam continued. 'Though she must do it quickly – Will Harcar was murdered at Kerr's inn yesterday.'

'Harcar?'

'When Sir Walter returns I shall advise him to close Kerr's inn and tavern.'

'My sister!'

'She chose to stay there, Andrew. It is not in your keeping. Your duties lie here.' The abbot gave Andrew a reproving look. 'You are still seated.'

Despite the bile rising in his throat, Andrew obediently rose, bowed to Abbot Adam.

Inclining his head graciously, Adam smiled. 'By the way, Master Thomas at Soutra Hospital has requested another chaplain. The English soldiers do not feel that one is sufficient. A delicate situation, assigning a canon to hear the confessions of those some consider invaders. Give it some thought, if you will. I need your advice on who might be discreet, trustworthy in that role. God go with you, Andrew.'

'And with you, My Lord Abbot.' It was not by his own will that Andrew departed soundlessly, but by the will of Abbot Adam.

When all his brothers were snoring, Andrew paced back and forth in his small cell. He had thought his new resolve would break the hold the abbot held over him, but he still behaved like a puppet. It must be a spell. The man was in league with the Devil. It was not natural that Andrew became dumb when Adam commanded him.

And now the abbot knew Margaret sought Jack's murderer. Someone in the abbey was spying for him. But Andrew could remember no one so near except the servant who had summoned him when Hal arrived.

❦ 14 ❧

SO MANY QUESTIONS

As she turned onto Cowgate, Margaret thought her eyes betrayed her. But no, the smiddie fire was lit, and a man bent over it hammering a piece of metal while another pumped the bellows.

'Dame Janet's son and her daughter's husband,' Hal said at her exclamation. 'Work went undone for two weeks. Davy never liked others to take up his work.' As they reached the door of the house, Hal withdrew to talk to the men.

The young woman who had stood beside Janet at the grave answered the door at Margaret's knock. Fair, with soft brown eyes and apple cheeks, she kept her left hand on her stomach in the protective gesture of a woman with child.

'Come in, do. I'm Tess. Mother is out at the kitchen. I'll fetch her.'

Margaret stepped past the fire circle to the large loom that had been pushed against the far wall to accommodate the mourners earlier in the day. The cloth that Janet had begun on Saturday was already several feet long. The wool was undyed but the pattern intricate.

Hearing the door open behind her, Margaret turned to face Janet, pushing down her welling anger by reminding herself that the woman had buried her husband this day.

'What think you of the cloth?' Janet asked, her eyes on the loom rather than her guest.

'It is lovely.'

'It will be one of my finest.' Janet glanced back at the door, as if to see whether anyone had followed her. 'Has Tess been telling you what a perfect wean she will have, and how many more are to come?' Her voice was taut, anxious.

'She seems happy.'

'I've never seen a young woman so taken with carrying a bairn.' Janet sat down heavily by the fire. 'I worried how her mourning might hurt the bairn, but Tess is too absorbed in the wonder of her stomach to linger long on Davy's death.'

Margaret took a seat across, so she might see Janet's eyes. 'How many children does Tess have?'

'The one in her womb so far. I pray it lives.' Janet crossed herself. 'The first is so often the worst. And Tess won't take failure in birth in stride.' At last she brought her eyes to meet Margaret's. 'But you've not come to talk of my Tess.'

Margaret was relieved to arrive at the point. 'I am grateful to you for seeing me today.'

'One day is no better than another. I have felt in my bones Davy was dead these two weeks.' Janet pressed her palms to her eyes for a moment, then dropped her hands in her lap. 'Maud quieted after you left. She is ever a prickly woman, even in the best of times.'

'I have so many questions.'

'Aye. And you are angry with me.'

'My uncle has spoken to you?'

Janet averted her eyes. 'He thought the less you were told the safer you would be.'

'My coming to Edinburgh put me in danger's way.'

'You must remember you have both changed since he lived in Perth. He did not expect such a stubborn lass.'

'He said that?'

'Aye, he did. Still, I have my own mind about it now I've met you. Ask me what you will.'

'You saw Roger four days ago?'

Janet nodded.

'And his wound?'

'The wound, aye. I thought it a brand at first glance. But they were cuts, not burns. He told a tale of being attacked by a wolf.'

'Do you believe that?' Margaret felt her throat tightening. If she could have seen to his wounds . . .

'No.' Janet sighed. 'Men count us such fools sometimes. But I did not challenge the tale.'

'Why did he come to you?'

'He came to the smiddie to see about having a horse shod. He had not yet heard Davy was missing.'

Margaret wondered whether Roger knew now that Davy was dead. 'Why did he run from me? Who were the men with him?'

'I know not who would have been with him. As for his running, I should think he did so because it is not safe to be seen with him. He has done much to anger the English.'

'Uncle told me Roger supports Robert Bruce. I'd think that would please the English. His father has been a loyal subject. They say this youngest Robert Bruce is much favoured by King Edward.'

'You sound like Davy. He distrusted the Bruce and believed Balliol would return to save us.'

'You did not share your husband's beliefs?'

'Och no, not in that. John Balliol and the Comyns surrendered to Edward. We need Robert Bruce to drive Longshanks out of our land.' Janet leaned towards the fire, stretching out her hands to the warmth.

'Robert Bruce and his kin have done worse than surrender to Longshanks, they fought on his side against us,' said Margaret. But she noted that Janet's eyes were sad, her gaze unfocused, the argument apparently falling on deaf ears. 'I cannot understand how Roger was drawn so deeply into this.'

Janet glanced up. So she had been listening. 'I never thought to ask,' she said. 'I supposed it was his nature.'

'Trading is his passion. Leave governing to those with nothing better to do – that was his belief. At least I thought it was.'

'Something changed that to be sure.'

'These troubles have touched us all.' Margaret felt in that a kinship with Janet. 'So your Davy was involved in all this?'

'At Comyn's beck and call, he was. He and Harry were of a group who worked to return Comyn's kinsman Balliol to the throne.'

So that was James Comyn's cause. 'I did not know James Comyn's part in all this.'

Janet pressed her red eyelids with her fingertips. 'Such a waste!' she whispered, breathing unevenly for a moment. Then she dabbed her eyes with her apron. 'John Balliol does not wish to be king. They say he is in Hertford, where he is allowed a huntsman and ten hounds. I think he is grateful to have escaped.'

Margaret wearied of such hearsay. 'John Balliol tried to rule, but the nobles of our country are too divided between the Comyns and the Bruces, or care only to protect their own lands. And then at Dunbar so many of the king's commanders were taken by the English. King John had no sure support.'

Janet's eyes widened with surprise. 'A fine speech. Do you speak so to Roger? Perhaps that is why he told you little.'

Margaret's face grew hot. She was grateful for the flickering firelight. 'No. He has not heard such speeches.' She could not imagine what Roger would think if she argued such a thing with him. Perhaps, like her father, he would patiently listen, then tell her why she was wrong and consider it settled. 'What did Maud mean about Jack?'

'He talked too much when he had a head full of ale. And drank with the wrong men. The night before Harry and Davy were killed he sat at a table in the tavern with Harcar. They left with a flask of brandywine.'

'She believes Jack killed Harry and Davy?'

'No. They were executed by the English – quietly, not in public. It happened at Holyrood.'

Margaret remembered Andrew's reluctance to talk of the deaths. 'Their bodies were in the Tummel.'

'They were dead before their bodies were thrown in the river, I am sure of it.'

'What happened at Holyrood?'

'Comyn's men – Harry, Davy, and others – were to steal something from the abbey, something they believed was Balliol's by right. They dressed in the habits of black friars. Harry and Davy went ahead, gained entrance, and were to signal the others to enter. But the English soldiers were waiting for them. The others realised that their fellows had been caught and slipped away. From the first some said Harcar must have learned of the plan from Jack.'

'Do you believe that?'

'Murdoch and Roger accomplished a mission for Robert Bruce that same night. It was quite favourable for them that on that evening the soldiers from the Edinburgh garrison were watching the abbey and not Leith harbour. And were looking for men wearing black habits.'

'Jack would not have betrayed his own countrymen,' Margaret said, shocked that anyone would make such an accusation.

'No? Well, we may never know. I thought it possible – it was my impression he would do anything for your Roger.'

'But there must be other soldiers guarding the harbour.'

'Oh aye.' Janet shook her head. 'It is just a feeling I have.'

'Did Comyn's men murder Jack? As revenge for Harry's and Davy's deaths?'

'So I believe, though I would call it execution.'

'Balliol against Bruce, and Longshanks' men reaping the benefits of their animosity.' Janet was right, it was a waste – a waste of good men.

Janet rose, folded her arms in front of her. 'I am sorry to tell you about Jack, but in truth I wonder you had not heard of it before this morn.'

'In the tavern they stare, but say nothing. Old Will and Mary the brewster are the only two who have spoken to me.'

Janet shook her head. 'Both full of talk but little substance.'

'Mary said my uncle's chambermaid has returned.'

'She is right about that, but then a mother would ken such a thing.'

'Belle is her daughter?'

'Aye. Don't look so. Your uncle would not thank you for bringing her back to Roy. Things have been peaceful at the inn since Belle left.'

Tess quietly entered the room. 'Mother, you must rest, eh?'

The light spilling from the back door of the tavern attracted Margaret. As she stepped within, folk looked her way, and by ones and twos and threes they ceased their talk until silence filled the room. But not before she had heard, 'Dame Kerr,' 'Murdoch's niece,' 'she *is* married to a Sinclair, after all.' Being the subject of gossip was not new to her – not with a mother like Christiana, and she had given the folk of Edinburgh much to gossip about. But antagonising everyone was the very worst thing she could have done. She might just as well depart for Perth. Yet Janet had befriended her.

Murdoch rose to join her. She expected him to send her upstairs, but instead he invited her to sit with him by the brazier in the middle of the room. He shouted for Sim to bring them ale.

Mary the brewster, her face shiny from the heat, nodded to her. Margaret wondered about Mary's daughter Belle, but heeding Janet's warning she said nothing.

A man who looked like a MacLaren, with the family's red hair though no beard, stared candidly at her. His companion, nodding over his cup, took no notice. The men at the table near the door resumed their game of merrills.

Gradually the volume expanded. The talk was of soldiers and William Wallace.

'I'll lose custom for you,' Margaret said.

Murdoch's scarred right brow lifted. 'Folk come here for gossip. They're curious about you, now they'll have time to watch you. Did you see anyone leave at your arrival?'

It was a pragmatic reassurance, which she could accept. 'What are they saying of Wallace?'

'He's killed the sheriff of Lanark and some of his men.'

'Why?'

'He says he's fighting the English for John Balliol. Heselrig was a good target. But some say Heselrig attacked Wallace's home. There's also talk of a lass killed by soldiers.' Murdoch took a tankard from Sim, held it out to Margaret. 'Drink, Maggie. Drink to our freedom for a few days, weeks if God's smiling on us. The garrison has joined the hunt for Wallace and his men. The war has begun, but until the fighting reaches our door we are out from under the eyes of the English bastards.'

Margaret still lay abed the following morning when Celia came up to announce that Rosamund the laundress was below.

'Dame Janet sent her.'

Janet must have suffered a prick of conscience. 'You know where the bedding is,' Margaret said. 'Fetch it for the laundress. Tell her that when she has finished it, there is more.'

Celia took Margaret's gown from the peg on the wall, shook it out, returned it to the peg. 'She asked to speak with you, mistress. She said she does not take her work from servants.'

Margaret managed a weak smile. 'Rosamund must not understand the importance of a lady's maid.'

'You laugh at me.'

'I laugh at nothing and no one at the moment, Celia.' But they did need a laundress. 'I'll go down to her.'

'I'll tell her to wait, then return to help you dress.' Celia flew out of the room before Margaret could object. This lady's maid nonsense must cease. Margaret was fully capable of dressing herself. It was a matter of wanting to.

But Celia returned quickly, dressed Margaret, gathered her hair into a netted coif so that her wimple fitted comfortably.

'I prefer a cap,' Margaret argued.

'You should look as respectable as possible when hiring a maid,' Celia said, standing back to check her work.

'I feel like an old woman padded with clothes against the cold. But it is no matter.' Margaret took a penny out of her scrip in case she decided to hire the woman. 'Let us go down to Goodwife Rosamund.'

The laundress was a small woman with a sharp chin and angry eyes – a match for Celia. 'Dame Kerr,' she said with a curt bow. 'I am Rosamund the laundress.' She glanced down at the stinking straw on the tavern floor and sniffed. Margaret caught her eye. Rosamund blushed and dropped her head.

'If I hire you, you need not come into the tavern,' Margaret said. 'The tavern kitchen is out in the backland. Celia will show it to you.'

'Yes, mistress.'

'My uncle said you are the laundress for the priests at St Giles', and that you do some weaving for them. Do they no longer need you?'

Rosamund lifted her chin at the question. 'I do only the laundry now. They have given the weaving to someone they judge needier than me.'

'Is this woman needier?'

Rosamund regarded Margaret as if wondering how best to answer. 'She has but one other mouth to feed – I have three bairns and my husband unable to walk. Agnes Fletcher lost her husband, lost her wean, and is sickly now. For that her sister gets half my work.'

The name pricked Margaret's interest. 'You speak of Besseta

Fletcher.' She had forgotten the presence of Alan Fletcher's daughters in all the confusion of the past days.

'Aye.'

'She is a weaver?'

'So she says.'

Bess the young weaver had her eye on Jack, that is what Old Will had said. 'I wonder at the priests risking someone new when they were pleased with you. They were pleased with you?'

Rosamund sniffed. 'No one has ever complained about my work. It is knowing the Comyn that helped her. Perhaps more than knowing.' She bobbed her head and raised an eyebrow, letting Margaret know she might imagine the worst. 'He is oft seen there.'

And once more James Comyn was involved. Margaret nodded to Celia, understanding Rosamund's inference all too clearly but unwilling to pursue gossip spread by one with a grudge. 'Fetch the linens and accompany Rosamund to the tron to weigh them.'

Celia went off to retrieve the bundles from the lean-to.

'A farthing a pound,' Margaret proposed to Rosamund. It was a generous offer.

Rosamund's face softened. 'Aye, mistress, that is fair.'

Margaret handed her the penny as arles. Even in times such as these one should bargain in good faith. 'Do you have someone to help you carry the laundry?'

'I have a cart. It will do.'

A proud young woman. 'When you are finished, there is more of the same. I cannot promise to keep you steadily in work, but it is better than a private household.'

'God bless you, mistress.'

Margaret nodded to the laundress and went out into the backland to find Murdoch. He should know of the deal. His kitchen was empty. She stood by the window, thinking about the Fletchers. More pieces to the puzzle, but she still saw no clear shape. Besseta, who seemed unwilling to speak with Margaret, was a friend to James Comyn – mistress if Rosamund was right – and daughter to the man who had arranged for Jack's journey here. If the Fletcher sisters knew of the plan for Holyrood, Jack might have heard it there. But she could not think why they would know, or why they would have spoken in front of him. The stakes of this game were too high, and no one seemed to have trusted Jack.

The black cat rubbed against her legs, butted his head against the hand hanging idle at her side. She crouched to pet him.

'Well, Agrippa, what do you make of it?' she whispered.

The cat purred and presented each side of his neck in turn, then the top of his head.

'Should I beware James Comyn, or should I trust him? He is my king's kinsman.' And he seemed to be the link in all this.

Leaving the kitchen, Margaret was thinking where to look next when she noticed Roy's voice raised in anger, answered by a woman's voice. Concerned that Celia might be at odds with the cook again, she hurried to intervene.

Geordie and Sim sat outside the tavern kitchen, leaning their heads against the wall of the house, eyes closed, listening.

'Whoring queyn, why would I take you back?'

'You love me is why. I went with him for your sake. For the wean's safety.'

'You carried no bairn of mine when you left with your farmer.'

Sim opened an eye, elbowed Geordie. They stood up with guilty blushes and moved away from the house.

'It's Belle and Roy,' said Sim. 'Her farmer left her for soldiering.'

By now Margaret had guessed that. 'Does your master know she's here?'

Geordie shook his head. 'The master's in his storeroom.'

The padlock was not on the door. Margaret pushed gently. The door swung open with a faint creak. To one side of the door an oil lamp on a shelf illuminated part of an aisled room. The pillars and the walls were stone. But from without, the undercroft looked wooden. Murdoch's secret. Several chests rested on trestles in the centre. On one of them burned another lamp. Barrels stood in a neat line beyond the chests. In the far aisle yet another lamp burned. Against that wall hung what looked like a tapestry. She stepped farther into the room, drawn by the flickering colours, looked up. The ceiling was plastered.

'What are you doing in here?' Murdoch roared.

Margaret dropped down into a crouch beside one of the chests, startled by the loud sound in this dark place.

'I know you're here, Maggie.'

Her heart pounded. Best to stand. He must know where she was. But she could not make her legs move. This was his secret place and she was trespassing.

Beyond the chest by which she crouched was one with a thistle carving on the side. She knew that chest. It was her father's. He had taken it with him to Bruges.

Murdoch's footsteps approached. He must be by the barrels now. She wished she had not been such a fool as to hide.

He grabbed her by the back of her gown, dragging her up to her feet.

'I told you not to bother with this room.'

He was so close she could smell the garlic and ale on his breath.

It took her a moment to find her footing. 'I was looking for you.' She shook out her skirts. 'Geordie said you were here.'

'What did you need of me?'

'I've hired Rosamund.'

'You broke into my storeroom to tell me that you hired a laundress?' he shouted.

'I did not break in. The door was unlatched.'

Murdoch ran a hand through his hair. 'How much?'

'A farthing a pound of laundry.'

'You're robbing me!' He walked away from her, then turned, hands on hips. 'Why did you hide?'

'Because I could see I was being a fool.' She pointed to the deeply carved thistle. 'That's my father's chest.'

'Aye, it is Malcolm's.'

'Why is it here?'

'My brother brought it to me for safekeeping while he is in Bruges.'

'What is in it?'

'Records of his trade, his lands and possessions.' Murdoch folded his arms before him. 'Now you'll be going out that door behind you while I see to the cruisies.'

As Margaret left the storeroom she met a young woman coming down the alley pouting and muttering to herself. Her dress was of good cloth, loosely laced up the front with the cleft between large breasts well exposed. She would give birth by midsummer by the look of her. She wore neither mantle nor shoes. Dark, lustrous curls tumbled down about her neck from a threadbare cap. Her colour was high – perhaps from her encounter with Roy. She had a rosebud mouth and blue eyes heavily lashed. Noticing Margaret, she paused, smoothed the front of her gown.

'Dame Kerr?'

'Aye. And you are Belle, I think.'

The blue eyes rounded as Murdoch came out the door behind Margaret.

'Count everything you give that laundress, Maggie,' he said as he closed the door. 'God's blood!' he exclaimed as he turned and saw Belle. 'Has Roy seen you?'

'Master Murdoch—'

'There's no welcome here for you, Belle. Get you gone.'

She pouted prettily.

'Go!'

Belle's bottom lip trembled and the great eyes welled with tears, but she raised her chin. 'You'll come begging. You'll see. You need Roy, and he needs me.'

'I don't need Roy, and there's your mistake. I'm a better cook than he is.'

'Hah!' she said loudly, and headed off down the alley to the High Street.

'I must see to Roy,' Murdoch said, and left Margaret standing by his storeroom.

The padlock was still not on the door.

~§ 15 ઠ~

HONOUR

Margaret must have flustered Murdoch more than she had guessed. Or Belle had. But Margaret had no time to question God's purpose in throwing this temptation in her path. Her uncle might realise his mistake at any moment. She slipped through the storeroom door, pulled it to. Darkness. She felt round the inside of the door, hoping the padlock would be hanging on a hook as it did in the kitchen. Nothing. Crablike, she moved to the opposite side of the door, felt round, found the padlock.

But it would be of no use to take it. Murdoch would know she had it, and he would replace it. He seemed to need many locks – no doubt he hoarded a goodly number.

A noise outside the door alerted her. She pressed back against the wall, watched the line of daylight grow along the items to the left.

'Mistress?'

'Celia?'

The maid stepped into the room pulling the door closed behind her, opened the shutter on a lantern.

'How did you know I was here?'

'Whatever you want to see, do it quickly. Your uncle is in the tavern kitchen with Roy.' Celia produced a twig, lit a lamp from the lantern.

Margaret made her way around the chests, past the barrels, to the tapestry on the far wall. There were several, hung one over the other. Loot, she guessed. Beneath them sat another chest. She knelt down, lifted the lid, inhaled a lavender scent. A woman's gown lay on the top, made of scarlett, the costliest wool cloth.

'Someone is coming!' Celia said.

Beside the woman's chest was a smaller one, a size that fitted behind a saddle. Margaret had seen Roger strap it on many times. It was locked.

The light dimmed behind her. Celia had blown out the lamp by the door. Margaret shuttered the lantern. The door opened slowly.

'You must be more careful about the wick if you wish to be a spy, Maggie,' said Murdoch. 'It is still smoking.'

She opened the lantern shutter, unwilling to be locked in here as a lesson.

'Do you have the key to Roger's lock?' she asked.

'What took you to his chest so quickly?'

'It is where you were standing.'

Murdoch shook his head. 'I do not have the key. For all I did for him, the man still does not trust me.'

'I don't believe there is a lock you cannot pick.'

'Come out of there. I must get back to Roy. That whore has him in a drunken rage, destroying the kitchen.'

Andrew prayed that the Almighty would grant him the freedom to prove to himself he was not the puppet of Abbot Adam. He was done with that. He intended to warn Murdoch of the abbot's intention to close the tavern. And he must talk to Margaret – there were things she must know. His honour towards his family was so far intact, let it remain so, please God. He had borrowed a pilgrim's robe and wide-brimmed hat that had been left at the abbey by a hastily departing guest. So disguised, he passed out the gate without notice. Once in Canongate he forced himself to continue up the road at a solemn pace.

He felt exposed walking alone, without Matthew. He had not realised how accustomed he had become to the young man's presence, that now to walk by himself seemed unnatural, something all would notice. Matthew was a good lad, quiet and self-effacing. He wished more than anything to be a canon, but he seemed incapable of learning to read. His eyesight was good enough. Alas for Matthew, though the lad might be correct in his assertion that his parish priest did not know his letters, an Augustinian canon must be able to read and write. His best hope was as a lay brother in one of the Augustinian hospitals. Perhaps Soutra.

In all his agonising over this venture, Andrew had not thought about Abbot Adam's mention of Soutra the previous day. A confessor for the English soldiers. Andrew could think of no one in the order he would recommend for that duty – it might be a death sentence if this conflict did not end soon.

In fact it might be Andrew's. It would be in character for Abbot Adam to turn the request into an order. Once committed even further to the English cause, Andrew would find it impossible to retreat to his private preference. No one would believe him. No Scot would trust him.

Neither would any Englishman. After all, a priest, though he was God's anointed, was yet a man with man's frailties. Only God knew who might break the seal of confession when tortured.

There were no guards at Netherbow. Wallace had done this much for the town, a moment of calm, while the garrison marched south-west to Lanark. Andrew thought back to the ferry crossing, the last time he had seen Wallace. His bearing had seemed different then from the deferential man who had attended the meetings from which Andrew was shut out on that humiliating trip to St Andrews. As if Wallace was already envisioning the battles ahead.

Murdoch frowned at Andrew as he appeared at the steps leading to Margaret's chamber. 'Do you look for me, pilgrim?'

Andrew took off his hat.

'Holy Mother! Why do you wear such garb?'

Andrew told him why, and of the abbot's threat.

'You crossed your abbot just to warn me of that, nephew?'

'No. I must talk to Maggie.'

'She's above.'

Margaret stared at the patch of sky out the small window of her chamber. Seeing their things side by side had turned the knife in her heart. Roger had gone to Berwick and brought Edwina here before answering Edward's summons. And afterwards he had returned. But now that Edwina was gone and Margaret was here, Roger avoided the inn. She was less to him than Edwina of Carlisle was.

There was a knock on the door. She opened it to find Andrew in pilgrim's garb. He was hollow-cheeked, looking tense and weary.

'Why are you dressed so?'

'I must talk to you.'

'My ears are tired, Andrew. We'll talk another day.'

'No. There may not be another day.' He pushed past her into the room.

'I cannot bear more terrible news, Andrew.'

He stepped out of the pilgrim's robe, laid it and the hat on the bed. 'There are things you must know.'

'I pray you—'

'About the incident at Holyrood. And other matters.'

That caught her interest. 'Tell me about that night.'

'I arrived back the next day, in the midst of the confusion. What I know is second-hand.'

'The abbot confides in you.'

'No more, Maggie. He did then. But no more.' Andrew fingered the bed curtain. 'Have you heard what happened on Sunday?'

'Heselrig. Wallace's attack.'

'Aye.' Andrew turned. 'It has truly begun, Maggie.'

'What, Andrew?'

'The routing of the English.'

'It will take more than Wallace the thief.'

'You must get that out of your head. He is a brave man, fighting for our king.' Andrew sat down on the bed. 'Do you remember how we played in our parents' bed when we were little? It was a ship, a vast estate . . .'

'. . . a castle, a cave.' A sweet memory. But Andrew was not given to reminiscing.

'Family comes first after God, Maggie.'

He had truly changed since Sunday. 'I am sorry we argued.'

'I would not have brought Jack's body to Dunfermline if he were not now part of our family.'

'And I have thanked you for it.' She drew the curtains aside, sat down beside him, took his hand. So cold. Like the dead. Yet he was sweating. 'Andrew, if this is about Roger, he did not die on the border. I did see him last week.'

'So said your messenger. You have this on good authority?'

'I do. He was also seen by another.'

Andrew pressed her hand, drew his from hers, touched the side of her face. 'That is good news, but you do not look glad.'

'He is working for Robert Bruce. I do not know how I feel about that – or why he did not tell me. If he does not feel he can confide in me, how can he love me?'

'Roger is not good enough for you, Maggie. But if he is caught up in the fighting, God help him.'

Margaret did not repeat the prayer. 'Why were you dressed so?'

'I come here against my lord abbot's wishes, but that does not matter. I do not honour him. I do honour and love you. All my kin. Even Murdoch, because he has welcomed you here.'

'Why this change of heart, Andrew? Why have you disobeyed your abbot? What will be your penance?' Margaret feared the serious consequences of disobeying such a powerful abbot who might draw on support from Longshanks to punish Andrew.

'God has shown me the true way, Maggie. Do not think of my

penance. I can bear anything now. But I need to tell you everything. I may not see you again for a long while, Maggie. So hear me out.'

Her stomach clenched. 'Why won't you see me?'

'Hear me out.'

The tension in Andrew's voice silenced Margaret. She crossed her legs beneath her on the bed.

'I must begin at the beginning. You will know everything. You can be my judge and jury.'

'Me?'

He put a finger to her lips to silence her. It was like a children's game. Secrets in the sheltering curtains of the great bed. But this was real and he frightened her.

'I write Abbot Adam's letters. His is a prodigious correspondence. I was honoured to be chosen.' Andrew laughed as he said the word 'honoured'. 'By his dictation, I am privy to his thoughts, his arrangements.'

'And he is King Edward's man.'

Andrew shushed her as he nodded. 'This is difficult for me. Let me speak as it comes.'

'I meant nothing.'

'He is King Edward's man, and with access to many documents that should have been in the royal archives of Scotland but had been scattered among the abbeys. When King Edward ordered that the Stone of Scone, the emblems of the King of the Scots, and the royal archives be sent to Westminster, Abbot Adam saw his chance to improve his status. As he handed over the archives in his care, he informed Edward that there were other documents. He offered to send emissaries to collect them from around this kingdom. Edward did not trust that – he wished his own soldiers to go. But he needed someone who could both read and be trusted to attend them.'

'You, Andrew?'

He looked her right in the eye and acknowledged it. 'The soldiers were not by their nature gentle, you understand. When the clerics and their lay servants fought to protect the items from the English, they were brutally subdued. And I stood by, mute with fear. I am anathema now among my countrymen. I am Judas.'

'Why do you—?'

'I had a choice, Maggie. I might have refused my abbot, taken my punishment. But I am weak.'

'You took a vow of obedience.'

Andrew pressed his hands to his eyes. 'Our Lord God granted us free will with which to choose the path of grace. When I saw what was happening I realised that this was the work of Satan. Lucifer.' His voice was hoarse with emotion. 'Yet I was too weak to rise against him.'

Margaret could see Andrew truly believed he had done wrong, though in the eyes of the Kirk she was not so certain. 'Did many die?'

He shook his head. 'At least I do not have that on my conscience. It is the dishonour I cannot bear. I did not know how unbearable it would be to me until it was done.'

He was quiet again. His eyes closed, he seemed to be praying. Margaret wanted to comfort him. It was difficult to keep her silence.

'You asked about that night at the abbey,' he said at last. 'When Harry and Davy died. I will tell you. Only today I learned of the last link. I believe it was Harcar who betrayed them to the sheriff. On Jack's information.'

Dear God, another who accused Jack. 'Do you know that?'

'I know that Abbot Adam paid Harcar for something recently. And there is talk of Jack and Harcar drinking together.'

Margaret bowed her head. Although she had never met the men, she still found it hard to think of Jack being responsible for Harry's and Davy's deaths.

'The abbot told the brethren of Holyrood to expect several Dominicans in the evening, and to allow them entrance. What he did not tell them was that some of the supposed Dominicans purposed to create chaos and draw the brethren away from their fellows, who would come in after them to steal the documents that had been collected in the abbot's chambers for the couriers. Harry and Davy were caught before the others arrived.'

'How did the intruders know where the documents resided?'

'I do not know how it was planned.'

'Were the men murdered in the abbey?'

'No. The soldiers dragged them away to execute them.'

'This happened the night before you returned from St Andrews?'

'Yes. I believe they thought I had gone to St Andrews for the last documents, that someone would be travelling south with the archives soon.'

'Were you still gathering documents?'

'No. The abbot sent me to St Andrews to complain to Bishop Wishart and James the Steward, who were meeting there, about my rough treatment by King Edward. I was to say I had been forced to accompany the soldiers in gathering the documents, that I had helped them because I was weak and feared for my life, which was of course true.' Andrew pressed a hand to his forehead. 'I was to beg forgiveness.'

'But you had done what your abbot wanted. Why did he seek then to humiliate you?'

'He saw my misery and thought to use it, that I would be quite convincing and would gain their confidence and, perhaps, access to the talks from which he was excluded.'

'What happened?'

'I went to St Andrews, was told that the bishop and the steward were unable to see me. I stayed for a few days, but my reputation had preceded me and I was shunned by all, to them I was a traitor. And then I understood the other piece of my abbot's plan – he sought in this way to show me that I could never go back, I could never desert his cause, for no one would believe me. So I went to Elcho and confessed to our mother, the *blessed* Christiana, one who could not deny me an audience.' All Andrew's bitterness went into the word 'blessed'.

He had always believed in Christiana. Obviously that had changed. 'Why did you confess to Mother?'

'I wanted absolution.'

'Did she absolve you?'

'No one can, Maggie.'

Neither of them moved for a long while. A church bell tolled, but Andrew noticed it only as it ceased. What it had signalled he did not know, did not care. But it woke him from his breathless wait for Margaret's response. It was as if he had expected that she would shrive him when his mother could not. Yet more so than after his meeting with Christiana, he felt lighter of heart, having confessed all to his sister.

Needing activity, he eased off the bed and crossed to the window. Behind him, in the shelter of the curtained bed, Margaret began to sob. She had been right. He did not comfort her, he burdened her. She had received yet another sorrow to add to her burden.

'I should leave you now,' he said. 'You have what you wished, all that I know.'

He heard her rise and approach him.

'What is happening here?' she cried. 'Has God forsaken us?'

As Andrew turned, Margaret put her arms round his chest and hugged him hard. His throat tightened.

'He has spared Roger, Maggie. Is that not cause to rejoice?'

'This is not a time of rejoicing.'

He kissed the top of her head, held her.

She quieted. Took a few shuddering breaths. Leaned back to look up at him. 'I understand now why you did not wish to tell me.' Though her voice was hoarse from her outburst, she spoke with a calm that heartened him.

There was a knock. 'Father Andrew!' It was Matthew's voice.

Andrew opened the door, finding his servant anxiously pacing. 'You should not have left the abbey.'

'Abbot Adam is aware you are outwith the abbey and he is not pleased. There will be a reckoning, he says. Soon you will be missed at vespers.' Matthew's voice trembled with the enormity.

'Peace, Matthew, you say I have already been missed. Vespers will not matter. I shall come soon, and I thank you for your message. But it would go better for you if you return at once.'

Matthew shook his head.

'Go now, lad. I command you.'

'My fate is yours, Father Andrew.'

'It is a foolish loyalty.'

Margaret had joined Andrew at the door. 'I should think you would thank him, not rebuff him.'

Matthew made a good effort to smile, though it turned out almost unpleasant.

'If Matthew returns in your company, Andrew,' Margaret added, 'it will be clear who detained him and that he did not add loitering or another adventure atop his time away from the abbey.'

Andrew began to argue, but stopped, not trusting his judgement at the moment, still wondering whether he should have burdened her with his story. 'I will not be long now, Matthew.'

'Go down to the tavern,' Margaret said to Matthew. 'Tell Sim that you are thirsty. So are we.'

As the lad disappeared down the steps, Andrew realised he feared for him.

Margaret closed the door. 'What did Mother see in your future?'

'That I would go through fire.'

'That you had or that you will?'

'Will.'

Margaret left the door. Hugging her arms to her, she stood with head bowed.

Andrew felt detached, as if a spectator, watching brother and sister. How quiet he must seem, standing there, awaiting his sister's conclusion. Like a dumb ox waiting to plough. Yet there was nothing for him to do now but return to the abbey, learn his penance. He had given his warning to Murdoch. He had confessed to his sister.

'Mother is mad, it is no message from the Lord,' Margaret said.

Andrew watched her as she went to let Matthew in with a tray and three cups of ale.

'I will sit on the landing with mine,' the lad said, leaving them quickly.

Margaret poured the ale. Only now did Andrew notice how her hands trembled, how she bit her bottom lip as if trying to contain some overwhelming emotion.

She handed him a cup. 'Did you hear what I said?'

'I ken you think Mother's visions madness, but I believed her, Maggie. Her vision saddened her.'

'I cried when you told me what you have suffered. A sad, frightening vision is mother's way of weeping.'

'No. It is more than that, Maggie.'

'Is it because she predicted fire that you return to the abbey? Leave it.'

'I took vows, Maggie.'

She walked back and forth. 'You know too much. You are a threat to the abbot.'

'It is my place. Just as you will return to Roger, though he has deceived you and abandoned you.'

She paused before him, her eyes searching his. 'Why are you so certain he has abandoned me?'

'Remember that first trip Roger made, immediately after your wedding? He came to Edinburgh. And when I saw him—' Andrew stopped. He should not tell her this now, when it was of no use to her. And the expression on her face – he had never seen her look so defeated. 'Is it not clear to you that your husband has a life about which you know nothing?'

'That is most clear. But I do not fear for my life with Roger. You

179

should do so with Abbot Adam. He is powerful. He tricked you into an act for which you feel great shame. Shame which threatens him. Do what he fears you will do. Denounce him. Another order would take you gladly. And by denouncing him you would show others your true worth. Run while you can.'

'I might have refused at any time. Those who shunned me at St Andrews saw my true worth.'

She turned from him.

'I am sorry, Maggie. I should not have said what I did.'

She shrugged. 'After they execute William Wallace, what then?'

'I do not think Wallace will be easily caught. This is the moment I have feared. Now there will be fighting all about us.'

'And you have truly decided John Balliol is the rightful king?' Margaret asked.

'I believe it now, with my whole heart.'

'I, too, have come to believe that. Though Roger supports Robert Bruce.'

So Sir Walter was right in his suspicions. Andrew was glad he had not known that yesterday. 'What will happen to the two of you?' He did not think a couple would easily resolve such a deep divide. But Roger had already done so much damage to his marriage by neglecting his wife. 'Had he been a better husband, might he have convinced you of the right of his cause?'

'I doubt I shall ever know.' She still faced away from him, but he heard the pain in his sister's voice and ached for her. 'So we are agreed on this one thing, eh?' she said with forced gaiety as she slipped back down on her stool and took up her ale.

'Aye, Maggie.'

They drank to that.

≈§ 16 §≈

WE'LL BE BOUND

Margaret and Andrew walked slowly down the stairs to the backlands. He had made it clear they might not see each other again for a long while, but he would say no more than that. It was strange – though she could feel her brother was frightened, he carried himself straighter than he had of late, as if he had resolved something. She envied him that.

When they reached the alley he leaned down, kissed her on the cheek. 'You need not walk me out to the High Street, Maggie.'

She stood on her toes to kiss him on the mouth, then hugged him tight. 'I'll pray for you, my brother,' she said as he drew away from her. 'God go with you.'

'And with you, my sister.' His face was pale against his dark hair, his eyes sad. 'I pray for your sake Roger returns safely.'

'With a change of heart, eh?' She forced a smile.

He closed his eyes, bowed his head to her, then moved towards the alley. She withdrew to the stairs, suddenly unwilling to watch him cross over the spot where Harcar had lain, fearful she might see a sign of his own death as he touched it.

'Do not look so forlorn,' Murdoch said from the doorway of his kitchen. 'Despite the robes, he is not off on pilgrimage.' He stood with arms stretched out, his hands pressing either side of the archway as if holding it up. 'Did he tell you the abbot means to close me down?'

'Aye, he told me.' Margaret turned away.

'Come in here, Maggie. We've something to discuss.'

'Not now, Uncle.'

'I've news of Roger.'

The words hit her in the stomach, making her gasp. She pressed the heels of her palms to her eyes, steadied herself, fought to recapture her breath.

'Maggie?' Murdoch had quit the doorway, stood at her side. 'Are you taking a turn?' He touched her shoulder.

'Where is he?' she managed to ask.

'Far from here, Maggie. Word came through one of his men.'

She dropped her hands, pressed them to her sides. 'I was not expecting word from him. Go in, I'll come after you.' She waited until her breath was nearly back to normal, then followed him.

On the small table beside the window Murdoch had set out two tankards and a pitcher of ale. That did not bode well. Margaret dropped down onto a stool. 'He is alive, then?'

Murdoch filled her tankard before he sat. 'As of Sunday he was, aye.'

She did not touch the ale. 'He is with Robert Bruce?'

Murdoch glanced away. 'The messenger did not say. Roger's orders are that I send you away from here, Maggie. Back to Perth, where you will be safer.'

That stung. 'Where he will not risk seeing me.'

Murdoch frowned in surprise. 'No, I—'

After all this time, after he had seen how his appearance shook her, this was Roger's message. Anger rushed through her. 'How dare he!' The power of her anger brought her to her feet. The ale sloshed in the tankards and the pitcher.

'Maggie—'

'How dare he order me away!' She swept her full tankard to the floor. Her face burned, her breath came in gasps. 'He can order his Englishwoman about, but not me!' She was choking on bile.

'Edwina of Carlisle is dead, Maggie.'

She heard it faintly, through the roar of her blood. 'Good riddance.' She raised her hand to strike the pitcher off the table. Murdoch lunged at her, pinned her against the wall behind her.

'Stop it, Maggie! She was nothing to him, I've told you that.'

She struggled to free her hand, trying to slap Murdoch in the face. But he was far stronger than she was.

'Roger wants you safe, Maggie. This is no place for you, I've said it over and over.'

Through clenched teeth she managed to say, 'Go . . . to . . . hell.'

Murdoch suddenly released her, backed away. 'What's gotten into you, lass? What did that brother of yours say?'

'Something has happened, I don't know what – he says I'll not see him for a long while.'

It was plain Murdoch had not heard that. 'Then all the better that you go away.'

'Och aye, far more convenient for you.'

'Maggie! You must calm yourself, lass. You're wrong if you feel—'

'You can't even begin to ken what I feel. First my father runs, then my husband abandons me. Andrew – God knows what's happening to him. And now you would ship me back to where I have no one. No one, Uncle.'

Murdoch dropped his head, momentarily silenced.

Margaret caught her breath. 'Did Roger say he had seen me?'

'Aye, and he was sorry he could not come to you, but it would be dangerous.'

'And yet when Edwina of Carlisle—' She stopped. The woman was dead. 'So it was her body they found on the border?'

'Aye, it was.' Murdoch wiped his forehead with his sleeve. 'You'll go to Dunfermline, to your goodmother.'

'We'll see about that.' Margaret gathered her skirts and pushed past him and out the door. She heard him shout her name as she ran past the chambermaid's hut, the tavern kitchen. Once beyond the inhabited buildings she slowed to a walk, pressing her hands to a stitch in her side.

The clouds had lifted, the soggy rooftops steamed in the late afternoon sun. She squinted against the light. A deep, wrenching sob doubled her over. She sank down onto a rock, buried her face in her hands, and wept until it was too painful to weep any longer. When she was certain she had rid herself of the lump in her throat, she slowly lifted her head. The world swam before her, but after a time it righted itself as her breathing slowed.

How dare he order her back to that empty house. Christ, what a heartless man she had married. God had abandoned her and her brother, that was plain. Her mother's prophecy for Andrew was coming true, but those for Margaret – how pathetically naïve she had been to wonder even for a moment whether they might come to be.

Perhaps it would be better to leave this place. It would not be so awful to return to her goodmother's house. Edinburgh was a dark town choking with suspicion and hate. If ever she had done a pointless thing it was coming here, searching for a husband who did not wish to be found by her, grieving over another man who had not been the man she had thought him, seeking help from a selfish, spineless thief. She would be better away. She took some deep breaths, gazed around, wondering whether anyone had witnessed her collapse – not that it mattered.

Beyond the tavern kitchen stood a few sheds, then a paddock outlined with wattle hurdles. Behind the house that faced Cowgate was an old shed with a collapsed roof. Agrippa sat on the crumbled roof material, cleaning himself. His fur was a deep red-brown in the sunlight, not black at all.

Like Andrew's hair. Oh, what a handsome man her brother was. And so unhappy.

So was she. She wondered what her mother would make of her prophecies now – fighting alongside the men, holding her babe in her arms, her husband by her side. If the contrast were not so painful Margaret might laugh at it. Her goodmother had been silly to believe Christiana. And what would Katherine make of all this? Pray God she did not turn Margaret away. Her stomach clenched to think on it. A week ago she would not have feared rejection there, she would have been confident of being received by her goodmother with open arms. But Katherine might prefer not to know all Margaret had learned of Roger and Jack. That would require a silence Margaret feared she could not maintain. And once told, there would be no erasing it.

And so to Perth? She had a house there, at least. Yet there were rumours that William Wallace was in Scone a few miles upriver – that would not make for a safe or peaceful place.

Margaret had risked everything in coming here to seek out the cause of Jack's death, she had not seen that before. And still she could not name Jack's murderer. Well, as long as she was still here, she might continue to work at unravelling Jack's murder; perhaps she might learn something of use to her. It was obvious she had only herself to depend on. She still believed there was more to Jack's death than Comyn's men seeking vengeance. There was the loom weight. And Besseta Fletcher, daughter of the man who had sent Jack to Edinburgh, was a weaver.

Margaret found Celia in their chamber, spinning. The bedchamber seemed chilly and dim after the sunshine.

'Was it darksome news, from Father Andrew?'

Margaret hesitated by the door. She had come to a decision, but did not know how to begin. 'Thank you for coming to my aid in the storeroom.'

'I was gey glad to help. Did you find something of use to you?'

Here was the invitation Margaret sought. She sat down across the table. 'It is time you knew everything.'

Celia pursed her lips, dropped her eyes to her spindle. 'We'll be bound if I do.'

'Aye. But you've already risked danger to help me. You've already bound us.'

The maid lifted her dark eyes to Margaret's. 'Tell me.'

Not knowing how much Celia already grasped, Margaret began from the beginning, with the loom weight. It was a long telling, punctuated by pauses when Margaret lost her way in her own thoughts. Celia listened with rapt attention. At the end, there was silence.

Margaret felt as if she had confessed her sins. Andrew must have felt this way.

'I am sorry for any trouble I have caused you,' Celia said at last.

'You've helped. Surely you can see that.'

'What will you do?'

'My husband wants me to go back to Perth and wait there until he has nothing better to do than resume his business and his marriage. But before Murdoch finds us safe passage, I wish to see the Fletcher sisters. I want you to accompany me on a visitation tomorrow. I thought we would offer one of your remedies to Agnes. And while you have them distracted I shall look at Besseta's loom weights.'

The warm day allowed Andrew to do his copying in the cloister, away from the abbot and his knowing eyes – though he could not escape his words. Andrew was making a fair copy of a letter Abbot Adam was sending to Bishop Wishart regarding some old business. In an incidental remark at the conclusion Adam complained of Andrew's treatment by the English soldiers. Andrew had protested the passage when taking notes this morning, but Abbot Adam said his feelings were too delicate on this. Andrew cursed as a cat jumped up onto the table and jarred his arm.

'Damn you!' He jerked the parchment out from beneath the cat's large white paws. The cat hissed at him and retreated to the corner of the table. Andrew disliked the creatures, and they knew it.

'Cursing Griselda.' The abbot softly chuckled. 'It is no wonder she torments you.'

A chill ran down Andrew's back – he had not heard the abbot's approach. He put down his pen and rose to bow to the abbot.

'Forgive me, My Lord Abbot. She surprised me.'

'As have I, apparently. Return to your work. I did not mean to disturb you, merely to ask you to see me after Nones.' The abbot nodded to Andrew, then, calling to Griselda, walked slowly away.

Andrew broke out in a sweat. Adam played with him like a cat its prey. This morning he had been certain the abbot would challenge him about his absence the previous afternoon, but he had not mentioned it. All was as usual, the abbot dictating, Andrew scribbling. If Adam did not broach it at their next meeting, Andrew must bring it up himself. He could not bear this game.

In the warmth of the sunny afternoon the upper storeys that leaned crookedly over the High Street blocked the air. But it was her mission, not the spring sunlight, that had Margaret sweating as they turned down the alley to the Fletchers' door. She prayed for success, raised her hand, rapped sharply. Waited.

'Someone is there,' Celia whispered.

Margaret nodded, rapped again.

Besseta opened the door just enough to peer out. The room behind her was dark, as was the shade of mid-afternoon. 'Margaret. So you have found me.' She peered out farther. Her neck looked fragile beneath the cap that covered her hair. 'Who is with you?'

'Celia, my maid. She is skilled with herbs and roots. I thought if she could see Agnes, she might be able to mix something to help her.'

'Agnes is sleeping. She must not be disturbed.'

'Perhaps if you described Agnes's illness to us?'

Besseta shook her head, began to close the door.

'I have an excellent sleep potion,' Celia said.

Besseta checked the movement of the door. 'A sleep potion?'

Celia pulled back the cloth on the basket she carried, lifted a packet.

Besseta opened the door wide. 'It is a hellhole in here,' she said, stepping aside as if to let them see for themselves. But their eyes could not adjust to the indoor dimness so quickly. 'You are welcome if you do not mind it.'

There was no question of refusing the offer. Margaret stepped within, Celia following on her heels.

It was not a pleasant room, but hardly deserved the comparison with hell. A loom at the far right caught the north light from a high window – surely not enough light in which to weave for long in most seasons. A tattered cloth covered an interior doorway to the left of the window. Though the house sat on a hill dropping off north and east and should have excellent drainage, the beaten earth floor smelled damp, and the warmth of the day made pungent various cellar odours. Margaret prayed that Celia would not wrinkle her nose. But if she had, Besseta did not notice.

Margaret wandered towards the loom as Besseta and Celia arranged a bench and stools. The weights tied to the warp were larger than the one she had in her scrip. But on the floor near the loom were several piles of loom weights of various sizes. The smallest were much like the one Jack had clutched in death.

By the loom sat a wool comb. On an impulse, Margaret grabbed it, concealing it behind her back as Besseta joined her.

'I had no idea you did such delicate work.' Margaret touched the unfinished piece of weaving on the loom. 'Did you weave the mantle you are wearing?'

'I did. Useless thing.'

'But quite beautiful.'

They moved over to the arranged seats, near the unlit brazier.

188

'It would have been of more use to me to have carried down a larger loom.'

Margaret sat on the bench. 'You brought it from Perth?'

'I did.' Besseta perched at the edge of a wobbly stool. 'I needed something to keep my hands busy.'

'While you sat with Agnes?'

'Aye. Though I did not expect to be here so long.'

Celia moved her stool back slightly, so that Besseta would need to turn her head all the way to her left to see her.

Margaret was close enough to see that the fluted edge of Besseta's cap trembled.

'I understand Agnes was widowed, then lost a bairn.'

Besseta fidgeted with her hands. 'It has been a terrible time.'

'She was fortunate to have you here.'

Besseta looked down at her hands, quieted them. 'I seem to mind you are staying with your uncle?'

'I am. In fact, it was from the laundress I hired for his inn that I learned of Agnes's misfortune.'

Besseta looked up sharply. 'What else did the laundress say about us?'

'She grumbled that you took from her the little weaving work she had, for the priests of St Giles'.'

'Rosamund.'

'Yes.'

Margaret tried not to react as Celia slipped away, through the inner doorway.

'You will be satisfied with her laundering,' Besseta said, 'but do not depend on her weaving.' She tried a smile.

'I am glad to hear that I have not yet made a mistake with her.'

'It seems a strange time to journey here – with the English at the castle.'

'I hoped to hear news of my husband, Roger. He has been gone for some time.'

Besseta's head shook quite noticeably now. 'Oh.'

'Forgive me,' Margaret said. 'You have your own troubles. I should keep mine to myself.'

'How – how did you find my parents when you left Perth?'

'Your mother wore a lovely new cap to market with a pale ribbon woven into the border,' Margaret said, 'and she looked bonny. I have not seen your father since Jack departed.'

Someone knocked on the outside door.

Besseta rose so abruptly she tipped over the stool. It clattered as it rocked to a halt.

Celia came through the curtained inner doorway and slipped back onto her stool as Besseta answered the street door. Margaret dropped the wool comb into her scrip.

'Dame Fletcher.' It was a man's voice.

'Master Comyn. How strange to have so many visitors in one afternoon.'

'Who is here?'

'Dame Kerr and her maid.'

Margaret and Celia exchanged a glance and rose.

Besseta opened wide the door. James Comyn filled the doorway, bending slightly to enter.

'Dame Kerr, forgive me for intruding on your conversation.' He studied her face, then Celia's. Glanced round the room.

'You did not intrude at all. We must return to the inn.' Margaret turned to Besseta. 'I pray you, send word to me at the inn if there is anything I can do.'

'The potion?'

Celia handed Besseta the packet. 'That is enough for ten nights. Mix it in wine or ale. Sparingly.'

Comyn gave Besseta a questioning look as he nodded to Margaret and Celia.

'What did you see?' Margaret asked when they reached the High Street.

'There is a room back there with a locked door.'

'Probably Agnes's chamber.'

'A pallet lies in the hallway just beside the door. Mistress, the odour back there is that of a sickroom and something else.'

'There are many unpleasant odours in that house.'

'I should not like to spend a night there. It is far worse than the inn. What did you put in your scrip?'

'A wool comb. I'll show you when we are back in our chamber. But first I want to talk to Janet Webster.'

Janet's door was open to the warm day. The weaver had pulled the loom beneath a panel in the roof that had been propped open. She stood on a bench pushing up the weft with a wooden sword, the light revealing the lovely pattern of the weave.

'Good day to you, Margaret.'

'Might we talk?' Margaret asked.

Janet tucked the sword in her girdle, stepped down off the bench with a grunt. Her brow and upper lip glistened with sweat from the warm sun.

'Surely I've told you all I know?'

She sat down on the bench. Margaret pulled over a stool. Celia sat on the bed in the corner nearby.

'We have been to see Besseta Fletcher,' said Margaret. 'James Comyn arrived while we were there. He seemed – I felt that he came to watch over her conversation with me.'

Janet sighed. 'Celia, will you hand me that pot of grease on the shelf beside you?'

Celia passed her a small earthen pot. Janet scooped some of the grease out with her fingertips and rubbed it into her hands. 'Comyn might be right to be concerned.'

'I don't understand.'

'Agnes's Tom, like my Davy, was Comyn's man,' she said. 'He died on a mission for Comyn. I expected trouble when Jack Sinclair arrived.'

'Why?' Margaret could not imagine Jack caught up in Comyn's battles.

'I told you – Jack wished to be like Roger, even in his support of Robert Bruce,' Janet said gently.

'Jack was on her father's business,' Margaret insisted.

'And why do you think he agreed to travel in such times?'

'For Roger.'

'That, and Besseta. Jack stayed at the Fletcher lodgings here. It was said they were to be wed.'

He clutched the loom weight in his hand. Besseta's loom weight. Margaret closed her eyes, trying to make sense of all the noise in her head.

'You did not know they were lovers?' Janet asked.

'No.' Even had she noticed them arm in arm she would have thought little of it. Jack was that way with all women. 'Besseta and I had not spoken much for many years.' Margaret was trying to absorb all this, reason her way through it.

'Someone at the Fletcher lodgings must have been indiscreet in Jack's presence,' Janet suggested, 'talked of the plans for the raid on Holyrood.'

Margaret nodded. 'Jack was holding one of Besseta's loom weights as he died. Might she have killed him, I wonder?'

Janet shook her head. 'I cannot imagine a woman cutting up her lover's body like that.'

'I can't either, but *someone* murdered him.'

'Aye.'

'Comyn seems very worried about Besseta talking to me. Perhaps he or one of his men murdered Jack?'

'If that were so, and Besseta kenned, she would be eager to tell you, I think. Vengeance.'

Perhaps Besseta would have told Margaret had they not been interrupted. 'What do you know of Comyn, Janet?'

'Little more than what your uncle has told me. He once brought me a lovely piece of plaid and the wool to make another – the piece was charred on two sides. I think of the odour of burned wool when I think of James Comyn, smelling that all the while I copied the pattern. That was our only true encounter.'

'Is he married?'

Janet dipped her fingers in the grease again. 'Old hands dry so quickly, even handling wool.' She shook her head. 'Murdoch says Comyn loves the wife of another.'

'He is wealthy, that I ken.'

'He has worked for it. He does favours for his wealthy, more powerful kin.'

'What sort of favours?'

'You can be sure his efforts for his kinsman John Balliol do not go unrewarded.'

'I thought therein lay his honour, that he was committed to his kinsman's right to the throne.'

'It has become that, I think. But it began as a mission for another.' Janet rose, pressed her hands to the small of her back, arched to consider the light coming through the roof. 'I must get further today.' She glanced down at Margaret. 'Do you really think Comyn murdered Jack? Is that why you are so curious about him?'

'I don't know. I hoped to learn something I could use to keep him away from the Fletchers tomorrow. I need to speak further to Besseta.'

'Ask Murdoch to help. He's taken in ill part the cruel murder of Jack Sinclair.'

'He doesn't behave so.'

'He thought if he seemed indifferent you would give up your mission. Tell him this will allow you to leave all the sooner.' She tilted her head, studied Margaret for a moment. 'Murdoch tells me you pick a lock as well as he does.'

Much good it had done her. She would do better to unlock the secrets of the men in her life.

Back in their chamber, Margaret drew the wool comb from her scrip. 'This I did not show Janet.'

Four long, narrow bone prongs with tapered edges. If one were to stab at flesh and drag the prongs down they might make a wound like Roger's. It nauseated Margaret to hold it.

'I believe this is what someone used on the side of my husband's face.'

Celia crossed herself.

NOT A MURDERER BY NATURE

Abbot Adam knelt at his *prie-dieu*, his Pater Noster beads wound in his long, slender fingers. Andrew, settled into his customary chair, folded his hands in his lap, bowed his head.

Adam rose, still holding his beads. They swung in rhythm to his graceful walk as he joined Andrew. His eyes twinkled. Like Griselda. Cat and master were of a kind, Andrew thought. But quickly the abbot's expression changed to one of sadness.

'Father Andrew.' He shook his head as at a troublesome child. 'You disobeyed your lord abbot.'

'My Lord—'

The abbot put up his hand, silencing Andrew. 'Of course you have prepared an excuse, and you might even believe it. But it does not change the matter of your disobedience.'

'I pray you forgive me, My Lord Abbot.'

'Forgiveness comes in many forms, Father Andrew. Apology and a penance of prayer or fasting.' Adam tilted his head back, studying the ceiling. 'That would be the easiest path for me.' He lowered his head, smiled briefly at Andrew. 'For I do love you, Andrew, like a son you have been to me.' He dropped his head, moved his beads through two Hail Marys, whispered tranquilly. 'I have been praying over it, you see.'

'I believe the Lord would wish me to help my sister.'

'You took a vow of obedience.'

Andrew said nothing, but he could not take his eyes off Adam's face, nor could he hide his loathing.

It was the abbot who looked away first. He shook his head over his beads. 'I was mistaken about you, and now I pay the penalty.'

Make your point! Andrew wanted to shout. But he did not. He sat and suffered, as ever a pawn in his abbot's hands. Except that he ceased to listen.

Until the abbot roared, 'Have you heard anything I have said?' His colour was high, his eyes burning.

'I was praying, My Lord Abbot. You seemed to be arguing with yourself, and I thought it more polite not to listen.' Andrew trembled as he said it, but the abbot's look of disbelief offered a strange comfort.

Adam's expression soon turned to scorn. 'You wish to make me think you mad so that I will not send you to Soutra? I see it now. It will not avail you.'

So he had been right, Soutra was to be his sentence. It shook Andrew, but he was determined not to let the abbot witness his fear. 'How soon do you send me?'

'I cannot say. Perhaps tomorrow, perhaps next week. I must pray over it.'

Soutra. 'I shall be confessor to the English soldiers?'

'Do you have an objection?'

My life! My name! But Andrew chose not to answer that aloud. 'For how long, My Lord Abbot?'

'For ever, if it suits me.'

Eternity stretched before Andrew.

He did not bother to wait for more of Abbot Adam's scorn or venom. Bowing respectfully, he rose and left the room. He walked slowly. There was no hurry now. His fate had been decided for him. To the abbey kirk he walked, hands tucked in his sleeves to hide his trembling. Within the kirk he knelt at Our Lady's altar.

Help me, O Mother. Help me open my heart to the English soldiers. Help me hear their confessions and give them absolution. Help me see them as God's children. In this he could disappoint Abbot Adam by staying alive. And if he found a way to help John Balliol's cause, all the better.

The wool comb sat on the table between Margaret and Celia as they ate.

'How do you know that was the weapon used on Master Sinclair?' Celia asked.

'If you had seen the wound, you would ken.' Margaret pushed away from the table. 'But was it Besseta who wielded it? Or Agnes? And why?'

'You must eat.'

'Besseta trembled so. What if she takes too much of the sleep draught?'

'She will curse me for the time spent at the midden. There is little valerian, but much mallow root in it.'

'Celia!'

Margaret expected laughter. But Celia did not smile. Her great dark eyes were quite solemn, her pale face pinched as usual. 'It was a way in, that is all.'

Margaret did not know quite what to make of her new ally, whether she would later regret the lesson in lock picking she must give her. But Celia's assurance comforted Margaret enough that she could eat, fortifying herself for a negotiation with Murdoch. She went in search of him after supper.

She caught Geordie headed to the tavern with a trencher.

'Is my uncle in the tavern?'

'No, mistress. In the kitchen shouting at Roy.'

As Margaret approached, she could hear it.

'The crops have been trampled by the troops,' Murdoch bellowed. 'We must conserve, damn you.'

'You've coin enough for extra mouths and laundry,' said Roy.

'You'll be the ruin of me, you and your temper. Feel this floor –

that's where the oats have gone. You wonder why I don't trust you with a key?'

She decided to wait until morning.

The dawn brought fog from the firth but blue patches showed through the low clouds promising another sunny day. Margaret attended Mass to pray for guidance.

Afterwards, she found Murdoch in his kitchen. He sat with his chin on one hand, thinking. Grim thoughts, by the look of him. The cook fire needed stoking.

'Do not touch it,' he warned as she leaned towards it.

'So you are not ill?'

'I don't like the heat.'

It was far from hot. She settled beside him.

'I have not meant to cause you trouble.'

'You're not the faultour. It's that Belle.' Murdoch pressed his palms against his thighs, stretched his back. 'Been to the kirk?'

'Aye.'

'Well, it's not the scent of my cooking that drew you here. What is it?'

'I tried to talk to Besseta Fletcher yesterday. But James Comyn interrupted. I do not think it was by chance. He must be watching her.'

Murdoch took off his cap, scratched his head. 'Why Besseta Fletcher?'

'I thought you might ken – he is your partner.'

'I ken as much as I need about him. He contributes to my stores, I turn a blind eye to his dealings in the tavern.' He replaced his cap, leaned towards her, eye to eye. 'What are you after?'

'She and Jack were lovers. His body was found close to her lodgings. I would speak with her.'

He sat back with a grunt. 'Let it be, Maggie.'

'After I talk to her, I'll let it be.' She held his gaze.

'You expect me to help in this?'

'I'll not be bothering you much longer. I ask just this favour, that you find a way to keep Comyn away from her house for a few hours today. Will you do it?'

Murdoch considered. 'He's truly watching it?'

'I believe so, Uncle.'

'What's he up to?' He stared at his bare feet for a few heartbeats, then looked up through his uneven brows. 'You'll tell me what you learn?'

'Aye.' As much as suited her.

'I'll start an argument he'll not wish to walk away from. Midday. Go then.'

Margaret thanked him, rose to leave him in peace.

'And Maggie.'

She turned.

'Have a care.'

Besseta's eyes were shadowed, but wide and staring, her cap crumpled as if she had slept in it, though she did not look otherwise as if she had slept.

'You are back?'

'I worried about the sleeping draught – that you might not measure it properly,' Celia said.

'It is untouched.'

'Agnes did not need it?'

Besseta flinched, began to close the door.

'I pray you,' Margaret said, 'I have something to ask of you. I could not yesterday, not with James Comyn here, but he is busy with my uncle now.'

'What would you ask of me?'

'May I come within?'

Besseta glanced back into the room, hesitated, then opened the door. She looked weary to the bone.

The seats were still arranged as they had been yesterday. The weaving on the loom had not been touched.

Margaret settled on the bench. 'I saw my husband a few days past, Besseta. Very near this house.'

Besseta separated her hands, clutching her skirt on either side. 'I thought he was away.'

So she had known of Roger's previous presence in town. But of course she would – from Jack.

'He had a terrible wound,' Margaret said. 'Four long slashes on his left cheek. He told Janet Webster he had been attacked by a wolf.'

'A wolf?' Besseta whispered, nervously smoothing out her skirt.

'But I did not believe the wolf story. And now I think I have found the weapon used against him.' Margaret brought out the wool comb from her scrip.

'My wool comb?' Besseta shook her head, glanced over at Celia. 'She mocks me.'

'Why should she do that?' Celia asked.

'Besseta, what happened here?' Margaret asked.

'I shall scream.'

'For James Comyn's men?'

Besseta jerked her head towards the door. 'What do you mean?'

'They watch this house.'

'What?' Besseta jumped up, hastening to the window to close the shutter. 'Why do they watch?'

'Why did you slash my husband's face? What did he do to you?'

Besseta stood by her loom, shaking her head. 'I know nothing.'

'But you do. Else why would this house be surrounded by James Comyn's men? I must know, Besseta. Why did you injure Roger?'

Besseta checked the door, resumed her seat. 'Jack is dead. Why should they care?' she asked dully.

'Harcar is dead too,' said Margaret.

Besseta hugged herself and began to rock. 'God grant him a long, frightening plunge into the eternal flames.'

'Why?'

'I know nothing.'

'What do you know of Harcar? You must know something to condemn him to hell.'

Celia began to rise.

'Don't you move,' Besseta commanded. 'You are taking advantage of my hospitality, both of you. Prying. Spying.'

'You give me cause, Besseta. You attacked my husband.'

'Why should I not protect myself?' Besseta cried. 'He shook me. He shouted and shook me until I thought my head would snap off. Then he dropped me like a sack of goods.'

'What was he shouting?'

'"Jack loved you!" Of course Jack loved me. He was my life and I was his. Of course he did. But Roger would not listen. He would . . . not . . . listen. I grabbed the wool comb and when he yanked me up again I raked him. I aimed for his eyes, but he moved too quickly.' Besseta was by turns sobbing and shouting by now.

Celia rose.

'Yes, see to Agnes if you can,' Margaret said softly. She did not know how she could speak so calmly. Her heart was pounding so hard it almost deafened her. Roger so violently attacking a woman? 'Why was he angry, Besseta?' She could not see how Jack's love for Besseta would drive Roger to lose control so.

'Jack is dead,' Besseta sobbed. 'Nothing will bring him back. Nothing.'

There was a noise behind the draped doorway, a little cry.

Besseta's head shot up. 'What is that?' Her eyes were wild. 'Do not touch her!' she shrieked as she lunged for the doorway.

Margaret grabbed her.

'Do not give her water!'

Besseta's body was so taut in Margaret's arms she wondered how the woman could still summon the breath to shout.

Celia suddenly burst from behind the cloth, her cap slightly askew, her hands flung out, palms forward. 'Do not come, mistress.'

'What is it?'

'You did not feed her!' Besseta shrieked.

'Of course I did not feed her,' Celia said in a quiet but tremulous voice. 'She is dead. And has been for many hours, by the looks of her.' She said more quietly to Margaret, 'The lock on the door was simple, as you hoped.'

'Hold her,' Margaret said, shoving Besseta at Celia.

Margaret took up the lamp, ducked through the curtain. The light danced on the wattle walls, no daub to smooth the surfaces. The odour was stronger back here. Celia had left the door ajar. Margaret stepped within. The sound of her skirts brushing against the door made her jump. Was Agnes still breathing?

Only the woman's arms and head were visible above the covers. The mouth was slightly open, the eyes staring. At Margaret? She crossed herself and moved closer, the lamplight flickering and giving life to the lyke of Agnes Fletcher. There – did her eyelids blink? Did her lips move?

Margaret forced herself to breathe and stand still long enough to prove to herself that the lyke was not stirring beneath the light. The cheeks had collapsed inward, the eyes had sunk in their sockets, the long bones of the fingers seemed to stretch the paper-thin flesh. Margaret hesitated, then pulled down the sheet, searching for wounds or scars that would explain the woman's death. Agnes lay naked beneath the covers, her hip bones protruding, her knees like growths in the middle of her skinny legs. Just months ago this woman had carried a child in her womb. There were neither bruises nor wounds, no signs of boils or infection.

Besseta had starved her, of both food and water, Margaret guessed. How could she do such a thing? Besseta had been a gentle child, God-fearing. And she had come all this way to care for Agnes. But though Margaret could not fathom what might turn one sister against the other in such a horrible act, she could think of no other answer. She must be missing something.

The atmosphere in the room choking her, Margaret said a brief prayer over Agnes and then gratefully withdrew.

Besseta was now sitting on the stool on which Celia had sat. She stared at the floor, shoulders hunched.

'Shall I go for a priest?' Celia asked, hovering close to the seated woman.

'Father Francis,' Margaret said, making a great effort to keep her voice calm. 'Is it Father Francis you would like to see, Besseta?'

The woman shook her head. 'No one.'

Margaret nodded to Celia to go. Devil or not, Besseta's fate was not in Margaret's hands.

She forced herself to resume her seat across from Besseta. 'Come, tell me what happened so that I can know what to do.'

Besseta raised her eyes. 'You have seen her?'

Margaret nodded.

'She is at peace?'

Why would you care? 'She is.'

A long, indrawn breath. 'I knew that Agnes hid their robes and the men themselves when they asked, but I did not think she cared so much.'

'What robes? Friar's robes?' asked Margaret, confused.

Besseta glanced at the outer door. 'James Comyn is truly watching?'

'His men, yes. Why, Besseta?'

'I loved Jack so. You can't imagine what it was like. I woke and he was twitching and shaking in my bed. But his blood was all over me, all over the bed, all over Agnes. She had slit his throat. She had killed my Jack. My God, my God,' Besseta moaned, burying her face in her hands.

The truth was so unexpected, Margaret took a moment to absorb it. Agnes Fletcher. Dear God. Margaret crossed herself. Agnes Fletcher had murdered Jack. Those gaping wounds – a woman's work. Just weeks ago that emaciated corpse had summoned such strength. Sweet Jesus, Agnes had done that to Jack. Margaret was strangely numb – she could not summon the hate for the woman that the act deserved, not having seen Agnes's shrunken shell. She wished for a strong drink, for both her and Besseta. She could not imagine what it was doing to the woman to relive the horror. 'Do you have anything to drink in the house?'

Besseta shook her head.

Awkwardly, with trembling hands, Margaret searched through Celia's basket. She said a silent prayer of thanks to find a flask of wine. She drank a little, then handed the flask to Besseta. 'Come. Tell me everything. You must long to. You must tell someone.'

Besseta began to drink greedily. Margaret pulled the flask away. It would not do for her to sleep.

In a little while, the wine composing her enough to speak, Besseta began to pour out her tale. Margaret sat quietly, urging when the woman hesitated, nodding when the huge eyes stared into hers.

Agnes and Tom, her husband, had been staunch supporters of Balliol, deeply involved in Comyn's campaign to restore his kinsman to the Scottish throne. And even after Tom's death, Agnes had remained committed to the Balliol cause. While carrying her child she could do little, but she did what she could. When Besseta arrived, unlooked for, to care for her widowed, pregnant sister, Agnes had tried to continue in secret, but soon enough had to tell her sister what she was doing. Until Jack's arrival all was well, though Agnes's deep mourning after Tom's death caused her to sicken and lose the child. She began to slip away. Besseta slept with Agnes in the bedchamber, Jack on the pallet in the small anteroom.

Several days before Davy and Harry were to slip into the abbey Agnes had taken out the friars' robes to air them and steam out some of the wrinkles – they must look like proper friars to gain entrance to the abbey. Agnes was beginning to regain her strength, but the work exhausted her. Besseta finished the chore for Agnes while she napped, and Jack began asking questions about the plans.

'I told him too much. I did not realise the danger at the time, but the following day I saw him talking to Harcar in the market square. I had heard the rumours that Harcar sold information to the

English and told Jack to avoid him. But Jack laughed at me.

'Harry, Davy, and two other men came the afternoon of that awful day to take their robes. James Comyn came with them, to thank Agnes for all she had done for them. Jack and I were told to stay in the bedroom. He persuaded me that as we were soon to wed we could bed. He used all his charm to woo me. Such sweet words . . .' She was quiet a moment. 'Sometime, I don't know when, Agnes listened at the door, heard enough to understand Jack had betrayed them. Comyn had returned to tell her what had happened at Holyrood, she had just learned of Davy's and Harry's deaths, but I noticed nothing but Jack. He was so beautiful.' Besseta glanced up at Margaret.

'Yes, he was like an angel,' Margaret whispered. 'What could Agnes have heard?'

'Jack said Harcar owed him some money, and as soon as he had it he would take me away from here. We would go to Carrick. Jack would fight for Robert Bruce. And we would have more riches when the Bruce became king. I was frightened, and I suppose I knew in my heart that he must have betrayed my trust – and that of my sister. But I loved him and I chose to trust him. I believed him when he said all would be well.'

Quite a damning conversation. 'What happened then?'

'We fell asleep. Agnes was mad with grief over Harry and Davy, and now she knew it was Jack who had sold the information that had condemned them. Sometime in the night—' Besseta stopped, staring at the horror as it unfolded in the air before her.

Margaret handed her the flask. Celia and the priest should be here by now. She prayed their arrival did not silence Besseta.

'He was already dead when Agnes slashed his stomach open, I think he died with her first blows. She was shouting the names of Tom, Davy, Harry, and "my baby". Would that I had killed her then.'

Margaret jumped as the door opened. Celia, Father Francis and a clerk entered. The priest carried the sacrament. He was tall, his robes hanging loosely from broad but fleshless shoulders. His bald hawk face was solemn.

Besseta shrank from the priest.

'Where is Agnes?' he asked.

'I will take you,' Celia said, leading him through the inner doorway.

'He will curse me,' Besseta moaned.

'Did you starve your sister?' Margaret asked.

Besseta's nod was jerky, as if uncertain. 'I fed her a purge and then gave her nothing to eat or drink. I did dampen her lips when she slept, though she ordered me not to. They were so dry they cracked and bled. I could not bear it.'

Margaret crossed herself. 'Agnes asked you to withhold food and water?'

Besseta looked surprised. 'She was not a murderer by nature, Margaret. She could not live with what she had done. To me, to Jack. She asked me to help her die.'

How would God judge that? Margaret wondered. Who was guilty, Agnes or Besseta? Both? Neither? Margaret took a deep breath. 'How did you get Jack's body out to the tron?'

'I wanted all to see what Agnes had done. I dragged Jack out into this room. Agnes was hysterical. I locked her in the bedchamber with Jack's blood soaking everything. I prayed that his spirit would rise up and kill her. But Comyn returned. He had been uneasy about Agnes, and he took charge here. He took Jack out to the tron late that night. He took the bloody mattress away, brought another.'

'How did Jack come to be clutching the loom weight?'

'I pressed it into his hand to have with him in the grave.'

⊷§ 18 ⸖⊶

Remember This

In the long shadows of late afternoon the inn alley was dark, smelling of damp and urine. Margaret and Celia had left the Fletchers in the hands of Father Francis and two neighbour women who had agreed to prepare Agnes's body.

Margaret's stomach was queasy, her head pounded. Had she guessed at Besseta's suffering she would not have pushed her so. But now she had the answers – once her mind could grasp all that she had heard.

'I'll go and prepare a cool compress for you,' Celia said.

'What of you? This has been no easier for you.'

'I'm not ready to think about it. I want some work, to keep my hands and mind busy.' She headed for the tavern kitchen.

Sim lounged in the doorway of the tavern.

'Dame Kerr, Master Murdoch asked that you go to him as soon as you returned. He is in the storeroom.'

From forbidden to invited, that was puzzling, but perhaps now that she had seen the room Murdoch felt he did not need to hide it from her, as long as she was not left alone to explore. She wondered whether he had lured Comyn with the chance to see his spoils. 'Is James Comyn there?'

'Aye.'

Margaret had mixed feelings about having so divined Murdoch's ploy. Perhaps she did have some of her mother's Sight, though it was pitifully late in showing itself – she'd had need of it long before this.

Sim followed her.

She tried to compose herself to talk to the two men. The inn yard was quiet, dusty and dry in the sunlight. Just days ago she had picked her way between muddy puddles. How quickly the saturated earth gave up its moisture. Like Agnes's body. Margaret shook the thought away, opened the storeroom door. A lamp burned within, but all was silent.

'Uncle?' she whispered.

'Have you found what you seek?'

It was a whisper. A man's voice. She could not tell whether it was Murdoch. She took a step inside. Hearing a sound behind her, she was about to turn when someone pushed her by the small of her back. She fell to her knees. The door thudded closed behind her. The lamp winked out.

Jesus, Mary and Joseph, watch over me. The dark closed in around her. She fought panic, trying to think what to do. She felt a trunk in front of her, used it to help her rise without losing her direction.

'I'll ask again.'

A scream caught in her throat. The voice was very near to her left.

'Have you found what you seek?'

It was James Comyn. He was now so near he might reach out and touch her. She took a step to the right, her heart pounding.

'What have you done with my uncle?'

'Has Besseta satisfied you?'

She tried to remember how many steps forward and to the right it was to a pillar she might put between them. She took a step, bumped the toe of her shoe against the trunk.

'I advise you not to explore in the dark, Dame Kerr, Murdoch has been shifting his treasures. But come.' He grabbed her by the left elbow. 'I'll guide you to a well-lit place.'

'I prefer to remain here.'

'But a moment ago you were moving.'

Her eyes had grown accustomed to the dark, which was not as complete as she had first thought. There was a glimmer of light in the left corner of the far aisle.

She tried to pull free of him.

'Do you wish me to carry you?' He reached for her waist.

'No.' She pushed his hands away and began to move towards the light. He caught her when she stumbled. 'Why are you doing this?'

'Why did you want me out of the way today?'

She explored the next step with her toe before moving forward. 'I wished to talk to Besseta Fletcher. Without you.'

'Why?'

'I had questions about Jack. And Roger.'

'What has she to do with your husband?'

They had reached the corner by the tapestries, where a lamp burned. Comyn's blue eyes were pale in the flickering light, his face shaping and reshaping with the movement. She wondered where the draught was coming from.

'Celia will come looking for me,' Margaret said.

Comyn said nothing. The dimple in his chin was sinister in this light.

'Where is my uncle?'

'Where is your allegiance, Dame Kerr?' His voice was disturbingly caressing. 'Murdoch wavers according to his comfort, but what of his niece?'

'You know why I'm here. To find my husband.'

'Perhaps. Yet you consort with English soldiers.'

'I did not choose to walk with them.'

'You do not prefer Longshanks?'

'John Balliol is our consecrated king. Longshanks' soldiers do not change that.' Knowing her loyalties were the same as James Comyn's did not comfort Margaret at the moment.

'What of Robert Bruce?'

'I don't trust him.'

'What of your husband's involvement in the Bruce's scheming?'

'I have only just learned of it. I don't know what will become of my husband and me.'

'You risked your life in coming to Edinburgh, seeking him.'

She would not risk her life for him again. 'My uncle is sending me away. I'll trouble you no more.'

'Murdoch cannot send you north. The Forth ferry is in the hands of the English and their forces are swarming through Falkirk and Stirling.'

So she was trapped here. She sank down on a chest. 'Agnes is dead, did you ken?'

'Her death is not unexpected.'

Margaret saw the emaciated body before her. 'It must have been terrifying for both of them. That is on your conscience. You left them alone together, trusting no one, hating each other.'

'Besseta will not be blamed, if that is what you fear for her. Father Francis will say Agnes died of sorrow. There was nothing Besseta could do.'

Margaret thought of Besseta's staring eyes. 'That does not undo the horror of what she's lived through. It will destroy her.'

'I'll find someone to take her in.'

'How kind of you.'

'What will you say of Agnes's death?' he asked.

'Is that what worries you?' Margaret tried to chuckle. It did not ring true. 'I've no cause to tell anyone what I learned today. But for what you did to the Fletchers, I might have been your ally.'

The storeroom door opened.

'Maggie?' It was Murdoch.

She rose.

'What is this?' Murdoch growled.

'Remember this,' Comyn said. 'Remember how easily you can be silenced.' He gave her a little bow.

She forced herself to walk towards the door at a normal pace, negotiating the chests and barrels in the gloom. Murdoch muttered something unintelligible as she brushed past him.

By the time Murdoch came up to the chamber to ask after her, Margaret was lying down with a compress draped over her forehead.

'I hope he frightened some sense into you. You don't walk into a dark room.'

'There was a light. And Sim told me you awaited me there.'

'So he's in Comyn's employ now, is he? Well, God grant them joy of each other.' Murdoch paced away and back to the bed. He carried a rolled paper that he slapped against his thigh as he walked. 'There's been nothing but trouble since you arrived.'

'I have not been the cause of it. Why does Comyn have a key to the storeroom?'

'He doesn't.'

Another lock expert.

'You were to keep him occupied,' Margaret accused.

'I did. For a few hours. You were too long away.' Murdoch thrust the paper at her. 'You have a letter from the abbey.'

'From Andrew?' Margaret sat up.

'No. From Abbot Adam.'

Margaret's hands trembled as she broke the seal. 'Will you tell me what it says?' She handed it back to Murdoch. She could not read.

'Aye.'

It was difficult to hang together Murdoch's halting sounding out of the words. But by his tone and the word 'banished' Margaret understood it to be bad news. 'Andrew is banished?'

'Aye, to Soutra Hospital, to be confessor to the English soldiers. God help him.'

Was that not the work of his order? 'What is so terrible in that?'

'Longshanks' men are an invading army, Maggie. Once Andrew

has heard their secret sins, how can they let him go out among his own people? He could be dangerously knowledgeable.'

Margaret had forgotten what Andrew had said about the English, why they brought their own priests with them. 'Dear God have mercy on him,' she whispered.

'What has he done, Maggie?' Murdoch asked. 'For what is he so punished?'

She ignored the question. 'When does he go?'

Murdoch squinted back at the paper, moving his lips as he reread it. 'A week hence, says Abbot Adam. Until then Andrew is cloistered, cannot see or speak to anyone other than his abbot and a few chosen brethren.'

'You must do something,' Margaret said. 'Surely in that time you can think of a way to stop this.'

'So that I can join Davy and Harry?' Murdoch shook his head.

'At least I might see Andrew.'

'Ask Comyn.'

Margaret grabbed the letter from Murdoch. 'I'll ask him nothing.'

'There are times when it's best to bury your pride, Maggie.'

She lay back down.

Murdoch leaned down close. 'So Andrew is to be trusted by the English, eh?'

'Once at Soutra it won't matter, will it?'

Murdoch took the letter that lay by her side. 'I'll talk to Comyn.'

The dry spell had broken with a thunderstorm in the early evening. Rain drummed on the roof, wind rattled the shutters, the thunder claps and lightning bolts felt like God's ire loosed on Edinburgh. For Agnes's death? Andrew's banishment?

Margaret sat in a corner of the tavern, watching the gloom spread as folk talked of Agnes Fletcher's death, rumours of the fighting, north of the Tay for now, praise God, but that was temporary. Sim fought to avoid eye contact.

Murdoch joined Margaret.

'Comyn will find out what he can tonight.'

'Why would he do this for us?'

'He said you are a loyal subject of his king. He'll not let your brother go to the Devil if he can help it.'

'I don't understand him.'

Murdoch pushed a tankard at her. 'Drink this. From what he tells me of your day, you need it.'

He watched her lift her tankard. She trembled with weariness, but her mind was too unquiet to rest.

'I pray God you are satisfied now, Maggie, that you've asked your fill of questions.' He took a long drink.

'What will you do with Sim?'

'It's best to have one's enemies in sight. I can watch him here.'

Margaret studied her uncle's face – he was serious. 'Will you at least punish him?'

'Aye, I'll do that. I'll wait until he thinks I've let it go, then I'll get him. It will be a pleasure.'

'I'd prefer not to see him again.'

'You'll soon be away from here.'

'I think not. Comyn says the English have stopped the ferries.'

She saw that it was news to her uncle. But he quickly recovered. 'Then stay out of the tavern, eh?'

How wrong she had been to think she might trust Murdoch. His wife's family had been right to drive him out of Perth. He was a thief and a bully, nothing more. But if she was to survive, she must learn to live with him. Which was why she pressed forward with her plan rather than continuing the argument. 'I have been thinking,' she began, 'it seems to me if we are stuck with one another we should make the best of it.'

Murdoch eyed her warily. 'Go on.'

'When you were away, I managed the inn and tavern quite well, I think.'

'Except for the corpse in the alley.'

'Neither of us could have prevented that.'

Murdoch grunted. 'Perhaps not.' He squinted at her. 'What's your point?'

'I want to continue to manage the inn and tavern.'

'What?'

'It would leave you free to disappear whenever you choose.'

Murdoch glanced round at the tavern, then quietly regarded the floor for a moment. 'Why would you want to do that?' he asked at last.

'I want to stay busy. I want to feel I have a place.'

'You want the keys.'

'I don't need them.'

Murdoch snorted.

Margaret took a deep breath, lifted her tankard to him. 'Are we partners?'

He lifted his tankard, tapped hers. 'You've a place as long as you stay out of trouble.'

They drank to their partnership.

❧ 19 ❧

A VALLEY WHERE NIGHT ALREADY HELD SWAY

It was hours later that Comyn arrived, long after the tavern had closed. The knock on Murdoch's kitchen door was so light Margaret almost thought she imagined it. It did not even wake Murdoch, who had fallen asleep by the fire while they waited for the man.

Comyn stood in the doorway, dishevelled and wet.

'Your brother leaves in the morning.'

'Sweet Jesus. I must see him!'

'What? Who?' Murdoch rumbled, roused by her cry.

'It is James Comyn, Uncle. He says Andrew departs tomorrow morn.'

'May I come in for a moment?' Comyn asked.

Margaret stepped aside.

Comyn took off his cap, shook it, then his mantle, laid them on a bench. 'We have matters to discuss.'

'Aye,' Murdoch said, rubbing his face to wake himself. 'The abbot wishes to be rid of Andrew so quickly?'

'So they say.' Comyn turned to Margaret. 'I can do no more than help you speak to him before he departs. But tell me why I should make Father Andrew's leave-taking easier for him. Do you know why he is being banished?'

'Yes, I do.'

'Well, I don't,' Murdoch said.

Comyn ignored Murdoch, his eyes steady on Margaret's. 'Then tell me why I should care about him.'

'My brother is a good man,' Margaret began. She tried to think what she might say without revealing to Murdoch more than she wished. 'He is in thrall to his abbot in some strange way that seems to exceed his vows. I don't know why, I don't understand the power Abbot Adam has over him. But the abbot has treated Andrew cruelly and in doing so he has shown my brother that Longshanks' rule is a terrible thing for us. If Andrew were free, he would work to help your kinsman regain the throne. He believes now with all his heart that John Balliol is the king God chose for us.'

Comyn shook his head. 'How do I know I can believe that? He could just be saying that.'

'*I* believe him. He did not have to come to me and tell me what he had done. I think that was a part of a desire to do penance for it.'

'Penance for what, damn it?' Murdoch demanded.

Margaret realised the futility of trying to ignore her uncle. 'Abbot Adam sent Andrew to gather the royal documents held by several abbeys. To be turned over to Longshanks.'

'Has he no spine?'

'And what would you have done in his place?' Margaret retorted. 'He is under vows.'

'Enough,' Comyn said. 'I must get some sleep. And so must both of you.' He swept up his cap and mantle.

Margaret joined him at the door. 'At what time will he depart?'

'Father Francis will come for you just before dawn,' Comyn said wearily. 'Perhaps your brother does deserve to see that you hold nothing against him.'

She was puzzled. It was plain to her that she had not convinced Comyn. 'Why are you doing this for me?'

'You might be my ally, in time.'

Indeed she might – if he had not destroyed the Fletcher sisters. 'God bless you for helping me see Andrew.'

'Would that I had such a sister,' Comyn said as he turned to depart.

When he had disappeared out into the stormy night, Margaret turned to Murdoch. 'I do not understand your bond, you two.'

'We ask no questions.' Murdoch rubbed his face again. 'Go to bed, Maggie. We'll talk of this another day.'

In the dark, listening to Celia's steady breathing, Margaret worried what would become of her. She could count those she trusted on one hand – Fergus, Andrew, Celia, Janet in certain things, Murdoch in fewer. She could not see how she and Comyn would ever truly become allies. She wished they could – he seemed to be the one man who stood firmly by John Balliol and had the influence to help his cause. But this afternoon she had seen Comyn's dark side, both with the Fletcher sisters and his threat to her. And yet he had arranged for her to see Andrew in the morning. Her brothers – how she feared for them both. They would be constantly in her prayers. But tomorrow both would be beyond her reach. Not beyond James Comyn's, though. She pushed that thought aside. She had been disappointed enough with men who had seemed absolutely trust-worthy, Jack and Roger – she dare not take her chances with a man like James Comyn.

She had been her most gullible with Jack. He had won her heart as a good friend and a trustworthy factor, appearing more caring and understanding than her husband, than any man she had ever known. She had not loved him with anything close to Besseta's passion, that was certain, but she had loved him. That was why even after so many hints that he had betrayed Harry and Davy she had held on to the belief that Jack had been Harcar's dupe. But the things he had said to Besseta made it quite plain he had sought his own gain. Margaret could not find it in her heart to forgive him.

And Roger. Tonight his name conjured the scene Besseta had described, his shaking her, Besseta raking his cheek. Margaret had seen how his anger could explode, but she could not imagine what his attack on Besseta meant about his part in Jack's duplicity, whether Roger had set him the task or whether he had not believed Besseta's tale. If Roger were to appear at Margaret's door now, she could not predict how she would receive him. Even beyond the pain of his neglect of her, she questioned his honour as well.

The abbey courtyard echoed with the sound of water dripping from eaves, gates, trees. Haloes of mist circled the lantern light. The soldiers from Soutra were already mounted. The horses were restless, their saddles creaking, their breath rising like clouds.

Andrew stood beneath the eaves, watching Matthew secure the packs to the horses. Soon it would be dawn. He had taken his leave of the abbot a moment ago, his parting words to him expressing gratitude for the pleasant weather. Abbot Adam had looked bored with Andrew's barb. It would have been easier for Adam to have poisoned him and be done with it; this charade of sending Andrew to Soutra was solely for his sadistic pleasure.

Poor Matthew. His only offence had been loyalty to his master before his abbot, but the lad was to attend Andrew in exile.

The gate opened. A priest and another figure entered the courtyard.

'Who goes there?' Abbot Adam called from the doorway.

The abbot was frightened, Andrew realised. William Wallace had not yet been found. All on the English side in the conflict must be wondering whose throat he would slash next.

'Father Francis of St Giles',' said the priest, as his companion ran to Andrew, her hood falling back, exposing her hair.

'Margaret!' Andrew cried, reaching out to her.

'You did not think I could let you leave without a farewell?' She tried to smile up at him, but her eyes were already wet.

Andrew held her to him. God was with him, to grant him this moment.

'I shall pray for you,' Margaret said. 'You will be ever in my prayers until we meet again.'

He stroked her hair. 'And you in mine, dear Maggie.'

The soldiers called to him.

Father Francis pulled Margaret away, but she clutched Andrew's arm.

'We agreed, Dame Kerr,' said the priest, putting his hand over hers, 'you would see your brother to wish him Godspeed and then depart without trouble. You will only make it worse for him if you detain him. Think of your brother. Not yourself.'

Margaret stepped back, but did not take her eyes from Andrew.

'God watch over you, Maggie,' he said.

'And you.'

'God go with you, Father Andrew,' said the priest.

'Bless you for bringing her,' Andrew replied.

Margaret let Father Francis lead her off to the side as the company began to move towards the abbey gateway. As Andrew rode past the two cloaked figures, he lifted his hand to bless them, then dropped it, fearing his blessing might anger God and curse them.

But Margaret and the priest crossed themselves as if he had finished the gesture.

He believes he is cursed, Margaret thought. *My Lord God, show him that he is not. Forgive him.*

Father Francis watched her closely until Andrew disappeared through the gateway, staying her with a hand when she would move forward.

When the sound of the horses faded, he said, 'We must go, daughter. Before Abbot Adam puts us in chains.'

They were being watched by several of the larger brethren.

'I don't care.'

'I do.'

They trudged back up Canongate in the softening rain, saying little.

Murdoch had lighted the brazier in the tavern and opened the door to the wet morning. Margaret and Father Francis stepped within, stood close by the brazier, warming their hands.

The priest's hawk face was softened by a gentle smile that wrinkled the flesh from brow to chin.

'You gave your brother great comfort this morning.'

'I thank you for escorting me, Father.'

'I am the shepherd of my flock. I do as God directs me.'

They had just settled at a table far from the draught when Celia came in. Her dark brows drew a straight line across her pale forehead as she lifted Margaret's discarded mantle.

'Dame Margaret, you must have dry clothes.'

'I'll follow you up by and by, Celia.' She wished to talk to the priest.

Celia hovered for a moment, then withdrew.

'Father, you have helped James Comyn as well as my uncle – and Andrew, whose actions on his abbot's part I've no doubt you ken.'

'I have told you – I am the shepherd.'

'Would you have saved Will Harcar if you could?'

He dropped his head, shook it once. 'He was an enemy to all in this town.'

'Who killed him, Father?'

The priest ran his hands over his bald head. 'A loyal subject of King John Balliol.'

'MacLaren?' Redbeard seemed the obvious suspect to her now.

Father Francis bowed his head.

'Who was the Englishman?'

'The bait. He was no Englishman, but he convinced Harcar he

was. And offered him money for information.'

While MacLaren waited down below in the inn yard, ready to cut his throat. Margaret crossed herself.

'And Agnes Fletcher – what of her?'

Francis raised his eyes, searched her face. 'It is clear her troubles robbed her of her trust in God. But are you not truly asking, what of Jack Sinclair?'

'What of Jack?' she whispered.

'He is in God's hands. As are we all.'

'That is not a comforting thought.'

'No, at the moment He is the God of Abraham, a smiting, terrifying power.'

Margaret saw images of Andrew's drawn face beneath his hood, Agnes's wasted body, Jack's bloated lyke, Roger's wounds. She had no stomach for the ale Murdoch set before her.

'I'll leave you now, Father. Bless you for your kindness.'

'Go in peace, my daughter.'

Once in her chamber, Margaret threw herself down on the bed and let the tears come. Celia came to sit beside her, quietly holding her hand. When Margaret began to shiver and rose to warm herself at the brazier, Celia helped her undress. Then Margaret slipped beneath the covers and pulled the bed curtains to block the morning light.

On the road south the soldiers were uneasy all the day, glancing back at every sound, watching the hills. When they stopped to rest their horses Andrew wandered towards the brush to relieve himself. A soldier was immediately by his side, dagger drawn.

'My lord abbot would reward you handsomely for using that on me,' said Andrew. 'Say you were forced to subdue me.'

'Your abbot spoke well of you, Father Andrew. You do not know your own worth. We are sorely in need of you at Soutra: Father Obert is old, he falls asleep hearing our confessions.'

In the shadowy landscape of the hour after sunset the small party followed the road up to a height that gave them their first glimpse of the great Hospital of the Trinity astride Soutra Hill. It was just an outline in the deepening twilight. Except for the regular line of the high walls it could be an outgrowth of the stony hill. A spire was visible for a moment before they began their descent into a valley where night already held sway. Matthew began to pray aloud and did not cease until they reached the guard post at the foot of Soutra Hill.

Wind fanned the flames of the guards' fire into fantastic shapes. Andrew joined in Matthew's prayer.

⇜ 20 ⇝

WATCHING THE CLOUD SHADOWS

Margaret and Celia sat in Janet's house, talking quietly with the weaver as she worked the loom. The click of Margaret's cards made counterpoint to the slower rhythm of the shuttle. Celia worked on new sleeves for Margaret's best gown.

'What will Murdoch do about Sim?' Janet asked. 'He cannot trust him now.'

'Sim is still in the tavern,' Margaret said. 'Murdoch thinks it best to keep him in sight.'

Janet exclaimed at that. 'He'll regret that.'

'I've a mind it's the same reason he accepts James Comyn as his partner,' said Margaret. 'I've never heard a pleasant word pass between them.'

'I don't like James Comyn,' said Celia. 'He has dead eyes.'

'I think him a fine figure of a man, although I dislike his loyalties.' Janet stepped down from her bench, shoved it aside with her foot. She had completed enough of the cloth to reach it from the ground. 'I understand Roy has done little work and much damage since Belle returned.'

'My uncle is too patient with him,' said Margaret.

Celia shook her head. 'If Roy loves Belle so, why does he refuse to wed her?'

'It's the doubt,' said Janet. 'He would ever look at the bairn and wonder if it's his. And fear Belle would wander off again with the first man who promised a better life.'

Margaret stretched forward to turn a card. 'Rosamund thought Besseta and Comyn were lovers.'

'Don't listen to that woman's tales,' Janet warned.

'Oh, Master Jack was much finer than James Comyn,' Celia said.

Margaret was glad her head was bent over her weaving. Celia's comment had startled her. She had not thought before how Celia might feel about Jack, how well she might have known him. He had returned to his aunt's house so often.

'He was bonny, aye,' said Margaret. 'The bonniest man I've ever seen.'

Margaret and Comyn stood together over Agnes Fletcher's grave. They had buried her close by the Blackfriars kirkyard, just beyond consecrated ground – Father Francis would not go so far as condoning both suicide and murder, and neither would the Blackfriars. Besseta knelt, weeping as she planted a rosemary that the fathers had given her.

'Do you not wish you had spared the sisters what they went through in those rooms these weeks? Separated them from one another?' asked Margaret.

'It would not have saved Agnes. Or eased Besseta's pain.' Comyn was looking out over the graves to the kirk wall, where two friars wielded shovels, digging a hole for a young tree that lay beside them. 'They might save their backs for the grave digging. The dead will fill the kirkyard when Wallace and Murray join together.'

'Darksome thoughts.'

'It's best to face it.'

Margaret did not respond. She was waiting for the right moment.

'Have you found what you wished to learn here in Edinburgh?' Comyn asked.

The day had grown warm. Margaret pushed back her hood. 'Not

all of it. I would ken whether my husband had a part in this. If he encouraged his cousin to betray you.'

'It would have been a good use to make of such a man as Jack.' Comyn said it with bowed head, nodding slightly.

What a cold, bloodless man. 'Good use? He was Roger's cousin, they were brought up together like brothers. I would not use my brother so.'

'No, I don't believe you would.' Comyn glanced at her, saw something, turned to look directly at her. 'What will you do if Roger appears?'

Not liking the way his pale eyes searched her face she moved away from him, sitting down on the wall that bordered the kirkyard. Comyn followed, as she had expected, but she had regained her composure.

'Well?'

'I shall ask him whether Jack acted alone. I'll not shy away from that.'

'And if you don't like his answer?'

Margaret dropped her head. 'I cannot say.'

He did not pursue the question, for which she was grateful. After a brief silence, he began to rise.

She must spit it out. 'What you said about our being allies, what did you mean?' She met his pale gaze, prayed God her eyes stayed steady.

'What are you asking?'

The intensity of his regard made her heart pound. 'John Balliol is my king. I want to know what I might do to help him.'

'Truly?'

Slowly, she nodded. 'I do not want to look back on this time with regret.'

'What does your uncle say about this?'

'He is not to know.'

Comyn dropped his gaze, shook his head. 'You have a strange way with you, Margaret Kerr.'

'You will consider what I have said?'

He reached over, took her right hand, turned it over and back. 'You do not shy from work.' He looked up into her eyes. 'I will give it some thought.'

She withdrew her hand.

In a little while Comyn rose, took his leave.

Margaret sat on the wall for a long while, listening to Besseta's tearful farewell to her sister, watching the cloud shadows glide across the castle high above. After a time Margaret hugged herself, trembling with the import of what she had set in motion. She had done it. She had embraced her mother's visions as the best hopes she had. Pray God Christiana was right.

FURTHER READING

Geoffrey W. S. Barrow, *Robert Bruce and the Community of the Realm of Scotland* (Edinburgh University Press, 1988)

Elizabeth Ewan, *Townlife in Fourteenth-Century Scotland* (Edinburgh University Press, 1990)

Andrew Fisher, *William Wallace* (John Donald Publisher Ltd, 1986)

Marta Hoffmann, *The Warp-Weighted Loom: Studies in the History and Technology of an Ancient Implement* (Robin and Russ Handweavers, 1974)

Peter Yeoman, *Medieval Scotland* (B. T. Batsford/Historic Scotland, 1995)

Alan Young, *Robert the Bruce's Rivals: The Comyns, 1212–1314* (Tuckwell Press, 1997)

Alan Young and Michael J. Stead, *In the Footsteps of Robert Bruce* (Sutton Publishing, 1999)

An expanded list for the Margaret Kerr and Owen Archer mysteries is available on my website: www.candacerobb.com.

To find out more about Candace Robb's Owen Archer novels, read the Candace Robb Newsletter. *For your free copy, write to The Marketing Department, William Heinemann, 20 Vauxhall Bridge Road, London SW1V 2SA. Please mark your envelope 'Candace Robb Newsletter'.*

Also available from Candace Robb

A Spy for the Redeemer
An Owen Archer Mystery

Read on for an extract from the seventh Owen Archer Medieval Murder Mystery . . .

O n a May day that hinted at summer, such a day on which the people of York rejoiced in opening their doors to the warm, fresh air and found excuses to walk along the river in the sunshine, or to walk out on to the Strays to check on their grazing animals, Lucie Wilton and her adopted son, Jasper, were shut up in the apothecary, staring down at the mound of dried herbs a customer had just returned. The tension between the apothecary and her young apprentice seemed to suck out the air. Jasper's cat scratched at the closed shutter, begging to be released.

Jasper glanced over at Crowder and began to move towards the shutter. Lucie grabbed his hand. 'Crowder must wait. You are too easily distracted, that is the problem. If you kept your mind on your work rather than on the intentions of friendly neighbours, you would not have made such a mistake.'

Jasper yanked his hand from Lucie's and pushed his straight, sand-coloured hair from his forehead with an impatient gesture. 'Peppercorns for nasturtium seeds. It is a mistake anyone might make.' His tone was insolent.

Lucie resisted the urge to slap him. 'Any fool can tell the difference between the two, in scent as well as hardness. I cannot think how you made such an error. Look at me when I speak to you.'

Jasper met her gaze, then dropped his eyes, hunching his shoulders. 'It will not happen again.'

'It should never have happened at all. An apothecary cannot make mistakes. Have I not told you that if you are at all uncertain –'

'I thought I was pouring from the correct jar.'

'Because you were thinking of something other than the task before you. Taking down the wrong jar – you know what is in each jar. You clean them. You fill them.'

'I swear it will never happen again.'

'If it happened once . . .'

'I swear!' Jasper shouted.

Sweet heaven, if only Owen were here. Since Jasper's twelfth birthday he had increasingly withdrawn from Lucie, at the same time growing closer to her husband, Owen Archer. Though Owen disciplined the boy more often than Lucie did, Jasper seemed to respect his criticism while thinking hers unfair. 'If Owen –' she began, but finished with just a shake of her head.

Jasper clenched his fists, jutted out his chin. His colour was high. 'If the captain were here, what would he say about Roger Moreton?'

'Jasper!'

'Or your mistake –' He stopped, dropped his gaze.

'Alice Baker's jaundice,' Lucie said quietly. 'Is that what you were about to mention?'

Though the boy's straight blond locks fell over his face, Lucie could see how he blushed. 'I meant –'

'Best to say no more.' Lucie needed no one to help feed her sense of guilt over the woman's condition.

Someone knocked on the door. Worried that Maria de Skipwith had already spoken of the boy's error, Lucie picked up the parchment full of herbs and handed it to Jasper. 'Take this into the workroom and pick out the peppercorns.'

Jasper looked down at the mix in horror. 'How can I find them all?'

'It is not to give Mistress Skipwith,' Lucie said. 'It is to fix in your mind the look, the taste, the scent, the feel of a peppercorn.'

Jasper hunched his shoulders and shuffled off to the workroom. Crowder followed close on his heels.

Lucie approached the door, wishing she would find on the other side a messenger with news of Owen, announcing his return. In late January her husband had headed south to join Geoffrey Chaucer on a mission into Wales for the Duke of Lancaster. Lucie's aged father, Sir Robert D'Arby, had accompanied Owen, wishing to go on pilgrimage to St David's in thanks for God's sparing the family from the recent pestilence. None of the company from York had yet returned. This was the longest Owen had been away since they had wed. Lucie had not anticipated the difficulties such a prolonged absence would cause. And that Jasper would be most difficult of all – that had been an unpleasant surprise.

Lucie swore under her breath as she found the door locked. She had not wanted a customer to hear her chastise Jasper. But the shut shop might itself cause rumours. Mistress Skipwith had said she understood, Jasper was merely an apprentice and there was no harm done, just some sneezing, she would tell no one, the lad would never do it again. But tongues wagged despite the best intentions.

A monk stood without, in the black robes of a Benedictine, his head bowed beneath his cowl.

'*Benedicte*,' said Lucie.

The monk raised his head. It was Brother Michaelo, secretary to the Archbishop of York and her father's companion in pilgrimage. What did it mean, that he appeared alone? The monk's patrician face was drawn, his eyes sad. *Dear God, please let Owen be well.* 'Brother Michaelo. I did not know you had returned.' Lucie stepped aside, welcoming him into the shop.

'*Benedicte*, Mistress Wilton.' The monk bowed as he entered the room.

Lucie glanced out into the street before she closed the door. 'You are alone.'

'I am.' Michaelo drew a stack of letters from his scrip. 'Captain Archer entrusted these to me.'

'My husband is well?'

A nod. 'I left him well.'

Deo gratias. 'God bless you for bringing them,' Lucie said, though her heart was heavy as she took the letters. 'My husband is yet in Wales, then?'

'By now the captain had hoped to depart for home. God willing, he should be home before Corpus Christi.'

A month. Still so long to wait. But she had managed this long. 'And my father?' When they had departed, Sir Robert D'Arby had not been in the best of health.

Brother Michaelo lowered his eyes and crossed himself.

'Father,' Lucie whispered. She had thought herself prepared for this. 'When?'

'On the third day of Passiontide, Mistress Wilton.'

More than a month ago. Lucie, too, crossed herself. She began to shiver. When had the room grown so cold?

'I am sorry to bring you such news,' said Michaelo, taking her arm, helping her to a bench.

It should not be a shock, Lucie thought as she heard Michaelo slip behind the counter, pour water from the jug. He sat beside her, held a cup until she was calm enough to take it.

'I should not have encouraged him,' Lucie said. 'He had not recovered and it was so cold when they rode out, then such a wet spring.' Sir Robert had caught a chill the previous summer. Despite his sister's devoted nursing he had never quite recovered. A recurring cough and hoarseness had been particularly troublesome.

'You could not have foreseen the weather, Mistress Wilton.' The monk drew a scented cloth from his sleeve. 'Sir Robert found the journey difficult.' Michaelo dabbed at his eyes. 'But he never complained.'

'Is it for my father, those tears?' Was it possible the self-absorbed Michaelo had been moved by Sir Robert's death?

Michaelo raised his eyes. 'I have walked in wretchedness all the way from Wales – selfishly, pitying myself for the loss of my friend. For your father was joyous in death and welcomed his release.' Michaelo's voice rode the waves of his emotions. 'After you have read the letters, I shall tell you of your father's last days. You might find comfort in hearing of them. Come to me when you are ready. I shall be with Jehannes, Archdeacon of York.' He rose. 'Should I send for someone?'

'Jasper is near.'

'You are very pale.'

His sympathy brought tears to her eyes. 'I shall come to you at Jehannes's house as soon as possible – tomorrow, if I am able.' The archbishop's secretary bowed, turned and departed silently.

If I am able. Lucie moved to a stool behind the counter. Alice Baker and her jaundice, Maria de Skipwith and Jasper's mistake, Jasper's distrust of Roger Moreton. And now she had lost her father. Her eyes burned. Sweet Jesu, but she was tired.

She needed a shoulder to lean on. Someone to comfort her as she wept for her father. She needed Owen. But he was not here. Her instinct was to go to see her kind neighbour, Roger Moreton, but the foolish Jasper had decided Roger was wooing her. He could not see that Roger was kind to everyone, not just Lucie.

Her father was gone. She must go to Freythorpe Hadden and break the news to Phillippa, her father's sister and long-time housekeeper. Could she close the shop for a few days? Would Alice Baker start rumours about Lucie's incompetence while she was not here to defend herself? Alice's jaundice was not Lucie's fault – most people would know that. For most of her married life Alice had complained of sleeplessness and fluttering of the heart. It seemed hardly a week went by that she was not in the shop buying new ingredients for the remedies she prepared herself. Lucie guessed that it was the skullcap purchased most recently that, mixed with something else on Alice's crowded shelves, had caused an overabundance of the wrong humours and turned her skin and eyes yellow, her urine a peaty brown. The midwife Magda Digby had agreed with Lucie – skullcap and valerian should not be mixed. Magda had prescribed an infusion of dandelion root and vervain. Lucie had mixed it for Alice, but who knew whether the woman was drinking it? And what she had added to it.

Sir Robert was dead. Lucie noticed the letters in her hands. She had forgotten what she held. Ink and parchment. She wanted *Owen* here, not his letters.

'Who was it?' Jasper stood over her, turning his head this way and that to see what she had in her lap.

'Brother Michaelo.' Lucie noticed that the boy's nose was red and his eyes watery. He would remember the punishment. 'Did you find all the peppercorns?'

'Made me sneeze.' He wiped his nose.

'Good. It did the same to Mistress Skipwith. You did your best?'

He nodded. 'What did *he* want?'

Jasper despised Brother Michaelo. The archbishop's secretary had once threatened the life of someone the boy had loved dearly, Brother Wulfstan, the old infirmarian of St Mary's Abbey.

'Brother Michaelo brought letters from Owen,' said Lucie. 'And – news of my father's death.'

'Sir Robert?' Jasper whispered. He crossed himself. 'May God grant him peace.'

Lucie crossed herself, too.

Contrite, Jasper said, 'Go, read the letters. I can manage the shop.'

Lucie pressed his hand, glad of the truce, however fleeting. 'I *should* read these and think about what to do. You can find me in the garden if you have need.'

He gave her a lopsided grin. 'If Mistress Skipwith has told anyone of my mistake, there will be little to do.'

'She said she would not speak of it.'

As Lucie rose, Jasper said, 'I am sorry about her. It will not happen again. I swear.'

Lucie nodded, squeezed his hand again. He was young, bound to make mistakes. Perhaps she was too hard on him. But the guild would not tolerate more serious errors. Even this would have been punishable. 'Now mix the correct herbs and spices for Mistress Skipwith. When we close the shop, you can take it to her. There will of course be no charge. And you would be wise to thank her. She might have spoken to the guild master and had you in the pillory.'

The apothecary's garden behind the shop had been the masterwork of Lucie's first husband, Nicholas Wilton. It held not only the herbs one might expect in such a garden but also many exotic plants grown from seeds Nicholas had collected. Lucie chose a spot amidst the roses, near Nicholas's grave, well away from the noise of the children at play. But it was not of her first husband she thought as she stared down at the letters. She thought of Owen and his misgivings about Sir Robert making the pilgrimage to St David's. Owen had pointed out the hardships of such a journey, to the farthest west of Wales, even for a young, healthy man. They must depart while winter still froze their breath. Could she not see how dangerous it would be for Sir Robert, almost four score and in uncertain health, to attempt such a journey? Lucie had known Owen's arguments were sound. But when she faced her father, saw the yearning in his eyes, she could not forbid it. And in truth, had she the right? All Sir Robert had wished was to reach St David's. Lucie realised with a pang that she did not know whether he had reached the holy city. Brother Michaelo had said that Sir Robert had passed away in peace. Surely that meant he had completed the pilgrimage? It was this, the question unasked, that at last loosed a flood of tears. Lucie let them come. She did not even notice Kate, the serving maid, until she spoke.

'I saw Brother Michaelo,' Kate said, standing over Lucie, holding out a cup of ale. 'He looked so solemn. And then I saw you weeping. I pray that nothing has happened to Captain Archer.'

Lucie took the cup. 'It is Sir Robert. The chill took him at last.'

'Oh, I am sorry, Mistress. He was a good man.' The young woman shifted feet. 'Are those letters from the captain?' Kate had boundless admiration for the literate.

'They are.'

'Will he be home soon?'

'Brother Michaelo says the captain hopes to be home by Corpus Christi.'

Kate made a face. 'Still so long. But it is good to have his letters?'

'It is, Kate. I was going to read them now.'

'Oh, to be sure. I must return to my duties.'

'You will not tell your sister about Sir Robert in front of the children?'

Kate's older sister, Tildy, was with Gwenllian and Hugh near the kitchen door. 'Oh, no, Mistress Lucie. It is for you to tell them. I shall not even tell my sister.'

Lucie sighed as she watched Kate hurry away. Why did everything seem so difficult of late? When had she last laughed?

Roger Moreton had made her laugh last night, at supper – until Jasper insulted him. The boy's animosity was misplaced. It was true that Roger was a widower. His wife had died in childbirth – a stillbirth – the previous autumn. But his wealth and good reputation made him the hope of all parents of marriageable young women. Who would be his next wife was a topic of much excited conjecture in the city. Roger had no need to woo a married woman.

Lucie looked down at the letters in her hands. Where to begin? She untied the string that held them together. Owen had marked on each the place and date of writing so she might read them in order, and so follow his journey. In the first letter he mentioned Sir Robert's cough, his dizziness. The river crossings had been difficult in the early spring, from the border country to Carreg Cennen. There was much in the letter about Owen's mixed feelings upon returning to his own country, but Lucie skimmed to find news of her father. Owen wrote of constant bickering between Brother

Michaelo and Sir Robert, good-humoured on the monk's part. A later letter mentioned Brother Michaelo's tender nursing of her father. The monk perplexed Lucie – in the time she had known him he had metamorphosed from a self-serving sybarite to a trusted servant of the Archbishop of York. Practical changes, she had thought, still self-serving. But this tenderness towards her father – this was change of a deeper sort. God had watched over Sir Robert, to grant him such a companion on his final earthly journey. In the last letter, Lucie at last found the news that calmed her. Not only had her father reached St David's, but he had been granted a vision at St Non's Well, a vision that had given him the absolution he had sought over many pilgrimages. Sir Robert had died in peace, a happy man. Thanks be to God.

For a long while Lucie sat, head bowed, the pile of letters in her lap, remembering her father. Melisende, her ageing cat, curled up at her feet. Faintly Lucie heard her children's voices.

The church bells chiming Nones woke Lucie from her reverie. She must return to the shop. Gathering up the letters, she took them to the workroom, tucked them on a shelf that had once held wooden dishes and spoons when Lucie and Nicholas, and later Owen, had lived in this house behind the shop. It was Sir Robert who had given them the fine house across the garden. He had tried hard to make up for his earlier neglect. Lucie hoped her father had known, in the end, how much she had loved him.

Jasper raised his head as Lucie entered the shop. 'Does the captain say when he might return?'

'In his last letter he said he hoped to be home within the month. That was over a month ago.' She nodded towards the package he was wrapping. 'Is that for Mistress Skipwith?'

'Do you want to check it?'

'I should.'

Jasper unwrapped it. Lucie poked about with a mixing stick, found nothing amiss and handed it back to Jasper.

'By the time she has cooked this in lard it will be useless anyway,'

Jasper said glumly as he refolded the parchment and placed it on the counter.

'She believes that it helps her sleep. A little on the temples.'

Jasper hung his head.

Lucie hated seeing him like this. 'I shall close the shop while I am at Freythorpe Hadden. I must tell Phillippa of her brother's death.'

'I could go to Freythorpe.'

'You will stay here. It needs a woman's delicacy. And I need you to see to the stores, and the garden.'

'But the roads –'

'Take the remedy to Mistress Skipwith!'

Jasper grabbed the package.

'And hurry back. We have much to do.'

As Lucie walked out on to Davygate the next morning, a hooded figure stepped out of the shadow cast by the jettied upper storey.

'Have you found the counterpoison for my jaundice?' Alice Baker asked.

Lucie felt her blood rise to her face, her heart pound. It was not her nature to enjoy confrontations. 'I told you what I thought caused it and what you must do to undo it.' She repeated the advice, hoping this time Alice would hear it. 'An infusion of vervain and dandelion root. Nothing more. Then fast for two days, drinking only water, eating nothing. After that, eat moderately and take no medicines.'

'You have found no counterpoison.' A statement, made an accusation by her tone.

'That regimen *is* the remedy. I believe you mixed valerian with skullcap.'

'Have a care, Lucie Wilton. I could ruin you.'

Ungrateful wretch, Lucie thought. But she merely said, 'I cannot believe you wish to do that, Alice.'

Lucie glanced up at the sound of a door opening and shutting across the street.

'May God go with you, Mistress Baker, Mistress Wilton.' Roger Moreton smiled as he crossed the street from his house. Another man followed in his wake. Lucie mirrored Roger's smile – how did he manage to be there when she needed him?

'Master Moreton.' Alice Baker simpered, then remembered herself and turned so that her jaundiced face was in shadow.

Roger was a handsome man, clear-featured and solidly built. He always seemed delighted with life, his eyes twinkling, his colour high.

'Can you believe it?' said Roger rather breathlessly. 'Just as I mentioned your name, I turned, and there you were. Is it not so, Harold?'

'Quite so.'

'God go with you, gentlemen, Mistress Wilton.' Alice hurried off.

Lucie had paid no attention to Roger's companion. Now she looked up into the stranger's eyes. Sweet heaven but they were remarkably blue. He gave her an oddly formal bow.

'You spoke of me?' she asked Roger.

'I lied. But that terrible woman. She will insist on blaming you for her foolishness.'

'It is difficult to accept that one is a fool,' Lucie said. 'But I thank you. And you,' she said to the stranger.

He in turn glanced uncertainly at Roger.

'Forgive my discourtesy,' Roger said hurriedly. 'Mistress Wilton, this is Harold Galfrey. He is to be my household steward when I move to St Saviour.' Although he lived alone, Roger had recently purchased a large house in another parish in the city. It had increased the frenzy of the rumours regarding his choice for the next Mistress Moreton.

Lucie would not have guessed the man to be a steward. With his tanned skin and sun-bleached hair he did not seem one who spent his days inside, organising a household. Neither was his physique that of such a man. However, his attire was appropriate for a household steward. His clothes had been chosen with an eye to cut and fabric, and yet in such muted colours they would offend no one or call attention to him. 'You are fortunate to find yourself in Master Moreton's household,' she said.

'I am indeed, Mistress Wilton,' said Harold.

'I must be going now. I have much to do before I leave for the country.' She needed time to talk to Brother Michaelo as well as arrange for a Requiem Mass for her father. And though she had shut the shop, she hoped Jasper might catch up with replenishing the stores – so there was much to discuss. 'Thank you for rescuing me. God's blessing on your day.'

'Leave for the country?' said Roger. 'What takes you to the country?'

Lucie had no one to blame but herself for mentioning the journey, for knowing Roger, he would wish to hear everything and then offer assistance. 'I received word yesterday of my father's death, while on pilgrimage in Wales. I must go to Freythorpe Hadden to tell my aunt.'

'God rest his soul,' Roger said. 'I must do something. I shall accompany you.'

'You are kind. But I shall stay several days. You cannot leave your business so long.'

He nodded, frowning. 'But you need an escort.' He brightened. 'Harold is idle until I am in the new house. He shall escort you.' Roger looked pleased with his inspiration.

Harold looked perplexed.

Lucie had no time to argue. 'Thank you, Master Moreton. I shall consider your offer.'